SUGAR HALL

SUGAR HALL

Tiffany Murray

SEREN

Seren is the book imprint of
Poetry Wales Press Ltd
57 Nolton Street, Bridgend, Wales, CF31 3AE
www.serenbooks.com
Facebook: facebook.com/SerenBooks
Twitter: @SerenBooks

Ebook ISBN 978−1−78172−144−5
Print ISBN 978−1−78172−143−8
Kindle ISBN 978−1−78172−145−2

Cover image: Victoria Thorley
Internal images: mario hernández (narquoise.tumblr.com)
Typesetting by Elaine Sharples
Printed by TJ International Ltd

The publisher works with the financial assistance of
The Welsh Books Council

MIX
Paper from
responsible sources
FSC   FSC® C013056
www.fsc.org

for Kamau Brathwaite

And limbo stick is the silence in front of me
limbo

limbo
limbo like me
limbo
limbo like me

long dark night is the silence in front of me
limbo
limbo like me

From 'Limbo', by Kamau Brathwaite

… All children – whether good or bad – eventually find their way home…
The Brief Wondrous Life of Oscar Wao, Junot Díaz

For the last ninety years the drive had been growing narrower as the rhododendrons grew larger.
In Youth is Pleasure, Denton Welch

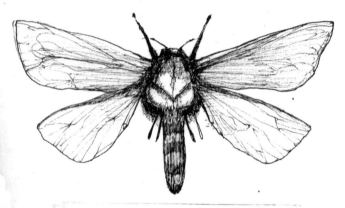

GHOST MOTH , male, hepialus humuli

Sunday, Easter Holidays, 1955, in Grandfather Sugar's House

1

When Dieter Sugar backed out of the long shed that edged the Hall's red gardens, when he ran through the graveyard with its tiny headstones to make a stumbling shortcut across the grass meadow where frilled daffodils bobbed like sprung Jack-in-the-boxes, when he sprinted past the black water of the ancient swimming pool onto the yellow gravel that made a sound like crunched sugar between teeth (and 'Sugar' was his name after all), when Dieter bounded up those grey steps, into the ancient house that he could never think of as his, when he shot through that cathedral-sized hall that smelled of marzipan (on account of the rat poison and not the cake his mother had told him), when he sprinted past the carved oak staircase and into the long room someone had named 'the reception', gliding to a stop on the polished floor, Dieter Sugar knew he was afraid.

He was petrified.

'What is it, Dee?' his mother asked as she unwrapped white tissue paper from small objects he had forgotten were theirs.

Dieter's words came out a jumble as he tried to tell his mother and sister what he'd seen. It was hard to put into words. There was a boy; there was a small boy and the boy appeared out of thin air, and he, Dieter Sugar, was sure this boy was something

9

different, he was almost certain this boy wasn't like any other boy he'd seen before.

To begin with, the boy wore something bright round his neck: a silver collar. It had writing on it, but it had glinted in the sun and Dieter couldn't read it.

It was his older sister, Saskia, who interrupted. 'Don't you have anything better to do than make things up?' The sharp snap of Saskia's voice echoed in the long room and she shook those things she called her 'heavenly hips'. (Dieter had once heard Saskia say her hips were more heavenly than a Knickerbocker Glory.)

'I'm not making it up. He just popped into the air, from nothing, and he stared at me and didn't say a word, and he looked so ill, and I felt dreadfully funny all over. There *is* a strange boy out there.'

Dieter pointed to the bay window and the wild red gardens. He squinted; it was all too bright in the countryside and he didn't like it. He didn't like this house: he hated the fact it was home now. London was his place to be. By the river: Churchill Gardens.

'He just appeared, and he wore a silver collar…' Dieter's voice tailed off.

Saskia latched onto these last words and snorted. 'Don't be silly, Dee. Boys don't wear collars. Vicars do and dogs do.' She glared at him and Dieter felt his fear settle, a burrowing toad. The points of the toad's wet, sharp feet, its warty sides, all dug deep into Dieter's belly; his breath went and he collapsed into his grandfather's lime-green armchair.

Dust puffed.

This reception room was green. Green silk wallpaper, patterned with gigantic open-winged butterflies and hairy moths, peeled just below the line of the ceiling; at times Dieter was sure he heard these insects flutter. Green velvet curtains held greener mould in their swags, and there, by the great gape of a fireplace – like a black mouth and such a long way away – was an even greener something Saskia called a *chaise longue*. It sat directly beneath the dead bulbs of a light Saskia had told him was a *chandelier* (Dieter was learning so many new words in this strange house, it was exhausting). As for the armchair he sat in, it was as lime green as the Mekon's face, and how Dieter hated the Mekon: Dan Dare's deadly adversary from outer space; evil, alien and so very, *very* green.

'Dee, you must listen to your sister.'

Dieter's head tilted at the sound of his mother's voice. Its tone had altered so much since they'd come to Sugar Hall. Of course it had the same part-English, mostly-German sound but now it was full of something both sticky and stuck, and Dieter didn't like it. Ma sounded like she was talking through a mouthful of condensed milk.

'You have to believe me,' he pleaded, kicking his legs out. 'A boy *was* out there, and he *did* wear a collar. It was silver and it shone in the sunlight—'

'So you do mean like a dog?' Saskia snorted again as she hopscotched on the parquet floor; the countryside had brought out the child in fifteen-year-old Saskia Sugar.

'I don't know, Sas, I've never seen a dog in a *silver* collar.' That got her, Dieter thought. 'And it was real silver, Ma, because it shone like your special necklace...' Dieter stopped. That silver necklace was sitting in the window of Kinsey's Pawn Shop, on Lupus Street, SW1. That was such a long thought away. It made Dieter think of walking with their suitcases from Number 52C, Shelley House, Churchill Gardens to the bus stop in the pink morning light because Ma couldn't afford a taxicab. It made him think of bouncing on the creaking springs of his carriage seat at Paddington Station as the train mushroomed smoke into the thicker smog, *shuuuu-tu-shuuuu-tu*, and the pistons pumped and the whistle shrieked like a woman falling from a bridge. It made him think of Ma's egg sandwiches that smelled like farts, and Ma turning and turning her wedding ring on her finger as the carriage rattled all the way to this horrid place.

Then he remembered something else about the strange boy: the boy hadn't worn clothes. When he appeared the boy was naked. Dieter didn't know why but he couldn't quite tell his mother this, so he said, 'Ma, listen to this, when I saw him he didn't have a shirt on, can you believe it?'

'Don't be ridiculous, it's cold out there,' Saskia sneered.

'It's true…!'

'Please, Dee,' his mother interrupted, 'be good, a good boy. Please don't make up these stories.'

Frills of wood shavings patterned the floor around Dieter's mother: and such a young mother she was.

At last her children were quiet.

Dieter watched her reach up and unwrap more forgotten things from the tea crate. Dieter didn't know why it was taking his ma so long to unpack; perhaps it was because things disappeared, things moved, in this house.

Like their shoes: like the figures in the paintings on the walls, like the ornaments on the mantelpieces; like the billiard table, Dieter thought.

And Ma's laugh: that had disappeared too.

His ma, his beautiful ma, she was so scruffy now. This awful house had done that to her. She wore a pair of Pa's old trousers with a belt and a dreadful green overcoat that swallowed her up. Dieter was used to her wearing pretty dresses patterned with bluebirds that seemed to fly up the short sleeves and flock at the little belt at the waist – and that dress made him want to sing, *There'll be bluebirds ovah, the white cliffs of Dov-ah!*

Not long ago Ma had been so glamorous.

Glamour was a word Dieter loved because he had read it in a thick-as-a-brick magazine called *Vogue* that Ma kept between her mattress and bedsprings at 52C Shelley House, Churchill Gardens,

SW1. 'Glamour' was a word Dieter loved because when you said it the words made your face smile at the first 'gla' and then they made you blow a kiss on the 'mour'.

'Gla-mour.'

Dieter liked that. He liked it so much he once practised the word in the bathroom mirror, wearing Ma's Siren Red lipstick.

'Gla-mour.'

It was London that had made Ma glamorous. In London, Dieter ran home from school longing to hug her. He wanted to smell the diesel fumes, the newspaper-scent that the city, his city had given her. Dieter wanted to smell this as the thud-thud-thud of her quick little heart beat through the satin and frill layers of her slips and dresses. Even Ma's name was glamorous; she was 'Lilia', she wasn't 'Vera' or 'Daphne'.

Now her heart had slowed to a dull thud and she smelled like the black damp that lurked behind the green silk wallpaper in this room: she smelled of the spores and the dust that danced busy as the flies in this ancient house; like the foxed pages of the ugly books that lined the bookshelves in the red library, like the silverfish, the earwigs; the living ones and the husky-dead.

Dieter looked across the long room at his newly drab mother and his puppy-fat sister and the toad of fear burped inside him. Saskia had begun to sing, 'Nearer My God to Thee', and Dieter closed his eyes. He didn't want to think about sadness today, about How It Was Before They Came to Sugar Hall, because How It Was Before made his muscles tense and his lungs shrink, and the thing that hung between his legs move back to where it had come from (and Dieter wasn't exactly sure where that was, he had tried to see in a mirror once, but for now he just knew it was inside).

He let his head drop back against lime-green upholstery and he thought of the Wee-Hoo Gang. That last afternoon in London, Dieter had stood on his dirt mound in the place they called the Wasteland and – as the smog came in from the Thames, and the cranes that were building, building, building chugged in the distance – he shook the dry hands of every member of his Wee-Hoo Gang, just like a grown-up leader would. His best friend, Cynthia Nurse, had cried.

'See you, Dee,' Tommy Perrot said as he wiped snot candles from his nose, and when none of them could see a thing because the smog was so bad, they held hands and walked in a crocodile all the way back to Churchill Gardens.

In the long, cold reception room of Sugar Hall, Dieter tried to picture his friends; he thought of the twins, Deuteronomy and Comfort Jones, running through the Wasteland crying 'weeeeeee-hooooooooo!' at the roofless buildings with their brick steps that led to doors that led to rooms that weren't there anymore – all because of the war, a war he didn't know or remember. (It was Mr Hutchins, his old Form Teacher, who had told the class they had a different war now, and this war was about bombs called atom and hydrogen; Mr Hutchins said that if this new war happened there'd be no bombsites because there'd just be nothing left).

How awful to have nowhere to play, Dieter thought. How awful it is to have no one to play with.

If he concentrated, Dieter could hear Billy Foley and Tommy Perrot make spacemen ray-gun noises; he could hear Cynthia Nurse and Precious Palmer flicking their skipping rope, singing, *'The wicked fairy cast a spell, cast a spell, cast a spell. The wicked fairy cast a spell, long, long ago!'*

If Dieter was with them, he'd be kicking about in the dust by the river until the sun set over Battersea Power Station and their different mothers' different cries and the smells of their different cooking were carried out on the dry wind, all the way from their beloved council flats, the brand-spanking-new Churchill Gardens.

A furry bluebottle hit against one of the tall windows in the long, green reception room and Dieter opened his eyes. If he crushed the fly he knew its guts would be yellow, just as he knew that being back home, in London, would make everything right.

'A boy *was* out there,' he whispered, 'he did wear a silver collar *and* you'll see, I'm going to make him my friend.'

December 1st, 1938
List of Articles (Lilia Fisch, aged 15)
2 pairs elastic stocking
2 textbooks (mathematics)
School Report (1938)
1 straw hat
1 pair galoshes
2 summer dresses
4 international reply coupons
1 in-between season coat
2 'shillings'

Lilia Sugar Stops to Think

2

Lilia Sugar loved to hear her children. Unfortunately Saskia had yet to grasp the fact that her gift did not lie in singing, and Lilia had retreated to the window seat of the library to escape her daughter's mauling of 'Nearer My God to Thee'.

If Lilia hadn't been so out of practice, she would have laughed.

She glanced up at the leatherbound volumes sitting behind dust-caked grilles. Lilia saw hard work up there. Still, in this house she knew that if she could clean it, she could sell it.

She thought about books.

The first book she read in English was *Jane Eyre*. At the time she was fifteen, she was Lilia Fisch just come to England, and *Jane Eyre* suited her very well. Of course she had already read the book in German: as a child in Demmin, and again during that last black year in Berlin, but Lilia would always remember the first time she mouthed those words in English and in England, sitting on the hard wooden bench of the tall and almost round Quaker Meeting House in Nailsworth. She remembered she had been quite alone, quite cold, but content; and her fingers on the white page seemed very red.

Nails-worth. At first it had seemed such a frightening word for a town.

Drizzle spat against the library windows and Lilia shuddered.

It had been a shock to discover that Nailsworth wasn't far; it lay out there – she tapped the window – over those fields and past the wide mud of the Severn River. She didn't care for that river; it was tidal, she couldn't swim it and so it was useless to her. She'd heard dreadful stories, too, of ponies stranded and sinking to their deaths in the slick mud of the estuary, of a girl who jumped in at high tide and was never seen again. No, Lilia didn't care for that brown churning river at all. She knew there was another behind them – the River Wye – she hadn't ventured out there but she did hope it was proper, calm water, for Lilia loved to swim. It made her want to laugh, though she didn't, the fact that rivers surrounded them.

Sugar Hall is an island, she thought, and we are marooned in this new home.

'Nearer my God to Thee!' Saskia cried from the staircase. 'Nearer to Theeeeeee!'

Home. It wasn't that. Sugar Hall was a dirty-grey square, spiked with fancy but useless chimneys. Two silly towers shot up from a porch decorated with stone roses and stone creatures that Dieter had insisted were lions, dragons and bears, but to Lilia they were rain-washed lumps that made her head hurt. Sugar Hall was the past, and Lilia did not care for the past. This was her husband's past; it was Peter's, and Lilia couldn't think of Peter, not today.

She dug her hands into the pockets of the army coat she'd found all those months ago in the boot room (the coat had got her through this winter so well she'd forgotten that it made her itch). Lilia lit a cigarette, breathing in as deep as a poacher on a cold night.

'Juniper, please come,' she whispered at the windowpane: smoke clouded the view.

In the rat-infested and freezing winter Lilia had been too busy surviving to consider loneliness; now she craved company, or the company of one person at least.

Juniper Bledsoe had arrived one day in February when the drive was still banked with snow. Lilia was standing at these library windows when she saw a figure on a white horse pushing through the drifts. Lilia thought it was out of a book. Still, she'd hidden behind the red curtains.

Lilia had always thought the English strange; either they were fawningly polite or they barged in like bulldogs. Juniper had marched into the hall and cried 'Haalllooo! Haaalllooo!' for so long that Lilia had to scurry out of her hiding place and open the library door. Juniper wore a long wax coat and trousers that flared above the knee, and for a moment Lilia thought it was another century.

'Ah! There you are!' Juniper said. 'Christ, it's an ice-cellar in this place. How *do* you survive, dear?' She barked all this as she slammed her riding crop down on the hall table and tugged off her leather gloves. 'I can only apologise that I haven't visited until now. Ill, you see. Damned pneumonia. This winter is enough to kill us all. But I can't tell you how thrilling it is to meet you at last.' She shook Lilia's hand with a grip that could crush bones and Lilia worried about her own hard, dry skin. 'Now where do you bunk up? Where's your warm retreat in this arctic place?'

'I…'

'I remember the old range in the servants' kitchen, kept me toasty after many a ride. Old Sugar didn't have the foggiest I was here.'

'Yes, the kitchen,' Lilia said and immediately she worried about how German she might sound, but Juniper hadn't flinched; she simply took Lilia by the shoulders and marched her along the passage towards the worn stone steps that led down to the kitchen. Juniper knew the house.

'By the way, it's Mrs Bledsoe to most, Juniper to you.' Her long wax coat creaked as she walked.

'Lilia.'

'Pretty name. Pretty altogether.' Juniper laughed. Lilia blushed.

Juniper; it was such a strange name. Lilia tried it in her head as they walked down the cold stone steps to the kitchen: Joo-nipper.

This first encounter had been so brisk, so English, that Lilia had been dazzled, and when Juniper slammed her holdall on the kitchen table and pulled out a large brown package that dripped blood, Lilia gasped.

'Beef,' Juniper said, and she waved the package in the air; blood sprayed. 'You'll embarrass me if you don't have it, dear. Larder the best?' Without waiting for an answer she walked into the back scullery. 'Ah, I see the old meat safe is still going. Good. Good. So, have you had a line of them? Visitors?' Juniper marched back into the kitchen, wiping bloody hands on her wax coat. Lilia took a cloth from the sink: there was a trail of dark spots into the scullery.

'Well? Visitors? Had many? While I was languishing in my sick bed?'

Lilia couldn't imagine this woman being ill at all: she was so thick and strong.

'I was hellishly ticked off, you know. Once I heard you were here, I wanted to be the first. Well?'

Lilia had to think while she crouched and dabbed at the blood. 'The vicar and his wife. They came…'

'What did they bring?'

'Margarine.'

'Frightful! Ghastly people.'

Lilia hid her smile and swilled the bloody cloth. She checked her face in the dirty basement window.

Juniper pulled out a chair, the legs squealed on the flagstones and she sat. 'Now, tell me, what on God's green earth are you doing here all alone, Lovely Lilia?'

Lilia opened her mouth; she didn't think she liked the nickname but she couldn't think of what to say so she blushed again.

'How about a little drop?' Juniper took a flask of whisky from her greatcoat pocket, she reached for two glasses from the draining board and as she poured she gave Lilia sound advice about the rats and the bats and the moles that were ruining a perfectly good lawn.

After a little whisky, Lilia took to Juniper more than she had taken to anyone for such a long time. Juniper had a strong nose with freckles and the tip of it seemed permanently red. Lilia thought this woman smelled of kindness, and it was a buttery, soapy smell.

'You'll die here, my dear, without help,' Juniper told her.

Lilia gulped her whisky, elbows off the table.

'Really. We must rally round. I know things have been terrible for you. Otherwise why would you come to this damned place?' Lilia swallowed. 'I could not stay at the flat, I could not remain in London.' She swallowed again. 'This house is for Dieter. It is his.'

'Yes, I see,' Juniper glanced about the kitchen. 'Where's the boy by the way? The heir.'

'School. They have opened the schools at last.'

'Heck! The *village* school?'

'My girl, Saskia, she is…'

'Didn't know about a girl.'

'She…'

'Is she Peter's?' Juniper was so direct Lilia had to swallow more whisky.

'No. She – she was before. Before Peter.' Lilia baulked at her husband's name; she hated to say it out loud. 'She, she is … she was born in the war.'

'You must have been pretty young.'

'Yes…'

'Do you have family, dear? Back home?'

Lilia drank.

Juniper was silent: for a small moment.

'Yes well, the war. There we are. The war. Still, we mustn't dwell, must we? Tell me, what are your plans? For this old place? You can't just rattle around in it.'

Lilia was numb with whisky, though for the first time in weeks – sitting at that kitchen table – she felt warm.

'You must have plans, Lovely Lilia. You can't take your eye off the quarry. You must plot and scheme with a responsibility like this.'

'I hate it,' Lilia said and she felt the burn of whisky in her throat.

Juniper didn't blink. 'I don't blame you. I'd hate it, too, but the point is, you came here, so you must have a plan to make it work. Do you see?'

Lilia was a little too cloudy to see, so Juniper spoke again about the rat problem and the cold winter. The two were connected. 'They come into the warm, evil blighters.' She also spoke of her time as a nurse in London during the war and Lilia nodded, trying to dodge any words that might take her back there. It seemed like Juniper Bledsoe was a countrywoman who had done it all, a woman who was bored at home now that her husband – who she admitted had loved her a little too much – was dead.

'Heart attack, five years ago. Dreadful. Mighty older. Almost a good innings.' Juniper sighed, 'Death duties,' she said. 'Will they swallow this place up?'

'I do not know,' Lilia shrugged, because even at this first meeting Lilia found she could only be open and truthful with Juniper Bledsoe.

'Have a solicitor?'

'Pardon?'

'Do you have a good solicitor, dear, looking into it?'

'I…'

Lilia found she had to be quick to finish her sentences with Juniper.

'Well you can use mine, good man. I'll arrange it. If you don't mind.' Juniper paused. 'And are things hard, Lovely Lilia? I mean,

22

did Peter leave you anything, apart from this horrid place? What I'm trying to ask, my dear is, is there money? Ghastly thing to talk about, but in these times, needs must. Can't stand pussy-footing.'

'No,' Lilia said. 'No, there is … there is really nothing.'

'You can't go back to London?'

Lilia bristled. 'No, I cannot. For today we cannot live anywhere else but here.'

'Yes, well, that is understandable.' Juniper drained her glass and slammed it on the table. 'I hope you don't mind me mentioning it, Lilia, but I am dreadfully sorry you know. It was awful what Peter did.'

Lilia nodded.

'He always was so put upon by that ghastly father of his. It really is quite sad. But, we're here and there we are. That's the way it is. I hope you don't mind me talking like this. Tell me about your children, dear.'

And so Juniper carried on, and on, and Lilia was soothed by the sound of a stranger's voice and by a stranger's whisky.

Juniper liked to visit at least three times a week now, and whenever she did Lilia would wave a tipsy farewell from the big stone steps of Sugar Hall, and for a very small moment all was fine.

Her cigarette was done; she spat on the tip, crushed it, and buried it in her pocket. Lilia looked up at the library bookshelves: she was onto 'D' and 'Dickens', and now she knew she was as bored as Lady Deadlock. She sorely needed Juniper and her whisky today.

Lilia tugged off her headscarf and walked to the huge spotted mirror on the library wall. She laughed: her Dieter was right, it was her hair that was the worst; two thick wedges of dark growth were bold at her crown while the rest of the blonde felt and looked like straw. Her eyebrows were thick, she hadn't a stitch of make-up on and her fingernails were black with dirt. Lilia unbuttoned the army coat and hung it from the bookshelf's ladder. She went up on tiptoes in her gumboots – a difficult manoeuvre – and examined herself.

She certainly wasn't Lovely Lilia any more: she looked a sight in Peter's old tweed trousers, rolled up at the ankle. Her body had changed too; she'd become wiry, stretched. There was no pleasing plumpness to her cheeks or her breasts. Lilia gripped her hands in tight at her waist, and turned, a profile pose: she had lost her bottom, too.

She was thirty-one. Surely it couldn't be over yet?

Lilia barred her teeth at her reflection, a warning dog. She wanted to howl, but instead she stuck out her tongue and blew a raspberry.

'Sugar Hall,' she said to her reflection, and suddenly her breath was white in the cold: she felt the hairs on the back of her neck rise.

Lilia spun around to look behind her.

There was no one there; of course there was no one.

She reached out to touch the wallpaper, black silhouettes of oversized butterflies stood proud on the blood red paper. Fleshy, she thought. Lilia felt movement beneath her fingers.

She jumped back and grabbed her coat from the ladder; she plunged her hands into the itchy arms and marched across the room, singing. It was an old song in an old language she had hoped to forget.

'*Bak, bak, Kuchn! Der Bekker hot gerufn,*' the words came quick and easy, and she knew why her daughter sang alone for hours in this house.

Saskia was scared.

'*Bak, bak, Kuchn! Der Bekker hot gerufn,*' Lilia cried, '*Wer s'wil gutn Kuchn machn…*' She cut off and hurried across the worn red rug as fast as she could, but the rubber of her gumboots kept catching on the bunched thread, pulling her back.

How to Write a Good Letter
HOW NOT TO BEGIN

Even one who 'loves the very sight of your handwriting' could not possibly find any pleasure in a letter beginning:

'I have been meaning to write to you for a long time but haven't had a minute to spare.'

Or:

'I suppose you have been thinking me very neglectful, but you know how I hate to write letters.'

Or:

'I know I ought to have answered your letter sooner, but I haven't had a thing to write about.'

The above sentences are written time and again by persons who are utterly unconscious that they are not expressing a friendly or loving thought. If one of your friends were to walk into the room, and you were to receive him stretched out and yawning in an easy chair, no one would have to point out the rudeness of such behaviour; yet countless kindly intentioned people begin their letters mentally reclining and yawning in just such a way.

Dieter Writes Two Letters

3

Sugar Hall, Sunday, about a quarter to three, April 17th 1955

  Dear Cynthia,

  How are you? I am very well...

Dieter chewed the end of his pencil. He liked to feel the wood splinter in his mouth.

I am very well and so are Ma and Sas (even if Sas is a silly old moo because she's singing on the stairs right now, it's awful) I hope your Ma and you are jolly good.

He was sitting at a desk in the yellow room on the second floor. Here, canary-yellow moths with intricate patterns on their wings danced on the lemon-yellow wallpaper. Dieter was used to the eccentricities of the wallpaper in this house, he hardly noticed now.

I still wish you were here with me, Cynthia, and now more than ever because guess what? This morning I found a strange boy in the sheds. He

frightened me, Cyn, but I want to see him again.
You'd tell me not to, you'd tell me he wasn't right,
I know you would, but there's no one else to play
with. He didn't speak but I know he'll be my friend.
Sas and Ma don't believe in him, but you would. I
am making it my mission to find out about him. I'm
going to be as sharp as Sherlock Holmes...

Dieter glanced up at the letter he'd already written: it was a thin thing with 'To The Boy In The Shed' on the envelope. He picked it up and sniffed it. Dieter knew that letters held secrets so he hated to read them. He also knew that letters kept people alive; at least they kept the *idea* of people alive — Ma had taught him that — so he had to write them and he had to read them.

Cynthia, he wrote, *I wish—*

Dieter dropped his pencil. He picked at the fluff of green baize on the desk top and he thought about Cynthia: Cynthia Nurse the best Wee-Hoo in the world; Cynthia who lived above him at Churchill Gardens, Cynthia who could use a slingshot, Cynthia who could run faster than Tommy Perrot; Cynthia who could recite her Bible off-by-heart, Cynthia who could hex you, too. Today was a Sunday so she'd be back from church with her ma, Mrs Nurse. Mrs Nurse dressed Cynthia in so much white on Sundays that the ribbons in her dark hair looked like snowflakes.

Dieter looked up at the grandfather clock in the corner of the room. *Bong-bong-bong* it said as the grandmother clock on the landing replied, *bing-bing-bing*.

Three o'clock.

Cynthia would have sneaked out by now, her white puffball dress and her ribbons hidden under her bed. She would have crept down the concrete steps of Shelley House, Churchill Gardens wearing her play dress and an old brown cardigan that was too big for her. The cardigan had leather patches on the elbows, and it was her pa's. Cynthia brought it over to England in the bottom of her trunk and she said it smelled of cherry tobacco and fried fish, and it was all she had left of her pa because Cynthia had come to England on a boat just like Ma had (and Dieter often wondered if Mrs Nurse and his mother had just sailed up the Thames, right by the Wasteland, and jumped off). Cynthia said she came from an island made of coral where fish could fly and a schoolteacher called Mrs Briscoe hit her with a cane. Cynthia called it *Bar-ba-dos*.

There were magic words on her island, Cynthia said, and she whispered them in Dieter's ear as they lay on the tar roof of Churchill Gardens.

'Duppy. Baccoo. Loup-garoux,' she whispered.

Duppy. Baccoo. Loup-garoux.

It rhymed if you let it.

Cynthia said it was a dangerous spell. She said it meant ghosts and bogeymen and werewolves. She said a duppy was the worst because it could make time stop still; she said a duppy wanted to steal your soul or your skin, sometimes both. In the heat of a summer city night, as they lay on their backs on the roof of the flats and giggled at the stars, Cynthia Nurse told Dieter Sugar everything she knew about duppies.

'They're mean. My mum said when she married my dad they left Jamaica because of the duppies, but the duppies followed them anyway.'

'My ma says ghosts are sad.'

Cynthia smacked her lips and kicked her legs free of her sticky nightie. 'Mean-sad. Duppies are mean-sad because they're ancient and if you're sad too long, you get mean.'

'How do you know?'

But Dieter knew Cynthia was right: there was sad and there

was mean-sad like those duppies she left behind in the coral-island home that was no longer hers – *Bar-ba-dos*.

'I think you get mean if you can't go to where you're supposed to,' Cynthia said and she squinted at the half-moon as Dieter stretched out in a starfish shape, his fingers and toes touching her on one side.

'Like where?'

'Like heaven or hell or just that place you're supposed to be,' she said, because although Cynthia was a church-girl, sometimes she had other ideas. 'Mum says duppies play tricks on us, she says they can steal our souls, trick us into swapping our soul for theirs, so all of a sudden we're them and they're us and they get to live again.'

'That's dreadful.'

'A dog howls in the night, that's a duppy.'

'Like Mrs Anderson's dog?'

Cynthia punched him. 'Don't be silly,' she cleared her throat. 'Just be careful, Dee. My mum says don't go out when the moon's full and stay away from the crossroads. That's where the duppies are.'

Dieter felt warm in that somewhere beneath his belly button as Cynthia whispered in his ear. 'Duppy. Baccoo. Loup-garoux. Duppy. Baccoo. Loup-garoux…' Dieter's nose twitched along with the night-sounds of London: the growl of cabs, the push of the Thames, the roar of red night buses, but Cynthia wouldn't stop. 'Duppy. Baccoo. Loup-garoux,' she whispered. 'And there's the heartman, too. He steals children's hearts and gives them to the devil. You wake up in the morning with your ribs open and an empty chest and you're dead.'

Dieter shivered.

'Duppy, Baccoo, Loup-garoux.'

'And these ghosts, they never go away, Cyn?'

'Mmm-uh. Never.'

'So even when you're dead you can live and live and live?'

'I suppose, if you're sad and mean enough. Though it's not really living, is it?'

Dieter felt Cynthia's hand in his and he wished with all his heart that she would live and live and live. Though even if she died, even if she was stuck neither here-nor-there forever, he knew Cynthia Nurse would never get mean. That night, Dieter made a promise to himself, and it was to watch out for ghosts, particularly the mean-sad ghosts.

'Duppy, Baccoo, Loup-garoux,' he whispered at the green baize desk in the writing room of Sugar Hall. He listened for the Hall's clocks: but they hadn't stopped; time wasn't standing still. Cynthia didn't need to worry; there was no duppy here. The boy in the shed was just different, that's all.

He looked up at the face of the grandfather clock: it was ten past three.

'Nearer my God to Theeee!' Saskia cried from the landing. 'Nearer to Thee! E'en though it be a cross that raiseth mee!'

Dieter picked up his pencil and thought of the letter-writing tips he'd read in Saskia's *Bumper Guide for Young Ladies*.

'If you are writing a letter, tell your correspondent where you are. Consider the scene to describe the scene…' it had said.

'Cyn, I told you there are strange noises here, didn't I? Ma says it's the forest behind us, but it isn't because trees don't scream…'

He stopped.

Dieter *considered* Sugar Hall.

This place was a sort of big that forced you to make up words that had you stammering, because it was gi-gi-normous, it was gar-ga-ga-gantuan. His grandfather's house was a million times bigger than their flat but not as big as Buckingham Palace. Maybe on the tops of his letters he should write 'Sugar Kingdom, Sugar World, Sugar Skies, Sugar Universe'. He thought of the first night here when Ma had to lay their coats on top of the bedclothes and they all slept in the same bed, huddled, because there was nothing but the scuttle of rats and the howl of something terrible outside that tickled the white-blond hairs on his head. That first night he had decided Sugar Hall was a Black Forest Gateau (the one Ma made when he was younger once she'd saved up enough ration tickets). Yes, this place was a Black Forest Gateau because it was made up of layers – of floors upon floors of rooms – and as Sas said, God knows what lurked in the shadows. Dieter wondered if God *did* know, though he suspected it was more likely to be the Devil, and that was why Ma had dragged a commode into their bedroom and locked them in every night.

Dieter decided to make a list of facts. It was going to be very long.

Cyn – since I last wrote these are the things I have found out...

1) In this house 21 doors are locked and 19 are open.

2) I have found a room stuffed with frightening things. Masks made of wood and animal heads are nailed to the wall. I saw three zebras, a lion, a tiger and a big black cow with horns. They have glass eyes and their skins are on the floor. The masks frighten me more than the animal heads.

3) In the same room are glass cases filled with butterflies and moths. The butterflies and moths are pinned down so they can't move.

Some of them are GIANT and bright but I don't like them.

4) Ma has locked this room up.

5) There is a front staircase and a back staircase. There are 62 steps to the back staircase because it goes all the way down to the cellar and all the way up to the attic. Ma said this was for servants.

6) There are 7 leaks in the attic rooms. Last month I counted 12 dead rats, 3 crows, a something I think was a cat, and piles of flies in the corners. I can't count the flies, there are too many.

7) Last week we had a bonfire for the dead rats. Ma wore a hanky over her face.

8) Saskia found a thing called a Priest Hole and she said that is for Catholics so they have somewhere to hide. Are you a Catholic, Cyn?

9) In the olden days people called Roundheads killed people called Cavaliers in our dining room (or is it the other way round?)

10) There are paintings of olden-day Sugars here. Ma says they are my ancestors. They are ugly.

11) We have been here for 77 days.

12) I can fit in the thing called the Dumb Waiter.

13) I have grown 2 inches.

14) There's a river over the fields in front of us that sometimes looks like the Thames, but I know it's not. Ma told me ponies get stuck there because the water goes away, but it always comes back.

15) I have found a boy in the sheds and he wears a silver collar round his neck. He's not a duppy, Cyn, honestly, he's a boy. He won't hurt me or stop the clocks.

16) I am lonely.

17) I wish...

Exhausted, Dieter let the pencil drop; his hand cramped. The truth was he had so many wishes they buzzed around him like gnats. He pushed himself away from the desk and marched to one of the tall windows; he gazed beyond the lawns to the redness of the forest of rhododendrons where you could get lost for days on an adventure; he blinked at the overgrown tennis court where you could win every tournament in the world, and then he stared at the swimming pool puddled with water, black as a pirate sea. Dieter had played all the games he could think of out there: but it was boring being a tennis champion with no opponent and impossible to rule a pirate ship without hands on deck. Dieter breathed deep. Sometimes breathing like this made the jittery feeling of loneliness go away: sometimes. He touched the windowpane. He tapped on the glass with his fingernails, tip-tap-tip. Tip-tap-tip.

Tip-tap-tip, the drizzle replied.

A small white moth, furry, crashed against the windowpane and joined in.

Flutter-flutter-tip-tap-tip. Flutter-Flutter-tip-tap-tip.

It was strange that here they were in his grandfather's house when there was no Grandfather anymore. Grandfather Sugar was dead, and when Grandfather was not-dead, Dieter never came to Sugar Hall.

He knew that part of it was on account of Ma and Saskia being not-recognised by Grandfather (which Ma said was the same thing as being ignored). He knew it was because Pa was Cut-Off, which meant Dieter was The Only Hope.

These phrases meant little to him; they were like, 'RGT HON'. Grandfather was a 'RGT HON' which sounded funny if you said it out loud.

Ri-git-on. Ri-git-on. Just like a frog in a pond; like the belching toad of fear that fizzed in his belly. *Ri-git on*, Dieter whispered.

Tip-tap-tip went his nails on the pane. Tip-tap-tip. Flutter-flutter. Ri-git on.

Dieter sighed and he placed his thumb and forefinger either side of the bridge of his nose. He pressed there just like Pa had whenever Pa took off his glasses.

Yes, it was all Very Complicated. It needed Thinking About.

'Grandfather Sugar is dead and this house is mine because I am the last Sugar left. My pa is dead and I've found a boy in the sheds,' Dieter said out loud.

Tip-tap-tip, said the drizzle as Saskia growled out that endlessly repeating hymn, her voice croaky at last, 'Yes, all my dreams shall beee! Near-er my God to meeee!'

'WAYS TO CATCH A RAT'

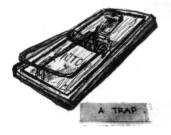

A TRAP

A GUN

POISON

A SHOVEL HEAD

Mr John Phelps Helps

4

In the yellow writing room Dieter's milky breath clouded the windowpane. He drew a circle with his finger then rubbed away the middle. Dieter was a boy on a ship, a stowaway hidden in a cabin with his first sight of land.

Ahoy there!

Through his porthole he saw the bright black and white cows that clomped twice daily along the path by the fence. When he'd first arrived, those cows had scared him to death, now he liked the call of the farmer. 'Hep, hep, hep. On girls, on girls. Hep!'

Dieter had learnt another new word: *silage*.

He spotted the dot of John Phelps on his black bicycle down by the Hall's open gates and he had to stop himself crying out, excitement knotted in him, because Dieter adored Mr John and he wished he could call him plain 'John', like Ma did.

Mr John wasn't old; Mr John had a fine head of strawberry-blond curls. Mr John was handsome, he made Dieter think of Dan Dare and he wished Mr John owned a uniform (even if he hadn't gone to war on account of his lungs). Mr John had no Pa, just like Dieter (though he said it was the bees that got his pa).

Dieter rubbed away the trickles of condensation on the windowpane; he wanted a clearer picture as his handsome friend pedalled up the long drive.

John visited because there were things that were difficult for Ma, and although Dieter knew John couldn't help Ma with every difficult thing, like sadness, he could hit the taps that dribbled green with a spanner; he could climb up onto the roof as Ma worried below, and he could bang until the gush of water stopped. Ma said if it wasn't for John Phelps they might be dead.

He watched as John left his bike against one of the grand pillars and bent over to take off those shiny bicycle clips; the ones Dieter wanted to steal, jackdaw that he was. From the window he saw John ruffle then smooth down his curls and then he saw him do something very silly, which was cup his hand over his mouth and sniff. A glossy raven hopped on the lawn behind him. This was Rosie, John's pet. Dieter knew that people usually had budgies or dogs or cats, maybe cockatiels or parrots, but John told him he'd had Rosie since she was an egg. Dieter watched Rosie hop-waddle with bowed black legs. Hop-waddle. Hop-waddle, like she had rickets (and Tommy Perrot's big sister had had rickets and Tommy said no one would marry Sheila now).

A door slammed at the back of the Hall; it was the servants' entrance because John said he'd never walk in the front. There was the sound of his hobnailed boots as they echoed up the back stairs and into the grand hall.

Saskia stopped singing. Dieter heard another door slam.

'Oh, John, so nice, you have come!' Ma shouted. Ma tended to shout at people who weren't her immediate family. Saskia said that Ma thought shouting would make her English clearer.

'You have come! Now you follow, down to the kitchen. Sit, have cheesed sandwich. Have tea. Dear John…'

Dieter reached out for a swatch of yellow curtain. He wrapped himself up in custard yellow and breathed in its damp, dishcloth smell. Dieter felt the hard hit of the fat coin sewn into the curtain's corner. The coin thumped against his ankle as he listened to Rosie the raven out on the lawn, skittish, chasing flies and butterflies and cawing her caw, because Rosie wouldn't ever hop over the threshold and into Sugar Hall.

It was time for work and Dieter was following John up the back stairs to search out the latest roof leak. John was wearing the leather gaiters that protected his ankles from the rats. They were only halfway up when John said, 'Hold on, son. Have to get my breath.' He sat on a narrow step and pressed his palm into his skinny chest. 'Give me a minute,' he said.

John had bad lungs. This wasn't the same as a bad arm that would get better: John said his lungs could only get worse, and he wheezed in the musty air of the back stairs.

Dieter sat next to him and saw a thin-skinned pulse shimmering on John's neck: it made him think of the baby rats, and he hadn't thought about them for so long. He'd found them the first week at Sugar Hall; they'd squirmed in a nest of tweed on the floor of a wardrobe. They were hairless and pink, their closed eyes black mounds. Dieter had picked one up to see every blood vessel, every one of those heartbeat shimmers as the baby rat's see-through skin pulsed. Dieter had held it in his palm and skipped down the stairs to Saskia. He'd found her in their makeshift bedroom on the first floor and he held out his hand, 'I've got a present for you. Look!' he cried, and Saskia screamed. The baby rat was terribly cold by the time he put it back in its tweed nest, it was so cold Dieter thought of hot water bottles and hot bricks, all the things they had to use in their own beds now.

As Dieter stared at the beating pulse on John's blushed-red skin, he couldn't stop thinking about baby rats.

'Want a proper listen?'

Dieter started. 'I beg your pardon, Mr John?'

'Come on, lad. You put your ear up and listen to me rattle.'

Dieter was shocked when John took off his jacket and unbuttoned his checked shirt almost to his belly button; he was shocked because not only were there a few long blond hairs on his chest but he wore no undershirt. And Dieter thought it was very peculiar that John pulled his shirt down over his smooth shoulders, rather than taking the whole thing off. It reminded Dieter of the ladies in the paintings here at Sugar Hall, the ladies in ballgowns with their white shoulders and the bulge of their bosoms showing just above their frilled bust-lines: except John was too thin for bulges and too handsome for frills.

'Go on, lad,' John said, 'listen.'

Dieter pressed his ear, then his whole cheek up against John's hot and bony chest. John's skin smelled of carbolic and boot-polish and the sound of breath in his chest was the sound you hear under the waves at the seaside (and Dieter had been to Camford Sands). It was a deep in, and then a whoosh! out. It was the tide's rattle; the click-click-clicking of broken shell and salt-worn stones pushed back and forth on the seabed: it was the sound of something that had saved John from the army and the war. Dieter was thrilled, he sat back and wiped his ear, wet from listening.

'That's quite strange.' He looked up at John's bird-egg blue eyes: they seemed sad. 'Mr John, are you younger than my pa is?' Dieter corrected himself, 'Than my pa *was*…'

'Aye, a fair bit younger than Master Peter, your dad, like.' John coughed. 'Younger than he *was*.'

'Were you Pa's friend?'

John chuckled, his lungs hissing. 'Master Peter was a kind man, mind. He'd give us his shoes, he'd write letters when letters were needed. When my mam worked here I were younger 'n you and I'd see Master Peter when he was home.'

Dieter tried to picture John in Pa's patent leather dress shoes; he wondered if they'd creaked as much as they had on Pa's feet.

'When did you last see my pa?'

It looked like John was thinking. 'Can't say for certain. A long time after the war.'

'Why didn't he bring Ma and Sas here?'

'Him and Old Sugar – that's your granddad – well, they didn't see eye to eye. It was sad your dad doing what he done.'

Dieter noticed John's eyes seemed a darker blue.

'Why do you think he did it?' Dieter asked, because no one talked about Pa and that morning at Churchill Gardens when the policeman and the policewoman knocked on their door.

John rubbed his face with his hands. 'Oh, I don't know, lad. Maybe it's like a fox or a rabbit in a snare. They're caught, see, there's nothing they can do, but they're still alive. So what they do is gnaw at themselves, they gnaw at that leg 'til it's off, and then they're out of the trap. They die but they're set free, see?'

Dieter didn't. He tried to but it was like a pea-soup fog and he thought that nothing would ever be clear again.

John took in a lungful of dusty air. He pushed his slim shoulders back into his shirtsleeves and grasped his knees to stand. 'Right,' he smiled, 'do you want me to show you a secret?'

'What is it?'

'Wouldn't be a secret if I told you now would it?'

'Please!'

'It's a special place your pa showed me. It's dangerous, mind,' he winked, 'Your pa and me, we'd dare each other and we'd both lose. Cowards we were.'

Dieter wanted to shout, 'My pa wasn't a coward! My pa was in the war!' but John's eyes twinkled so he didn't.

'Yeah, cowards.' John turned on the step, and then he was muttering something Dieter couldn't understand and walking up the last of the back stairs to the attic rooms. 'You coming, then? I'm only offering this once.'

The tall corridor was dark. Of course Dieter had skipped along here before, but now, as his eyes adjusted he saw a door with a round golden handle in front of him.

John tapped on the door with his fingers. 'There's a secret in here, lad,' he whispered. 'A mystery.' John was patting the door now, palm down, as if the wood was a wild animal he had to tame. 'Still warm,' he muttered as he put an ear to it. 'There's stories in here, lad, ancient ones.'

'What stories?'

'Can't say.'

'Why?'

'Just can't.'

Dieter thought John's eyes looked sleepy, as if he was being hypnotised.

'What is in there?' Dieter whispered. He stepped closer, took a deep breath and touched the wood. Heat pulsed through his fingers and he gasped.

They both jumped at the sound of footsteps: a sweet voice began to sing.

'*Bak, bak, Kuchn! Der Bekker hot gerufn!*'

'That's your mother,' John twisted his head at the noise and he stepped away from the door. 'Reckon we better keep this for another day.'

'No, please!'

'*Wer s'wil gutn Kuchn machn, der mus hobn sibn Sachn,*' the voice sang.

'What's she singing about?'

'I don't know. That's Ma's language. She sang that to me when I was a baby.'

The song filtered up through the rat-gnawed floorboards. John cocked his head, and Dieter reached out and touched the shiny brass handle of the door. He shuddered as the blond hairs on his neck stood to attention, 'Please can we go in?'

John was putting the key in his pocket. 'It's an old story,' he muttered. 'Better let sleeping dogs lie.'

'*Bak, bak…*' his mother sang.

'But I like stories, I like dogs.'

'*Bak, bak...*'

'Let's keep it like that then. Don't want to fret your mother.' John walked away, tick-tack-tick in his hobnail boots and towards the singing voice that was getting louder.

'*Putter un Salz, Milch un Mel, un Safran, Safran: macht dem Kuchn gel!*'

John looked back. 'Come on, lad, we've got a leak to find.'

Dieter sprang into a run, but in the opposite direction: back to the servants' staircase.

'Hey, where you off to?' John cried after him.

Dieter was jumping down the steps because he'd had a brilliant idea, and the idea was all thanks to John. It was because of John unbuttoning that shirt of his: though it wasn't the creamy look of his white shoulders that got him thinking, it was the fact that – even with his terrible cough – John had worn no undershirt, and that was something Dieter had found the oddest thing. It was almost as odd as the small boy in the shed wearing nothing at all.

Thinking about that Dieter saw how he could coax the boy out with something better than cake, better than Milk of Magnesia, or even *The Eagle* (for perhaps the boy couldn't read, just like Tommy Perrot).

For this something better, Dieter need his pa's trunk.

The London Times, April 17th 1955

Edwardian Boys, 'Teddy Boys' fight in Deptford, *The London Times* reports.

Rival gangs of youths sporting Edwardian suits with stovepipe trousers and velvet-collared jackets became embroiled in fighting last Saturday night. Trouble started when a rowdy party of youths and a few girls arrived in the area. A knife was drawn when a member of one gang objected to being jostled. Police broke up the fight with some 40 youths held overnight. 'It's becoming a regular occurrence with these gangs,' a local woman said (she does not wished to be named). 'Fines are no good for these gangs, bring back the birch is what I say.'

The Shirt

5

Saskia Sugar was slumped in a nut-brown armchair by the crackling fire. She wore her mother's midnight-blue dress; a blue beret pulled down over her ears. Her ankle socks were baby-blue and her sandals red. Saskia wore the only arresting colours in this room because it was a predominantly brown room and this was why Lilia Sugar had chosen it for their bedroom: plain brown was a relief in this house. Of course this wasn't meant to be a bedroom; encased in wood panelling, softened by brown rugs and brown velvet curtains, stalked by an oily rocking horse with dead-glass eyes in one faraway corner; this room had once been a playroom for generations of Sugar children.

There was a book on Saskia's lap – *Sense and Sensibility*. For the last two days Saskia had been telling her brother how she wished he were a sister, she'd even called him 'Marianne'. It had been worse last week when Saskia was reading *Little Women* and cast herself as Jo March; Lilia as Marmie, and Dieter as all the other sisters: prim Meg and pretty Amy and poor coughing Beth. Dieter had shot her with his Dan Dare ray-gun.

Saskia loved pretend. Saskia wanted to be an actress. Saskia kept a copy of *Forever Amber* under her bed.

'Oh my, how the days are long!' she cried from the armchair because she didn't like these Easter holidays: Saskia was a London girl and she didn't yet understand the boredom of the countryside. She let the back of her palm drop on her forehead: her beret fell to the floor and she left it there. Sometimes her mother called Saskia a slattern.

Dieter kicked the fire-grate: sparks sprayed. 'How long are you going to be in here?'

'Oh, dear brother, but for a kind word or a smile!'

Dieter screwed up his face. 'Don't talk like that, Sas.'

'Whatever do you mean?'

'Like that. La-di-dah.'

Dieter knew what la-di-dah was because he'd sat through elocution lessons with Mrs Channon who smelled of pilchards and lived three streets away from Churchill Gardens. Ma told him she didn't want him sounding like her or the Wee-Hoos or the West Indian girl, Cynthia Nurse. After his lessons, Dieter would skip down the pavement muttering, 'Mrs Chaynon smeeels leek tinned saylmon.'

Still, Dieter didn't sound as posh as Saskia did now.

He remembered how only a few months ago Saskia was standing out on the balcony of Churchill Gardens and yelling down at Flinty Smith, 'Jezebel! Bleeding Jezebel! I'll have ya!' because Flinty had got off with Jack Perrot, Tommy's big brother and Saskia's dreamboat. Now she was speaking like the lady on their first television set who said, '*All-eggs-arn-drar Pay-lace*', and she'd gone from worshipping a crooning Johnny Brandon to idolising a bellowing singer called Mario Lanza.

Dieter couldn't keep up.

If only Sas was a normal sister, if only she was the sort of sister who wore trousers and thick shirts (like some of the girls wore at the village school) then Dieter could play British Bulldogs with her. And if Sas was like Cynthia he could play everything with her and he could tell her everything, too. It could be brother and sister who whispered in their beds at night as Ma slept her high-pitched sleep: it could be them who said things like, 'Why did we come to Sugar Hall?' and, 'What's going to happen?' and, 'Don't worry, Dieter, I'll make sure everything is all right.'

But Saskia wasn't like that at all.

He kicked the fire-grate again and sparks flew up from the logs. 'You've gone funny since we got here, Sas.'

'I haven't *gorn* anything, dear brother.'

'Yes you have. You wear Ma's dresses and you walk about the place and sigh, and you wear that thing,' he pointed at her chest.

Saskia gasped and clutched her hands to her. 'All young ladies wear a brassiere!'

Dieter kicked the cold paraffin heater; he had taken to kicking things and he remembered how that heater had made his eyes water and his throat stick in the freezing winter: he kicked it again.

'In any case, Dieter, we are posh,' Saskia told him.

Dieter saw the commode in the corner of the room. 'We're not.'

'Our pa is in Debretts.'

'What's Dee-breads?'

Saskia raised her chin, *Sense and Sensibility* dropped from her lap. 'It is a book of posh people. There are copies in the library. Our pa and our grandfather are listed.'

Dieter didn't want to hurt his sister's feelings by stating the obvious, so he walked to his metal bed and sat down. This rattled the metal end of Ma's bed, which in turn rattled the metal end of Saskia's bed. Ma had squared the army beds she'd found, here in front of the fire, and John had put the furniture and the Modesty Screens behind them. This kept the big-room draughts out rather than the modesty in but at least the room seemed smaller, and they were thankful for that. At first Dieter hated sharing a room with his mother and his sister. All at once he saw things he didn't want to see, like Ma sitting on her bed, her knee up to her chest and her fingers smoothing a stocking up her leg (and if he wanted he could watch as she hooked the stocking to her suspenders with a little white clasp).

Dieter picked a scab on his knee as the sun came in golden, and light fell over Ma's things on her dressing table. He watched them glitter: her malachite hairbrush and mirror, her abandoned lipsticks. Light flashed on the silver frame that held the photograph of Pa, Ma and Saskia, who was a tiny girl on Pa and Ma's wedding day. Dieter had always been jealous of that picture because he wished he was there.

'I am not thought of, yet,' he whispered.

In that photograph his father was a handsome man because it had been taken before his father's hair went to black strands and his eyes went foggy. Dieter shook his head because the tight feeling was coming again, the one between his privates and his belly button. He picked up a shoe and flung it at his sister.

'Hey!' she cried.

'I said, how long are you staying?'

'Oh, forever and ever I expect; it was Papa's wish for us both to live here.'

'I mean how long are you staying in-this-room, stupid!'

Saskia leapt up in mock horror and ran to the window. She pretended to smoke a cigarette in long, flowing movements, puffing and sighing. He watched her unlatch and push up the sash window.

'Once we get this place up and running' – she blew imaginary smoke – 'we can have balls and tennis parties and hunts and we can play croquet. We could open it as a girls' boarding school, like Malory Towers.'

Dieter thought of the place mats they used for breakfast; the pictures of men on horses jumping hedges, dogs following, and the writing that said 'The One That Got Away!' and 'Tally-ho!'

'Oi! For Christ sakes!' Saskia was suddenly yelling out of the window. 'Them bleeding cows! Look at the mess they've done down there. I bloody hate them cows!'

Dieter smiled because Saskia's old voice was back.

She sighed. It was a proper sigh this time. 'Do you miss the flat?' she asked, her voice just her voice.

'Yes.'

'Me too.'

There wasn't anything else to say, so Saskia pulled the window down, picked up her *Sense and Sensibility* and marched out.

As soon as she was gone, Dieter leapt off the bed and ran to the far corner of the room, to his father's trunk.

It was a big leather bulky thing, a wardrobe in itself because you could stand it on its end, click the clasps and it would unlock. No clothes would fall out because these were neatly folded in internal drawers or hanging from a silver rail in tissue paper.

Dieter opened it.

He was stunned for a moment because it smelled of Pa, of Pa, of Pa.

He hadn't seen much of his pa, but he knew he smelled of old books and pomade. Pa smelled of lemon and car wax.

Pa.

It was getting harder to recall his voice. Trying to remember him was like being stuck in the smog. Dieter had to peer hard into the murk and wait for the figure to come to him.

He knew that Pa hadn't been a Pa who sat with them in the evenings listening to the wireless. Yet he had been a Pa who took them to Regent's Park, the Natural History Museum, the Victoria and Albert Museum, *and* for tea and scrambled egg at The Lyons Corner House on The Strand on Saturdays. He was a Pa who only ever kissed Ma on the cheek, never on the lips, when he said goodbye on a Sunday evening and left them for the week. He was a Pa who left small brown envelopes of money on the sideboard; he was a Pa who took them for a week's holiday every second week of July to Camford Sands, and came home with sunburn on his nose and shoulders.

Dieter had a shoe of his father's; a brown brogue without laces. He kept it under his bed. Cynthia's mother, Mrs Nurse, had taken most of his father's things for The Salvation Army. Mrs Nurse stood in their living room and told them, 'Where's sense now, children, keeping them? It's keeping sadness.' And she made a noise that sounded like, 'cuh dear, cuh dear'. And so the whole family had scurried about the flat pinching what they could and squirrelling it away before Mrs Nurse had the lot for the tramps. Ma had packed this trunk with Pa's shirts and wrapped his hairbrush and comb in her best silk dress. Saskia pinched Pa's tobacco pipe and shaving foam brush, coloured like the tip of a wolf's tail, and all Dieter got was one shoe. He often thought of the other shoe and who might have it; who at the Salvation Army had found a use for Pa's one brown brogue shoe, with its leather tongue hanging out?

Dieter fell into his father's shirts, mouth open, he swallowed the smell and then he lay beneath them: the shirts swaying from their hangers on the silver rail. Dieter considered each one. He particularly liked the look of a crisp white shirt; it was the smartest. He unhooked it, stood up, chose a pair of dress trousers and pushed the trunk shut. There was nothing to do now but put his plan into action, so he skidded across the room and ran out into a rat-infested passage. Dieter took big creaking jumps down the wide oak staircase at the front of the house, his hand catching on the cobwebs between the barley twist rails, the shirt gripped under his arm. He counted, one step, two step, three step, four, until he reached twenty-three and landed with a slap on the huge black and white tiles of the grand hall.

He ran out, through the porch, down the grey stone steps, and into the red gardens. At the tennis court he paused to watch blue tit parents flit from tall weed to tall weed, their fledglings beneath them peep-peep-peeping and giving that little powder-winged flutter. The babies looked so fat and helpless, but the parents were thin, like Ma, and it made Dieter sad. In the patch of lawn beyond the pool he heard a giggle; it was Ma. Mr John was saying, 'Six weeks and them seeds'll all shoot up, you mark my words. New life takes that long. You got to thin them out mind. You got to be harsh.'

They were still digging up the croquet lawn; planting, making plans.

April sun was shining on Sugar Hall and Dieter cursed himself because he had forgotten sandwiches. Any waiting, Dieter knew, had to involve sandwiches. That was why you had sandwiches at train stations and bus depots and sometimes on ships. Ma had come to England on a train and a ship and she told him that when she arrived at Harwich she was given a box in which there were two cheese sandwiches.

'Two cheesed sandwiches,' Ma said, eyes bright, 'and they were the best meal I have ever had.'

Fulham and Hammersmith Chronicle, Jan 4th 1946

Construction work will begin this year on the site to be named the Churchill Gardens Estate in Pimlico, London. Bombings during the war destroyed many buildings, and it is an ideal area for redevelopment. Two young architects, Powell and Moya won the competition held by Westminster Council. Churchill Gardens will be comprised of 1,661 dwellings, in flats and maisonettes, spread over 31 acres overlooking the Thames. It will be built as 36 blocks and completed in four phases; the first phase should be completed by the end of the decade. The flats will be heated by waste hot water pumped under the River Thames from Battersea Power Station. An ingenious device!

Lilia Digs

6

When Peter Sugar carried Lilia Sugar over the threshold of Flat 52C, Shelley House, Churchill Gardens, she screamed with pleasure. She wasn't a new bride, they had been married five years, but still she begged for this one little thing, this giggling lift into a new home. Lilia wasn't someone who liked to show herself, but as she stumbled into the bare flat and saw it so neat, so clean, so brand spanking new, so empty, it made her heart sing and her mouth shriek, 'Peter, oh, Peter!'

He set her down and picked one of her stray blonde hairs from the front of his coat. 'Sh! Lily, don't make a scene.'

She smiled because Peter suited her so well: he disliked intimacy as much as she did, but today things were different.

'I cannot help this! Look! So new and bright!' She marched off down a small corridor to the three bedrooms (three!): one for her, one for Saskia and one for Dieter.

'You will spend more time with us, yes?' she said and the words echoed off the bare white walls.

Lilia pushed open each door, crying out at the shiny new floors, the spick and span windows and the river view. She breathed in the smell of new paint and plaster. 'So beautiful,' she said to herself, and she erased the memory of their last flat, a dark Victorian terrace with a shared lavatory in the backyard. How a man like Peter Sugar could be so poor, she didn't know. He told her he was cut off; he said they had no choice. Lilia's fingers tingled on the handle of the bathroom door.

'Oh, Peter! Look! A bath! A lavatory!' Lilia couldn't help pointing and naming things as if she were an explorer discovering a new species. She touched the cold porcelain; it was bright and white and never used. How wonderful, she thought, we are the first: this is a new country, a new planet, fresh and clean. Lilia tried to remember the English phrase. Yes, this was a *clean slate*. Suddenly she regretted packing up their possessions from their last flat; Lilia wanted everything to be new.

She walked into the largest bedroom. She supposed that this would be her room, and their room when Peter was at home. It was so beautiful, empty like this. The golden floor and the bright white walls, the new windows and – was that...? Yes: it was a radiator. Lilia felt a happy lump in her throat.

Peter walked in.

'It is beautiful,' she said.

'I'm sure.'

Peter was in one of his black moods. He held his hat in one hand, ready to be placed back on his head. He marched up to the large window and stared down at the Thames. For a moment Lilia felt anger, she almost yelled, 'Well go, go then!' But she had learned over these years that with Peter Sugar everything was not how it seemed and this everything would just have to do. He had tried to tell her once, in his own way; he had said the words 'a certain kind of love' and 'marriage' and 'I would like a son'. At the time it had been more than enough for Lilia, for what else did she have? A ready-made daughter who needed a father, that was all. And anyway, didn't she think him quite the thing as the doodlebugs fell and he lit her cigarette in the darkness of the tube station – the Angel – didn't her hard heart flutter when she saw his wide gold signet ring? And when he spoke of Cambridge and a place called Sugar Hall, didn't her heart swell more? It had stopped swelling of course and she was so glad; in fact it reduced to quite a normal size a year after they were married and Dieter was born; when they still lived in Peter's shabby flat and he'd pawned the signet ring and never spoke of Sugar Hall again. Lilia's heart maintained a regular beat when he came home on Saturday morning and left Sunday night. Lilia's heart was quite immune when all Peter did was read *The Secret Garden* to Saskia on the days he was home, in fact her heart was fine, as long as Peter left the brown envelopes of money on the kitchen table before he left. They were kind to each other, she held onto that, and she asked little of his life, and he would entertain the children every Saturday and Sunday. Lilia had found herself quite content.

'It is so ugly,' he said, staring out at the Thames.

'What?'

'Well, it is, Lilia. You wouldn't understand.'

'What do I not understand?'

'Modernity. Like this.' His long fingers gestured back at the empty flat. 'It is ugly.'

Lilia bunched her hands into fists.

'And that...' Peter pointed out of the-soon-to-be-her-bedroom window, at Battersea Power Station, '...a monstrosity.'

'I like it. It is strong. Powerful.' Lilia bunched her fists tighter and glared at the tall chimneys.

Peter shrugged and placed his grey trilby on the crown of his head. He was looking so tired, she thought, she must save coupons and cook meat for him at the weekends.

'So, Lily, the movers will come later today.'

'Yes.'

'And I will see you on Saturday.'

She was still staring down at the rumbling swell of the Thames.

'Lily, did you hear what I said?'

She had forgotten him, 'Oh yes, Peter dear, I will see you.' She walked to him, her heels harsh on the new floor and she pecked him on one cheek. He always smelled so nice, his cologne fresh as cut lemon.

'Goodbye,' he said and he turned, his grey coat flowing as he walked.

'I will cook meat, beef if I can find!' she shouted after him. She counted up her ration tickets in her head, but the door had closed and he was gone. Lilia was glad the children weren't with her, she would pick them up later, but they would all be in by the end of the week. She turned on the spot, her arms out and she cried out, 'Wheeeeeeee!' She didn't care if the new neighbours heard; Lilia was happy.

Now she was finding the old spade went into the croquet lawn of Sugar Hall quite easily: like a hot knife through butter, she thought, and she smiled at the English phrase.

Digging. It was strange. Here she was digging up Sugar Hall's lawn: Lilia Fisch, Lilia Sugar, or whoever she was now. She pressed her foot down hard on the top of the spade John Phelps had found in one of those awful sheds; she tugged on the wooden handle and the red earth came away as easily as stewed meat from a bone. She felt the shadow of the Hall behind her, and the huffing and puffing body of John to her side. She liked John working at her side; at last Lilia was grateful for human contact.

'You see, six weeks, six weeks you'll see something,' he was saying and shaking a packet of seeds.

The spring sun struggled above them and Lilia noted the faded and crisp snowdrops and the fat buds on the rhododendron bushes that crowded this garden; she pushed her spade into the old croquet lawn and the earth came up redder than before.

Cynthia Nurse's Five Rules of the Wee-Hoos

1) You must die rather than tell our secrets
2) Any bad fights will be punished with The Wee-Hoo Snakebite
3) British Bulldogs, What's the Time Mister Wolf, Skipping and Murder will always be our favourite games
4) You must pass the tests to join the Gang. They are hard
5) A Wee-Hoo is a Wee-Hoo for life

A Murder

7

The long black shed smelled of creosote and setting onions. Dust danced. In this magic place Dieter had found twenty-three toothbrushes, thirty-one puttees and a green army jacket that had reached his knees because the army had lived at Sugar Hall during the last war.

He was sitting on the skin of an old air-balloon, Pa's white shirt and dress trousers in his lap. He'd found the balloon the first morning he woke at the Hall. This was the morning he'd dared to go out into the vast gardens alone as Ma and Saskia snored beneath dusty blankets and their overcoats. It was the morning Dieter first found the black water in the swimming pool, the weed-pitted tennis court, the little gravestones with the Roman names, and this line of long sheds.

Two of the sheds were roofless, rotting; three were padlocked shut, but this one was easy to open. He remembered it had been such an adventure for a first morning, and he'd felt like that orphan girl in that book his father liked to read out loud, *The Secret Garden*. Yes, Dieter felt like Mary Lennox: he'd felt brave and spiteful and he'd soon forgotten the *ye-ye-ye-ye-ye* of the vixen pawing the lawn for worms, he soon forgot the screeches of the early morning owls as he searched this shed for treasure and found the balloon crumpled in a corner.

What a find it had been!

He thought it was a parachute at first, and for a moment he didn't breathe because he knew that with a parachute comes a parachute-*ist*. He'd read about them in *The Eagle*. Parachute-*ists* were the soldiers who came down in enemy territory and said, 'Oh cripes, Jerry's on the loose!' and asked for bread and ham from French peasants who said, '*Oui*'. Dieter followed the strings, expecting to find a shrivelled old soldier attached, but instead there was a wicker basket. He had read Jules Verne's *Five Weeks in a Balloon*, the story of Samuel Ferguson flying across magical places called Zanzibar and Timbuktu, so he recognised this as an olden-day hot air balloon and the source of a great adventure. Once he wiped the decades of dirt from a patch he saw it had vibrant colours – blues and yellows and reds in banded patterns across its skin and Dieter was so excited he'd danced around that old balloon whooping, until the silverfish, the spiders, the owl pellets and the sunlit air of the shed danced too. This was the moment Ma had opened the shed door and screamed, 'Out, out, out! You must never, never! You stay in the house! I forbid it, Dieter!' Yes, she'd dragged him out and slapped his legs until he cried.

Ma had not hit him before.

Of course he sneaked back whenever he could. In fact Dieter was using Ma's mending patches and thread from her sewing-box because it was his Big Plan: he was going to use this balloon to fly back to London, to Cynthia and the Wee-Hoos, they would get such a shock!

On top of Pa's white shirt was his letter: 'To The Boy In The Shed'. Dieter was waiting and it was hard. To help he sang one of Ma's songs.

'*Putter un Salz, Milch un Mel un Safran, Safran,*' he tried. He had learned this song like he'd learned that other song, '*Frer-a jack-a, frer-a jack-a, dormey voo! Dormey voo! Somi lama Tina, somi lama*

Tina! Ding Dang Dong!' Dieter had no idea what the words meant, but still he sang, his voice clear and high and pure, '*Putter un Salz, Milch un Mel un Safran, Safran: macht dem Kuchn gel!*'

Sunlight crept out from behind a cloud and poured through the mildewed window: three Red Admirals twitched, trapped in cobwebs. Dieter tried to think of nice things, he thought of the green shoots of bluebells coming up in the wood behind the Hall. He tried to think what Cynthia would be doing now because she wouldn't be sitting in a stupid shed with a stupid shirt in her hands. She'd still be on the Wasteland with the rest of the Wee-Hoos, playing, *Dip, dip, dip, my little ship, sails on the ocean, like a cup and saucer, you are not it*; Tommy Perrot would be pinching Cynthia and saying, 'C'mon Cyn, let's have a go at sardines, go on, Cyn!' and Cynthia would be putting her nose in the air, her brown eyes flashing, because Tommy was the only one who wanted to do all those girl-and-boy things.

The Red Admirals twitched some more, and suddenly Dieter felt like crying. He was so cold his lips were numb and he decided to try another song because singing helped Ma and Saskia; he decided to sing something Cynthia had taught him, something she called a Calypso.

'London, is the place for meee!' he cried. 'London, this lovely citee! You can go to France or America, India, Asia or Australia, but you must come back, to London citee!'

His cry echoed in the empty shed, his breath coming out in puffs of white. Dieter thought about London: he thought of the broken buildings and the cracks, he thought of the wide spaces and the rubble, and he thought of all those adventures he was missing. He gazed up at the dust dancing and the cobwebs pulsing, and Dieter heard a noise.

'Pop!' it said. Then, 'Pap!'

There were sparks and a shimmer that had to settle. Then, by the window and the filthy crates, there was a boy's face.

The face was moving as if the boy was already standing up, but there was no body beneath it.

The Cheshire Cat, Dieter thought, as the face moved towards him. He gripped his pa's crisp shirt tight, he stopped breathing, but he was determined that this time he wouldn't run away.

The face was making a strange noise, as if tiny wings were fluttering in its throat. Dieter felt the balloon's skin crackle beneath him; there was electricity: a crackle beneath his bottom and a crackle in the air.

He's not a duppy, Cyn, Dieter thought, he won't hurt me.

'I – I brought you this shirt, these trousers,' Dieter said. 'I thought you'd be cold.'

Then Dieter wondered how the boy could use the shirt if he didn't have a body.

A hot breeze of golden sparks cut through the freezing air and suddenly the boy was all there: his chest, his arms and legs, his neck and around that a silver collar. The boy shook himself and stretched up: Dieter had never seen anyone so naked, not even himself. The boy walked from those filthy storage chests and it was soundless, but Dieter watched the pit-pat, pit-pat of his footprints in the dust. Pit-pat, pit-pat; like steps in the sand and no one there.

The boy was thin. He was small, but Dieter couldn't tell how old he was.

The boy hunched over and bent into a squat. His arms dropped, hands palm-up and circling in the dust like little fish. The golden sparks were gone and Dieter saw the boy was pale for all his blackness.

'Are you well?' Dieter asked and he wondered if Ma had ginger beer or ginger biscuits because that always helped him.

The boy's head fell to one side as if he was listening for something.

Dieter clearly saw that collar now; there was fancy writing on it and a delicate chain dangled from a silver link onto the boy's skinny chest. The collar was tight; creases in the boy's neck showed above it.

'What's that?' Dieter pointed.

The boy was blank.

Dieter laid the shirt and trousers on the floor and he stretched his finger out to the boy's neck and touched the metal. 'Oh,' Dieter said. 'Oh,' as a Corona-pop fizz crashed through his fingertips and up his arm. He felt faint. 'Oh.' Dieter shook his buzzing fingertips.

The boy sniffed.

Dieter felt a sickness that reminded him of sucking too many iced lollies. An odd bubbling came up in him as if he'd spent too long in the sea under a hot sun: he could smell it too; the salt of the sea and a warm sweetness.

Dieter roused himself.

'I live here. Do you, too?' he breathed. 'I live here with my mother and my sister, Saskia. She's miles older than me. Four or five years at least.' Dieter was surprised he didn't know exactly, because he didn't think of Saskia exactly at all. He picked up a garden cane and hit the ground with it. He decided to try his best Mrs Channon EL-O-CU-TION voice.

'My name is Dieter, Dieter Sugar, and we've been here for such a long time, since February. We came from London. Have you been to London? No? Well, anyway, that's my real home though they tell me this is too. It's my grandfather's house you see and my Pa is dead. I'm the only Sugar left.'

The boy's head jerked.

'But there are these things called duties and they might tear it down. That's what the old man said. That's the old man in that scabby office off Piccadilly. He was rude to Ma, so I hated him. I hated him and I hated the lady Ma made me see because I was down in the dumps. That lady smelled of animal skins and I bit her…'

Dieter hit the cane – snap-snap – the boy flinched.

'Sorry! That's a bit noisy isn't it? I do hate noise when I'm sick. Should I get you some ginger beer? No? Anyway, the thing is we're here because I've no cousins or second cousins or secret relations or anything, not on Pa's side. Pa had an older brother but he died when he was young. So I'm the last as Saskia doesn't count, even though she's my sister because my pa wasn't her pa.'

Dieter caught his breath but he couldn't stop, this was the most he'd said to anyone in months. 'But Ma doesn't like to talk about that. Ma doesn't like to talk about much. She won't talk about Pa. He died. He hanged himself. At Christmas.' Dieter was surprised how easily that came. 'Sas has another Pa, nobody knows where he lives, which I say is pretty careless. I think if he wanted to find us he could, he could send Saskia birthday presents or Christmas cards. I think he's a rotten Pa and I think Saskia thinks so too.' Dieter's throat clicked but the words kept coming. 'And Ma says we're an odd bunch because she has dark eyes and I have green eyes and Saskia has very blue eyes. Ma says we're as mixed as a litter of cats. Do you want to join my gang? We're the Wee-Hoos and we're the best gang on the Wasteland, you have to join…'

This talking was like eating a sliver of cake but wanting more until the cake plate is empty and your mouth and your cheeks are sticky and your stomach's a drum, and no matter how much Dieter hated what he was saying – all of the secrets that tumbled from his lips – he couldn't help but talk because the boy was there twitching his head like a marionette.

'I brought you a shirt and trousers,' Dieter finally whispered because the life had gone out of him. It was the feeling of chloroform – and Dieter had had his tonsils out – it was the feeling of a freeze moving along his veins. He looked at the boy. 'Who are you?' he said.

The boy didn't speak, but he did let his head fall to his other shoulder, and when he did this the small bones in his neck clicked and popped with the movement (because it had been so long). When Dieter heard this sound his ears whined, his chin fell to his chest, and his nose dropped splashes of blood onto his father's white shirt, and then the world was gone.

In the darkness Dieter might have heard a sniffing, a crack of more bones moving, and then the smacking of lips, perhaps the lapping of a tongue. He might have heard a soft moan, and then the hurried flutter of countless soft wings.

Sunday Pictorial, April 17th 1955

Blonde Model Accused of Killing Racing Car Driver

A blonde model, Ruth Ellis, has confessed to shooting her lover, 25-year-old racing driver, David Blakely, outside the Magdala public house in north London on Easter Sunday, April 10th. Ellis has made an appearance in court on April 11th and is currently held on remand. (Pictures p. 3&4).

John Phelps' Secret

8

'There now, steady. Let me get you up.' As John knelt to lift Dieter from the shed floor, the lad seemed to come to; then he was jerking, his legs little pistons kicking.

'Hey! Hey now, steady!' John wiped Dieter's bloody nose with his handkerchief. 'Head back. Hold it here, lad. Press down. Nothing to fret about.'

He let Dieter's head rest in the crook of his neck and their chests met: good-heart to tic-tacky heart. He felt the boy shiver against him. The shed was freezing.

'What have you been getting up to, then? We've been looking for hours.' John felt the lad's lips tremble against his neck. 'Steady. Steady. There now.'

'Is he still here?' Dieter whimpered.

'Who?'

'My friend.'

'What friend's that?'

'Did he take the shirt?'

'Now then.'

'Is he here?'

John saw an envelope on the floor, a man's white shirt with blood on it and a pair of smart trousers. A pity. Hard to get out, blood was. John saw what must have been the lad's splashes of blood in the dust, yet they were smeared as if someone had already tried to get them up with a damp cloth.

'He was here,' Dieter whispered.

In the darkness of the shelves John saw a sparking light. He frowned and an old feeling rose up in him like bad stew. 'It's just you and me here,' he said. Of course the boy was delirious, he was seeing things or doing that thing that lonely children do; he was making things up.

John felt Dieter straighten up in his arms.

'What's the matter with your cheek, Mr John?' he asked.

John had forgotten and suddenly it hurt: the wound was just below the eye, high on the cheekbone. When he'd walked up the feeble plank steps into this shed, Rosie was perched on his shoulder. Then, would you credit it, the damn bird pecks him hard in the cheek and flies off. John knew she didn't mean it; he'd had her from an egg. He knew this was a warning. Rosie was spooked.

'Come on now.'

'Tell him I'll be back,' Dieter croaked. 'He didn't hurt me. I just got a nosebleed.'

'This your shirt?'

'It's his now.'

'Let's leave it here then.'

Dieter was heavy in his arms or perhaps John was a little weak. Boy-breath warmed John's neck as he glanced once more at the strange light and those sparks in the air. He rushed to the door singing 'Onward Christian Soldiers' because it was a hymn that made him feel right and John Phelps didn't want to remember being afraid. He jumped down the steps to the grass and he felt a little better. He marched along the path, lungs rattling and breath cutting into him like a gutting knife, and John felt foolish: it was all imagination, it was all stuff and nonsense. Rosie must have felt foolish too because she swooped down from a fat oak, landed in front of him and shyly waddled to him like one of those American lady movie stars: hip-to-hip-to-hip-to-hip (except Rosie had a stick in her black beak).

'That's a sorry is it, girl?' John felt the burn of his gouged cheek.

Rosie bounced with him as he walked.

'Fair enough,' he said and he carried Dieter up through the red gardens of rhododendrons, through the graveyard patterned with small headstones, past the black swimming pool, the old tennis court pitted with yellow-headed weeds, and towards the great grey house and, because he was carrying the boy, John Phelps walked in through the front door.

John liked to hear his Christian name from Lilia Sugar's lips, but when she ran to him crying, 'John, ah, John, there is blood!' as he stood in the grand hall with her boy in his arms, he felt like her hero. His weak chest puffed as Lilia pushed him along the passageway and down the worn stone steps to the kitchen.

'John, John, quick, quick, John!' she cried and the words made him feel warm. Of course she was making a silly fuss, but he didn't mind.

His boots tapped on the stone (whenever John walked down to the kitchen he felt the tension of above-stairs leave him. It was foolish, but there you were.) He knew this kitchen – its black range, its long pine table. Years ago his mother had stood at that Belfast sink cleaning for the master while he sat at the table polishing silver. He didn't know how many years his mother had worked for old man Sugar, but she hadn't put a foot in the door since Lilia arrived. Few from the village had; they had their prejudices and that was that. They called her 'the German woman'.

John sat the boy on the spindle-back chair by the range and Lilia was on the lad like a rash, as if he was melting good as a block of ice in the sun and she was scooping up the water.

'Oh, my boy, my Dee,' she crooned and John watched her pick at the dried blood under the lad's nose. 'How? How?'

'He had a funny turn, that's all.'

'I do not…'

'He fainted,' John explained.

He knocked his head against the wooden Jenny above him. The drying clothes swung and he tried not to look up, but some of her *thing*s were there: so light, so delicate and intimate, dancing in the air. He saw Lilia's peach satin camisole; Lilia's coral pink nightgown and he blushed.

'Warm water, get warm water,' she ordered and John was happy to shoot off to the scullery for a bowl.

'I'll make a pot, too,' he called out, like it was just them and time for tea.

The mangle with its green arm stood with half a pretty red dress hanging out of it. John's gifts hung in here: two pheasants and three rabbits; he'd have to skin, pluck and gut them before they turned. He smiled because there was only him to help her with things like that. On the floor in the corners of the scullery he saw four stained enamel bowls. They were filled with dust, dirt, and dead woodlice: John remembered these bowls.

'Sprinkle them with sugar then, John,' his mam had told him, and she'd pour in warm water and leave them in the scullery corners. She told him it helped some, Mam said things didn't go missing so much, bells to locked and forgotten rooms didn't ring as often if she left out something sweet. 'Warm sugared water, that's his favourite,' Mam said, 'that'll keep him quiet for the night.'

Mam swore each morning that the bowls were empty.

John shivered in the dark scullery. He marched back into the kitchen, empty-handed.

Lilia was already wiping under Dieter's nose with a flannel.

'I'm all right, Ma. Really I am,' the lad was saying.

There were footsteps on the stone steps. John looked up and saw Saskia. He couldn't believe that pretty Lilia was her mother. He didn't much care for the girl.

'Oh, Ma, what's he gone and got himself into now?' she said.

John watched her jump the last few steps and land with a flat-footed thump on the flagstones. She pulled out a chair, scraping it across the stone. He leant against the sink and stared at her. John had found he could do this, because to this girl he was invisible.

She was laying out *The Sunday Pictorial* and eating something black because it had stained her lips and her teeth. He watched as she sneaked black coils of liquorice from her front pocket into her mouth and pushed the wad of chewed black sweet further in with her fingers. She smacked her lips and John saw black dribbles of spit collect, before her big tongue came out to soak them up.

John stepped closer; he could make out the headline on the girl's newspaper. 'Blonde Model Accused of Killing Racing Car Driver.'

John and his mam had heard about that woman on the radio: a woman who had taken a gun and shot a man on Easter Sunday. The radio called her Ruth Ellis and Mam had written the name down with her pencil. 'That's London for you,' Mam had said, and she switched the Bush off.

Lilia swooped down and snatched the newspaper.

'Ma!' the girl cried.

John watched Lilia fold the paper and place it behind the bread bin. *'Jetzt nicht, später!'* she said and he tilted his head at the strange words. Lilia turned back to her son, a scone in her hand. 'Eat, Dee.' It was a command. 'Eat.'

John knew he could watch this family forever.

Notice on behalf of the Borough of Harwich
14th December 1938

To Borough of Harwich residents

Please note that the first party of children have arrived on the 2nd December, with a figure of 198, age ranges from four to eighteen. At present they are housed at the Dovercourt holiday camp, established by Billy Butlin and opened for one season. On arrival the children were fed cheese sandwiches and tea. The children were all medically assessed before they left for England, and again by Dr Phelan and myself before leave to land was granted. All the children were stripped to the waist and heart, chest, eyes and throat examined. The children were found to be in a healthy condition and the majority compared favourably with the English of their own age. Arrangements have been made for the cleansing and delousing for any children that required it.

Yours truly,

Nurse Hayward

Dachkammer

9

It had been a long day and Lilia was glad night had come. Owls cried out like startled children from the cedar of Lebanon. The vixen called ye-ye-ye-ye-ye from the lawn as she did every night, black paws scratching for fat worms in the turf. Lilia had begun to note the habits of this place.

She'd decided to start on the top floor. She had a torch and rat poison filled her cardigan pockets. In her hand Lilia gripped the iron ring of keys she'd found hanging from those silent bells down in the kitchen.

Up here were the attic rooms.

She walked along the passage, trying each door, checking each lock. A single bat flitted above her head. A few months ago the bat would have petrified her. We get used to many things, she thought.

After the fright of today, after seeing Dieter in John's arms, white-faced but with that blood, Lilia was locking up tonight. She was securing the place. She was protecting her boy. There were so many doors and so many keys she simply wanted to shout, 'Get out!' along the passageways and down the staircases, but she knew it would take more than that.

It had started on their very first night here. Lilia had felt it as soon as she stepped over the threshold of Sugar Hall; she wasn't a fool. She didn't know, didn't want to know what 'it' was, but she'd wanted to run out of the front door with her children, she'd wanted to scream, 'No, not this!' But where else could they go? They had nothing, only this place and for how long Lilia had no idea, so if they had to share it then share it they would. They were squatters. They were maroons. Marooned in this great house among the trees.

Yes, these few months were not long enough for decisions. Her parents had made their decision in minutes. They had sent her to England, their Liliana, the youngest and so the one to go. She had been fifteen: her brothers nineteen and twenty-one. Lilia tested a key in an old lock and shook the memory away.

She opened the next door. As she switched on the light she checked for objects, for value. Oldness held no charm for Lilia, though she had discovered she could sell it and if she could sell it then maybe they could survive. In a house where objects moved, where they disappeared, what did it matter if she joined in, too? She'd started on the knick-knacks, the trinkets that wouldn't be missed because who was here to miss them? She had taken the train into Cheltenham one day in March, once the snows were manageable, with a small willow-pattern vase, two silver letter-openers, a red-faced Toby jug, and crested silverware wrapped up in a box held firm on her lap. She had walked the Regency streets searching for the Pawnbroker's sign. In the end she'd skulked into a small antique shop with her package. Now the dealers came to her, and only last week she had thrown caution to the wind and sold the billiard table. A large truck had rattled up the drive and Lilia thought she would be caught, she thought the neighbours would see, and then she had giggled because of course there were no neighbours here, just the black and white cows and the lone farmer who crossed their land twice a day crying, 'Hep, hep, hep. On girls, on girls. Hep!'

It was strange now to go into that long billiard room and see nothing but a low hanging light fitting, its green shades illuminating a space, because what do you call a billiard room with no billiard table? All these proper names and proper rooms and proper Englishness, it was nonsensical; all these ancient things gathering spite and dust.

Lilia tried another key.

These weeks, these months, they were too little a time for a new life.

She continued along the passageway. Not one of these damned keys worked.

Juniper had left an hour ago, and tonight Juniper had sat at the kitchen table and pleaded with her. 'I wish you would consider it, Lilia darling. Not for tradition and all that humbug, but just to get you out, to see people, to make you part of our little community.'

Lilia squirmed. 'I'm not sure I like these people.'

'Ha! Oh, you are a blast, a breath of fresh air!'

'But they have such dogs, you say…'

'The gentlest of creatures, foxhounds. Though you must be about yourself with working dogs, keep them keen. We have a splendid Master of Hounds…'

'Pardon?'

'Master of Hounds.' Juniper raised her eyebrow because Lilia had started to laugh and she couldn't stop.

When her laughter was exhausted they left dogs and talked of husbands. They talked a little of love.

'It must have been terrible for you, darling, ghastly,' Juniper said.

Lilia agreed.

Now in the attic, she listened to the rats scuttle beneath the floorboards and stamped hard. The noise echoed.

'*Raus hier!*' she yelled.

It was strange how it came to her quite easily in this house, her German, and her other language; the old songs of her mother's she had worked hard to forget. She had been unable to speak it for so long. Literally, the words wouldn't come.

She shone her torch on the next door, but it was wide open. The door had a round, golden handle. Lilia knew John called this the blue room, he had told her to leave this door be. That was his phrase: 'Leave it be, Mrs Sugar.'

Lilia walked in. She tried the light switch but the bulb flickered then popped. She started, but soon she was smiling at her skittishness and using her torch. Lilia supposed this room was called the 'blue room' simply because it was blue. Its walls were a blue that was brighter than John Phelps' eyes, bluer than the birds that twit-twitted in her kitchen garden. It was an ice blue. There were two small brass beds for older children, side by side. Lilia shone her light. The beds were made, not stripped. Patched quilts covered them and there were deep indentations in one, as if a something had crawled in here and nested. Lilia shuddered. She moved the torch to the only window; iron bars crossed it and the bright blue curtains were open, they trembled in the draft. Lilia inspected the corners of the room – it was odd that there was little dust. There was an open chest against one wall, overflowing with children's toys and books. It was eerie. A large spinning top poked out, a red fire engine, three porcelain dolls, a golden teddy bear, and against the wall a pair of stilts. On the floor she saw a small clown and a woolly monkey, both holding cymbals, keys in their backs. And there, a neatly arranged tower of alphabet blocks. Lilia tried to read the words they spelled out.

She stepped closer: she shone her light directly on them.

She saw his name amongst the letters.

'D-I-E-T-E-R'

She gasped.

Her beam of light flickered so she marched to the blocks and kicked them out of order. She shook her torch, the beam came back, but there was nothing but scattered letters now.

Lilia shook her head; she was tired, exhausted. Dieter had come up here to play that was all; she would forbid him to do this again. She gazed down at the chest of toys and made herself calculate how much they might be worth, she had heard that antique toys sold well. The billiard table money would be gone soon.

Lilia felt colder in this room, if that were possible. She shivered and she saw her breath come in white puffs in the torchlight. She balled up her free hand in her cardigan pocket, her knuckles rubbing against the pellets of rat poison as the freezing air tightened her chest. She stared at the fat and garishly striped spinning top and she wondered if Peter had slept in here as a young boy; it was a nursery after all. She thought of him in this bluest of blue rooms and her stomach twisted.

Lilia backed out.

Once she stood on the threshold she felt a little warmer, a little calmer, and she reached out to close the door. She pulled on the brass handle, but the door was stuck. Lilia directed her torch to the floor, she checked for carpet, rug, but nothing was caught. She examined the hinges; they seemed rust free. She tugged again, but the door truly was stuck solid. As her hand tightened on the round handle her skin tingled, and then she felt a sharp burn.

'Ahh!' she cried, but she wouldn't let go. 'Close!' she spat and she jerked her whole body with the effort. Lilia was going to fight and she pulled and she pulled again.

All at once there was no resistance and the door shut, the slam echoed. Lilia fell back on the passageway floor, bottom first.

'*Verdammt*!' she cried as her torch rolled along the ground.

The passageway was musty beneath her. There was a draft like cold breath up her skirt because she had changed when Juniper arrived. Trousers, she thought, I should always wear trousers in this old place no matter who visits; there is no shame in trousers. She touched her stinging palm, but the light was too dim to see. She blew on the skin the way she would blow on her children's scalds and grazes.

She lay there.

It is strange how we bury these things, she thought, and it is strange how and when they come back. At the oddest of times: when I am peeling potatoes, when I am polishing the silver. Lilia wasn't expecting this, not now, because as she stared into darkness all Lilia could see was the wind in his blond hair, the dancing wind teasing Peter's dead face.

Peter had died hardly a whisper of days ago. Was it one hundred and eighteen days: one hundred and twenty-two? Lilia had tried to wipe the memory of the police knocking at her door that morning, the policeman and the policewoman, and it had been so early, dawn just coming. She had tried to erase the memory of seeing Peter hanging from a rope, the birds flit-flitting from branch to branch of the London plane tree in the courtyard of Churchill Gardens. It was as if the birds were trying to wake him, to warn him. She had tried to wipe the memory as clean as she had wiped her surfaces in her kitchen at number 52C.

Peter had killed himself hardly a whisper of days ago.

The bank of water was gushing over her now. She had been holding it back for so long it was a relief. Lilia was panting, eyes wide.

She saw herself, fifteen years old and picking tired and mouldy winter berries from the hedgerow of the English holiday camp in Dovercourt. They had travelled so far to get there, through strange names; Hook of Holland, Harwich, to this place, to this England.

'Hook of Holland,' Lilia said from the rug.

She had been one of the eldest. Some were so small, such tiny children. She had had a baby thrust into her hands at Schlesischen station. Take. Take. Take, the parents had said. '*Nimm es, nimm es!*'

Her two brothers had looked bored, but her mother and her father were trying not to cry, hugging the life out of her on the platform.

'It's a holiday. It is a holiday, Lily.'

'A holiday,' her father told her, 'you remember that.'

'You will stay with nice people.'

'See you, sis. Take care of yourself.' That was Ari, she was sure: Ari her favourite brother, Ari who kept her secrets.

She hadn't thought of Ari for so long.

That evening at Schlesischen station she had been angry. She didn't cry. She held her nose up and didn't kiss them. She walked onto the train, she'd show them; sending her away like this. Then it was too late because the other children were crowded at the window and she couldn't see a thing. The train moved and her parents were gone. Lilia thought of her brother's cheeks, Ari's cheeks, they were like Dieter's.

Now Lilia was seeing it all: the moist, mouldy berries in the hedges at Dovercourt, those berries in her hand, in her mouth, and then the wind in Peter's blond hair and the birds in the London plane tree. There was the dark stairwell on Mülhauser Strasse, too, and the Quakers she'd lived with in Nailsworth – Mr and Mrs Dunbarr – the smell of their pigs, the sweet and sour taste of Mrs Dunbarr's gooseberry jam, and the silence of the cold Quaker meeting house. They were a kindness those meetings, sitting in that hall and watching the clock's brass pendulum tick – tick-tock, tick-tock – while she tried not to think. Then there was the day she had thrown herself down the steps of the farmhouse because suddenly she knew (it had been such a silly idea, but one of the land girls had told her it would do the trick, get rid of what she didn't want and get rid of it fast). Then four years later there was the scratch of a match on sandpaper in the silence of a blackout, she remembered the sound, there was a handsome man – Peter Sugar – lighting her cigarette in the tube station as they waited for the doodlebugs to be finished falling on London, the city that wasn't hers.

Lilia gasped.

That last part was like a silly film, and like a silly film she had edited out so much.

Yes, her mother's dimples, the Hook of Holland, John Phelps' blue blue eyes, the silence of the Quaker meetings in the cold meeting house, the kindness of Mrs Dunbarr's hands once Saskia was born and Lilia sobbed and told her about that dark stairwell on Mülhauser Strasse, the boy in the brown uniform and what he did to her (and it was something she hadn't told her own mother because where was her mother to tell?) Yes, there was this everything, and then there were the crowds at Schlesischen station, and waving at Mutti and Papa when she couldn't even see them. There was the train with all those children and the smell of fear and milk and sick. There was the journey and that boy who had died in her carriage.

But there were also those two cheesed sandwiches at Harwich, there was Dovercourt and the mouldy berries that had tasted so good and, yes, there was Peter. These pictures were coming all at once now. There was no grown Lilia, no little Lilia, there was just Lilia: Lilia in black and white, Lilia in Technicolor, Lilia throwing herself down the stairs of the farmhouse in Nailsworth, Lilia lying here on the rug of the attic in Sugar Hall, Lilia watching these moments of her life as if she were sitting in the 2 and 6s.

She wondered if the rats might crawl over her and eat her up. She wondered if at last she was mad. She listened to the scuttling and Lilia willed herself to let nothing else in: nothing but the noise of the rats.

On occasion, Lilia Sugar's will failed her.

The owls cried out again from the great cedar, and Lilia shifted her position, the small of her back settling into the floor.

'We are marooned,' she said out loud.

How she longed for the noise of London, it had drowned out so much.

Lilia knew that if Juniper could see her now she would say,

'Stand up and pull yourself together.' This wasn't a particularly English trait; Lilia's mother would have said the same.

'Stand up! Stop moping! There's worse, you know!'

She tried to think of worse, she tried to imagine worse until she felt a little better, and when she felt a little better, Lilia sat up.

Recently Lilia had read about old houses being flattened to the ground to build new; it was a new world after all. She had seen pictures of grand mansions crushed by machinery and wrecking balls simply because they were of no further use. Defunct: that was a new word for her. De-funct. Lilia reached out in the darkness and felt for the iron hoop of keys, for her torch, and she knew the wrecking ball wasn't a bad idea; not a bad idea at all. Suddenly she didn't care about the wilting daffodils and the growing bluebells and the red, moist earth here. She didn't care about the planting out and the fresh green shoots and the thought of tomatoes. Lilia wanted rubble and a wrecking ball, she wanted all this gone.

The boy had been watching the woman as she felt in the darkness for keys that would never lock these rooms. The boy turned his head, the bones in his neck unlocking.

The woman had been thinking such things. Now he saw the big machine and the stone ball crashing through the walls of Sugar Hall, leaving nothing behind but rubble and dust.

He liked this woman.

She is drowning, he thought, because now he could think. Since the child's blood woke him in the shed, he had begun to think and it was like shaking bluebottles from dustsheets.

This woman is drowning on air, he thought.

He crouched above her, taking in her breath, sucking.

Strange woman, but he liked her scent, and her taste.

She is sweet but she is bitter, the boy thought.

The clocks in Sugar Hall stopped, arms trembling on the half hour, and the boy smiled down at Lilia in the darkness.

The Cockchafer, Melolontha melolontha.

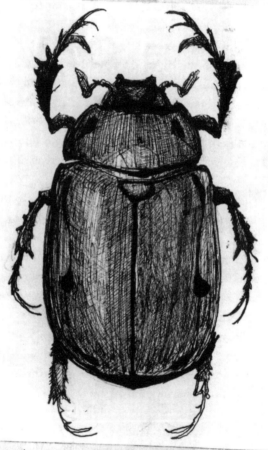

(Colloquial: Maybug, Mitchamador, Billy Witch,
Spang Beetle)

Maybug

10

Dieter wakes to the feeling of a hand in his in the darkness. The paraffin heater in the bedroom is dull and smoking; the wood fire is out. He squeezes the hand but suddenly there is nothing but air. He hears a faint giggle above the buzz of Saskia's snores. When feet slap the floorboards, Dieter sits up to the click and squeal of the latch as the door of their bedroom creaks open. He wraps his tartan dressing gown tight around him, gripping his toes into his slippers. The draft from the fireplace chills his back as he picks up a torch.

Dieter runs.

The colder air of the passageway wakes him. He hears soft footfalls on the staircase. He knows it is the boy from the shed because the boy comes to him regularly now, in fits and starts, flashes and moments.

This is different, Dieter can feel it, this is a game.

He wants to play.

'Ready or not,' Dieter whispers, and he switches off his torch and waits for his eyes to adjust. The bright moon shines in through the elegant hall windows, onto the staircase, and there is the boy in Pa's white shirt, it reaches almost to his bare ankles. Dieter smiles, shoves his torch in his dressing-gown pocket and bends his legs, poised to sprint. 'Race you,' he says.

He skids to the top of the staircase and tumbles down the steps, jumping onto the black and white tiles of the hall. Dieter hears voices echo up from the kitchen. It sounds like laughter; it's Ma and a deeper voice, Mr John, but why is Mr John here at night? Suddenly that doesn't matter and Dieter runs to the front door.

The vixen pitter-patters across the grass, eager to feed her cubs. She tenses as she sees Dieter beneath the porch's iron lantern; the owls in the cedar of Lebanon behind her fly up in retreat. Dieter is scanning the lawns for his friend but the fog from the river hangs above the grass. A huge bug crashes into his chest and he cries out, batting it away. It lands heavy on the porch and he watches it struggle, fat and hairy and brown like varnish; it sounds like an airplane's propellers.

Then Dieter sees something move; Pa's white shirt is glowing as the boy walks down the gravel drive.

Dieter follows.

In the downstairs kitchen you can hear the sound of teaspoons crashing against the Hall's finest bone china: sugar dissolves.

'You are kind to stay, John, to help.'

'Not at all.' John nods at the sandwiches. He hasn't been much help with the delicate work of mixing boiled egg with cress and cutting the loaves into thin slices. He pressed the butter in so hard he broke the bread. They have been boiling and cutting since Dieter was put to bed with hot milk and cinnamon. They now have four large silver salvers of egg and cress triangles. John watches Lilia takes out her packet of Craven A, she lights two: one for her and one for him.

'I cannot believe I let Juniper persuade me.'

'It's tradition.' John takes the cigarette, shy.

'It is?'

'Oh, yes.'

'How many…' Lilia starts at the bark of the vixen ' …how many hunters will come?'

'That's a horse that is, a hunter. And the folks who'll be here are called the hunt.'

'How many, then?' she rubs her thumb across a deep groove in the table.

'A fair few, I'd say.' John tastes the cigarette; he loves the feel of smoke in his throat, though his lungs don't.

The vixen cries out. Lilia gasps. 'Poor thing,' she says, and in truth she does feel like crying.

'Don't fret, last hunt of the season. She might get lucky. She'll have a rest after tomorrow. If they don't get her, that is.'

The black range sounds a loud pop of heat and Lilia jumps in her seat.

'Steady, Mrs Sugar.'

'Lilia.'

'*Lilia.*' John fidgets. 'Old houses make noises, it's what they do, *Lil-ia.*' He taps his boot on the slab floor as Lilia hums her off-key hum and smoke clouds swirl in the underground room.

John thinks of brightening the mood. She's always so sad, you see. He smiles because he feels like teasing. 'Have you met that Mr Churchill in London, then?'

'I beg your pardon?'

He winks, a full grin on his face. 'Thought you'd meet Mr Churchill, m'be the Queen herself up in London. Thought you'd be nodding at all them film stars, too. Elizabeth Taylor. Margaret Lockwood. I know them all, see, I like the Pictures.' He winks again.

'John!'

'It's nice when you laugh.'

Lilia pushes her chair across the flagstones and disappears into the cold scullery. For a moment John wonders if he has said the wrong thing.

'Glasses, please,' she calls out, and soon she is back with Juniper's latest bottle of whisky.

The golden liquid swirls in each cut-glass tumbler. She thinks John does a strange thing as he splashes whisky on the stone floor and mumbles something, but she doesn't ask what. They sit and they smoke and the liquor warms them in the hard kitchen chairs.

A fat bug clatters against the window above the sink and Lilia squeals.

'Jumpy tonight, steady!' John laughs.

'I cannot help! All day they do this. Those big insects, so ugly, crashing against the windows of the house.'

'Maybugs.'

Lilia drinks: it steadies her nerves. 'But it is not May yet.'

'Will be tomorrow. May 1st. They come a day early, mind.'

Lilia shivers.

'Don't worry they don't last long. Be dead by halfway through June.'

The bug, tenacious, crashes into the lit window again. 'I know this creature, John. We had them when I was a girl. *Maikäfer*.' She closes her eyes. Her fingers tap on the table as the bug taps at the windowpane. Lilia stubs out her spent cigarette and she begins to sing.

'*Maikäfer flieg … Dein Vater ist im Krieg. Deine Mutter ist in Pommerland. Pommerland ist abgebrannt. Maikäfer flieg!*'

John stares. He waits until the echo of her voice and the thud of the insect are gone: it is such a pretty voice, he thinks, but they are such strange words.

'What's that about then?'

Lilia opens her eyes. 'It is a simple song, for children. It is like, what is yours, ah yes, "Ladybird, Ladybird, fly away home, your house is on fire and your children are gone." My song means, "Maybug fly, your father is at war…"' she stops as the bug clatters against the pane. Lilia wants to change the subject; she gulps the whisky. 'John, you have always lived with your mother?'

'She's all I have.'

'You should marry, have a family of your own.'

'Oh, I don't look for that.'

'But it will look for you! You are a young man, you need family.' Lilia pulls back the greaseproof paper: she offers a sandwich to John and nibbles at a crustless edge herself.

The bug is gone.

'You know, there are times,' she says, 'I regret bringing the children to this place.'

'Fresh air. Good for them.'

Lilia tries to smile. 'Yes.'

'Will you stay, you reckon?' John feels nervous, waiting for the answer. The egg and cress helps.

Lilia is quick. 'I cannot say. This is for Dieter now, but I think it is too much. Such a silly old house. Expensive to run, and we live poor here, like peasants. Dieter was raised in a city. It is hard for us all.'

'Yes…'

'But I have you to talk to, John, and that makes me happy.'

He coughs on his whisky.

'Why do you…' she begins to ask but then she stops.

'What?' he smiles, the whisky clouding him.

'I have always wondered why do you not walk in the front door? You use this,' she points at the kitchen's back door, the one that leads to outside brick steps that take you up into the light of a kitchen garden and a small gravel courtyard where Lilia and John have just planted out tomatoes in clay pots.

'Just the way it is.'

'It is so strange.'

'Not so very much. And you're always down here. I come straight to you.' John blushes and Lilia looks away. She touches her hair; she's had neither the time nor the money to travel into town to the hairdresser Juniper recommended. It is a pity, but Lilia doesn't care, not yet.

'I would like for you to walk in the front door, always.'

'Can't say I'd like it,' John pauses, he looks straight at her, 'Lilia.'

'Then that is fair, it is your choice.'

'It is.' John drains his glass.

She is staring at the silver salvers. 'Will these sandwiches be enough, John? For "the hunt"?'

'I'd say it'll be plenty,' he lifts up a small triangle of sandwich, 'I mean you don't want to be galloping off after a fox with a belly full of egg, do you?'

They both laugh and it feels good.

'Be exciting, mind. Tomorrow. Been such a long time since we've had a crowd up at the Hall. Before the war, at least. Are you riding tomorrow – Lilia?'

She laughs, her eyes a little wild. 'Oh dear, no. I cannot. Peter, he told me. He said when he was a boy he goes out with them and the dogs they kill the fox and the man takes the blood and the blood is put on his face! Like savages.'

'Blooding…'

'This is a terrible thing,' but just as Lilia says this, she knows she doesn't believe it is *so* terrible.

'Quick death, mind.'

Lilia pictures big, slavering dogs. She stands, stretching her hands up towards the ceiling, and she walks to the range. Her knees click as she kneels to open a hatch.

'Here, let me do that,' and John is above her, his heat warmer than the heat of the burning wood. He is such a boy and such a big man, all in one, and the sound of his chest, it speaks to her, whispers to her, and makes her think of things she shouldn't.

'You cold?' he asks.

She is still kneeling. 'Yes.'

'Come here, then,' and his big hands are on her shoulders. She feels his jacket – warm with him – around her, and before she can protest she is guided to a chair and sitting with a glass in her hand, while John is on the flagstones in front of her.

It makes her think of dogs again, faithful ones.

'There *are* strange sounds in this house, John.'

'Old houses do that.'

'I hear the noises at night. I know there are unhappy things here.'

'How do you mean?'

'You must know, you have worked here many years…'

'Yes.' John puts his hand on the wooden arm of her chair. 'Best to let it be, Lilia.'

Whisky stings her lips, 'I am not frightened,' she cups the tumbler. 'It is only, what is the word? Queer. It is queer this place. That is a good English word, is it not? Yes. But places are nothing. It is the people, no?'

'Beg pardon?'

'What has gone, John. It is here, around us. Always.'

'That's what my mam says. She says them that have passed on are everywhere and we just got to learn to live with them and they've got to learn to live with us, see.'

'That is very true. I would like to meet your mother.'

The black range taps out the pulse of its heat: tic-tic-tic.

'I had always thought to fear the living,' Lilia says, 'not the dead.'

John coughs, his knees hurt on the flagstone, but he doesn't move. 'Lilia, if you don't mind me asking, how long were you and Master Peter married?'

It is such a sudden question, out of nowhere. She stares through her whisky-fug, at him at her feet. 'We met in London at the end of the war, but still there were bombs. We were in the underground, he lit my cigarette.' Lilia winds her hair behind her ear, over and over; she feels the throb of thinking right at the base of her neck and it pricks like pins and needles. 'You were here for the war, John?'

'Home Guard. On account of the lungs. Not proud of it.'

'There is no pride in war.'

'I dunno about that...'

Lilia laughs, but the throb grows stronger.

'If you don't mind me asking,' he says again, still at her feet, still staring up with those blue blue eyes, 'were you on our side, or theirs?'

Tic-tic says the black range.

John is as much a child as Dieter, she thinks.

Tic-tic.

Tic-tic.

'I left Germany a long time ago.'

Drip-drip says the tap that dribbles green.

'I didn't mean...'

'No, I have heard the question before. Please, do not worry. What is your word? 'Fret', yes, do not fret...' she reaches out to the arm of her chair and lays her hand on his. 'I came here months before the war began. Then, once it starts, I cannot go home. Many of us are here in England, and then the war starts and some of us are put in camps. Yes, John, in England. Two boys I know, they are taken. I was not. I worked, and for a good family. Quakers.' She coughs. 'It is funny. I don't tell anyone this. I don't speak of it, but,' Lilia breaks off; she takes her hand away, and drinks. 'I think, sometimes it is hard. Yes, it is hard to remember what you were. It is hard to remember what you are.'

John's knees click. 'Did Master Peter speak German?'

Lilia wishes John would stop asking foolish things.

'Peter...' it is so easy to say his name tonight, '*Ob Peter deutsch gesprochen hat?* Yes. That was his job. Translator. There was much work. War, it does not simply – poof! – end. War, it is bleeding. It is taking time. There are people. People are a war. Peter, he put people back with people. He tried to save, but sometimes.... It is like baby cats. Like kittens. Sometimes it is no good and people do not want to be saved. Do you understand me, John?' Lilia glances over at the kitchen table, at the bottle, and wishes she had more whisky in her glass.

'To be truthful with you, not all.'

'Maybe that is for the best. It is all so long ago. We must say this.' Lilia hugs herself, feeling warmth, such a rare thing in this place, but she wants to stop talking like this because it makes her shake. 'Please, tell me, what happens, John?' she whispers, 'tomorrow.' She watches him stand and rest his leg against the range; she wonders how he can stand the heat of the metal.

'They come up, 7 o'clock.'

'All?'

'Aye.'

'Men and animals?'

'Aye, women and children, too. And a few of those ladies they still ride side-saddle, never seen as how a woman can do that...'

'John.'

'Right, well they all come up on their horses, dogs and all.'

Lilia shivers.

'And we'll be here and I can hand out the refreshments,' John speaks like a gleeful waiter, 'and the master of the hounds has his hot port because he's partial, and the rest have their port or their whisky – Mrs Bledsoe said she'd bring that – and by this time the hounds are fretting, and the master of the house – which is you, I reckon – gives a little talk...'

'Oh no...'

'Well, I don't 'spect they'll be worrying about that, and then, well, they're off, and God help the fox. Bad time this late. Whelping.'

Lilia watches John's face; the heat from the burner has given him a flushed look and he seems lost for a moment, his head against a blouse of hers that hangs from the wooden Jenny. His blue eyes are – for a moment Lilia can't think of the word – yes, that is it – they are wistful – John Phelps looks wistful.

'And that's that,' he murmurs.

Lilia leans back in the spindle-back chair; she will sleep in it tonight. John's coat is around her and it smells of man, which to Lilia is tobacco. Peter preferred cologne on his hands and pomade in his hair. Peter liked everything clean. She thinks of the hunt. She wishes she hadn't let Juniper persuade her into it. 'The Meet', Juniper called it, and still Lilia doesn't know whether Juniper intended 'meat' or 'meet'. The meat. The meet. The hunt. The hunters. It makes little difference. It will still give her this night of sleeplessness, of ironing the children's clothes and hoping to God that the grand men and women on those horses won't laugh at her and her measly offerings; these dreadful egg and cress sandwiches, curling even now on the silver salvers on the table, salvers she will sell next week. She prays they won't laugh at her and her terrible hair with its black roots showing. Lilia wonders if she will still be drunk in the morning and then she wonders if the baying dogs will eat her and her children, and all for a damned silly English fox.

The boy is pulling Dieter's hand so hard it hurts. Dieter doesn't know how because the boy is so much smaller than him. And his touch, it makes Dieter feel so terribly sick, so terribly dizzy.

It's making him burp.

The moon follows them down to the faraway cowshed where the farmer milks twice a day. As they creep past the farmhouse a black and white dog on a thick chain barks, then whimpers. Then they are walking up the hill, looping back towards the Hall, and Dieter finds himself at the other end of the red gardens. It is such a strange way to come, he thinks.

'Where are we going?'

The boy says nothing as they march past the greenhouses – a forgotten village of shattered panes, rotten canes and weeds. They duck through an arch in a tall brick wall and into a small enclosure. This place is littered with small graves: Dieter knows because he often sits here. The stones are terribly old and some of the names have flaked away. Some are Roman, and Dieter once wrote them down in his exercise book: there is 'Romulus', 'Remus', 'Caesar', 'Caius', 'Pompei' and 'Scipio'; and then some are simply letters, 'D', and 'J', and a 'K'. He did wonder if they had been soldiers, centurions, poets; then he wondered if the headstones were so small because – he reasoned – people were smaller back then. Ma laughed when he asked this, and she told him that these graves were the graves of pets; she said this was a place where foolish Englishmen buried their dogs because Englishmen treated their animals better than they treated their children.

As the boy pulls him past the dark stumps of gravestones, Dieter imagines tall grey deerhounds in bright waistcoats beneath the ground; he thinks of white Scottish terriers in tartan kilts. Then the boy stops and bends down for a moment, trailing his free hand over the edge of one small gravestone. Dieter thinks of the time he visited a graveyard with Ma. It was before Pa died, before the fact of anyone dying had occurred to him, and he had been very little. He remembers how Ma knelt: perhaps this is what you did in a graveyard? She picked up a little pebble and placed it on the smooth top of a marble gravestone. Dieter remembers this and the fact that his new wool shorts had itched.

They pass a huge stretched-out yew tree and in front of them the forest of rhododendrons begins in red and pink. In the daylight these half-open flowers are red as a double-decker bus.

'Why are we going in here? I don't like the rho-de-do-de-den-drums,' Dieter whines but the boy drags him through the thick bushes: thin petals, moist leaves and stunted branches catch on his dressing gown, in his hair. He feels so sick and now he is frightened. When they make turn after turn in the dense shrubs, Dieter wonders how he will ever find his way out, and then suddenly, they are ducking through another arch in a brick wall. They are in the clearing with the swimming pool.

In the moonlight the water is shiny black and it stinks. Dieter knows there are things in there: three wooden tennis rackets, a cane chair and a parasol – shredded – and something dead he'd decided was a small dog because he spent an afternoon poking at it with a stick.

'I don't want to go in there!' he cries, tugging backwards. The boy lets go and Dieter's sickness lifts: he checks his nose for blood, but there is none. The moon shines on the boy as he walks to the swimming pool's edge. He rolls up the cuffs of Pa's white shirt and stretches his arms out at his sides.

'We're not *really* going for a swim, are we?' Dieter says, because the boy looks ready to dive in. Dieter struggles but he can't help it, he finds himself walking towards the edge of the pool until he is standing next to him; the boy is a magnet.

'I don't want to,' he whimpers. 'I don't want to jump into that.' Dieter stares down at the water; he wonders how deep it is.

There is a light hum in the air and something hits him square in the face. It isn't a punch or a slap but a bounce; something ricochets off his cheek as the hum turns into a rumble and the rumble glows bright green in the dark.

Dieter sees them – because they are a 'them' – buzzing together in a great luminous cloud, they are flying towards him. He squeals, but he can't move. He is frozen and they are on him now and he cries out, 'Mekon! Mekon! Mekon!' because Dieter doesn't know they are fireflies, little drops of toxic green. Dieter thinks they are aliens, outriders of the Mekon's army coming to suck the life from him. They fly in his mouth and he has to spit them out.

They fly onto the boy, too. They latch onto his outstretched arms, his hair, his bare legs, but the boy doesn't squirm. More come, all crashing straight into the boy now, until he is encased in luminous green and Pa's shirt glows.

Then the sound changes, something heavy is droning in the night air, and all of a sudden fat things are bouncing off Dieter's head. He squeals as they plop into the filthy water; they are the same fat bugs that have been crashing through the Hall all day.

Maybugs.

They hit Dieter in the chest, hard, and he has to slap himself to get the crawling insects from him. He teeters at the pool's edge. 'London, is the place for me,' he cries, 'London, this lovely city!'

When the moths come they sound like feathers. Some are tiny and plain, the size of a farthing, some are as large as rats and as bright as kites, and some are stuck with pins. They land in the grass and tickle their way over Dieter's slippers to his ankles, then up his legs, to his hips, to his chest, to his face: their soft furry bodies purring with speed. They thrum against his ears, tickle his hands, then sharp pins scrape across his skin. Dieter stumbles, trying to brush them away. 'Make them stop!' he cries. He's wobbling now, on the lip of the pool. 'Stop it! Stop it! Stop them!'

The moths like Dieter; they linger on his skin, whispering, leaving a bright dust before they take off, lazily, towards the boy.

Dieter falls back onto the grass.

More moths are crawling towards the boy's toes, their antennae twitching. They crawl over the green fireflies and the fat Maybugs on their way up his legs, past his belly and up to his neck, his face. The boy opens his mouth in a wide smile and insects push past his lips: they nestle close to his teeth.

They are Hawk, Hummingbird and Antler Moths. They are Garden Tigers, Emperors, Cinnabers, Bird-Cherry Ermine, Angle Shades: they are Lunar Hornets, Feathered Thorns, Diamond Backs, Scalloped Oaks, Map-Winged Swifts, Pale Bridled Beauties, Corn, Tapestry and Ghost Moths.

The ancient boy has woken them.

Their wings beat into blurs of colours. They leave their sparkling dust on the boy's skin; they give it life. He begins to move his arms, a conductor, as more insects pour from the sky. They land on him, covering him until he is as bright as the moonlight, until he is teeming with life; until the shimmer of the moths' wings and the glow of the fireflies' bellies are part of him.

'London,' Dieter gasps from the ground, 'is the place for me. London, this lovely cit-eeee.' He puts his hands over his ears; he is so afraid of insects burrowing into his brain. The boy is a shape now, made up of the scurrying, jumping bodies of insects. Dieter thinks of the moths and butterflies pinned down in the Hall, the ones preserved under those glass cases in that big room, and for a moment he wonders if these are the same ones, dragging their pinned bodies through the grass. Dieter wonders if they smashed the glass with their beautiful, beating wings to escape. Then Dieter hears a noise that makes his eyes roll to the backs of their sockets. He knows the noise is coming from the boy, and that is when he feels something tug at his belly button from the inside, and he faints where he lies in the grass.

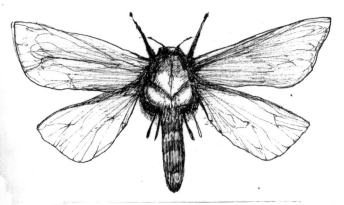

GHOST MOTH, male, hepialus humuli

The Hunt

11

The sun didn't take long to come up and Dieter didn't take long to open his eyes. A small white moth lay on the cuff of his tartan dressing gown. He watched it struggle – legs caught in the wool. When he flicked it off, it crawled through the dew-wet grass. Sun was bouncing off the red-brick wall, off the spoilt chrome rails that curved down the swimming-pool steps. Dieter rubbed his eyes.

'Are you here?' he croaked.

Small bright birds flitted up from grass to tree at the sound of his voice, and he sat up, dizzy and cold. As he stood the birds shrieked and flew off.

Dieter walked towards the swimming pool, his slippers sliding on the ancient turf. He squinted into the rising sun for a long while because he didn't know if he dared look down. He was afraid he might see the back of his friend bobbing in the black water and Pa's shirt ruined. Dieter took a deep breath and peeked. The water in the deep end was still black but now it squirmed because the surface was inches thick with insects. Moths fluttered, weak, their wings wet and stained with the black water. They covered the parasol, the old cane chair. Poor things, thought Dieter, but he was relieved, because there wasn't a body there (unless you counted the dead dog).

'Where are you?' he said.

He looked up at the trees. It was strange but in the daylight he wasn't scared anymore; Dieter was glad to have a friend, he was glad to have an adventure. It had been such an odd night that he wasn't sure what he remembered; what had happened. In the next moment he wondered if Ma had spent it out in the gardens, calling his name.

'Poor Ma,' he said, and he brushed himself down, turned to the archway in the brick wall, and began the long walk back to the Hall. He pushed himself through the fleshy leaves of the rhododendrons, hating their wet touch, but glad to be leaving this place. He ran through the pet cemetery with its stunted stones and he took the shortcut through the field. Here the faded stalks of spent daffodils bobbed about him like crisped Jack-in-the-boxes. Dieter slowed and let his hands move through the tall green ears of the new grass, and he skipped his stiffness out.

Dieter was running towards the house when he saw the colours, and when he saw all those people and all those animals in front of the porch steps he skidded under the larch trees.

There were so many horses: black, chestnut, dappled white, and they steamed in the morning air. There were so many people on the horses, in white and black and one man in a bright red jacket. And there were so many dogs. The dogs weren't quite brown or black or white, but spotty in all those colours.

'Aooooowoooo!' they howled, low and loose, like something was being ripped out from their bellies.

Dieter decided this was a search party, all for him.

The horses were brushed, their manes plaited into little buns that patterned the lengths of their glossy necks (Ma and Saskia did the same thing with rags in their hair at night, when they wanted it to curl). The people on the horses were smart too, and Dieter liked that. They wore black bowler or tall hats, the crispest whitest shirts with high collars and tightly tailored jackets in black or tweed. The man in the red jacket had thick thighs that hung either side of his horse's belly like fat brown sausages. Dieter watched the man's thighs grip as his black horse fidgeted, its tail swishing from side to side.

It was then Dieter noticed the children on the small horses. He fought the urge to jump up and wave at them. Dieter closed his eyes and listened to stirrups jangle, leather creak, soft nostrils snort, and molars grind metal. He listened to the voices.

'What a darling cigarette case, Hetty.'

'It was a gift.'

'Simply darling.'

'Has anyone seen her yet? Our lady of the manor?'

'Don't mock, Cyril, she didn't have to have us you know.'

'She's a project of Juniper's.'

'Yes, June arranged this whole thing. Trying to bring her out.'

'Rum little thing by all accounts.'

'Sh! Cyril!'

'Where *is* Juniper?'

'Inside with the Sugar woman. Not hunting today.'

'Oh. Pity.'

'Doubt this place or this new woman will be here in the new season. Too much for a filly to run.'

'Well, well. Let's enjoy today, Teddy. It is our last.'

'What-ho, here she comes.'

Dieter opened his eyes to see his mother walk out of the big front door carrying a huge silver plate of sandwiches; his belly growled. Mr John was behind her, holding silver goblets and two bottles on his plate, and as they walked down the wide stone steps towards the riders, the horses jostled. Dieter tried to keep track of his mother as she moved into the body of fidgeting beasts. He felt his insides contract, she looked so small; and then she disappeared.

'Ma…' he tried, and he saw Juniper walk down the steps with Saskia. They held big silver plates too, and as Juniper moved through the horses she slapped one on the shiny rump with her free hand and it moved out of her way, jumping from hoof to hoof. Dieter watched the riders lean down from their horses to take the goblets and drain them; they picked up the sandwiches and chomped them down in one gulp. Again, he strained to see his mother, to spot her head in the mass of steaming horses.

There was a sharp and high blast of something like a trumpet, the dogs howled and Saskia dropped her tray; the small triangles of white bread scattered.

Ma appeared from the throng. She rushed up the grey steps to the wide porch, her silver tray empty and her hair falling in her face; she stumbled.

The noise came again, and the man in red cocked his hat at Ma, turned his horse, and trotted off. The pack followed, and they were fast; they cantered across the grass and jumped the fence where the cows would march twice a day. Dieter heard the trumpet once more; a call to run, a root-toot-toot that blasted over the fields.

Then there was nothing but the ripe smell of horse, a ruined lawn, and a ringing in his ears.

A FRUITCAKE

CAKE KNIFE

A METAL FILE

A HAMMER

TIN SNIPS

A Hammer, a Fruitcake, a Cake Knife, Tin Snips and a Metal File

12

A wren zigzagged from bramble stalk to bramble stalk in the woods. Dieter looked down at his spoils; he was back at school so it had taken him weeks to gather these things.

Today he would do it.

'Which shall I use?' his fingers were on the cake knife. He looked up from bright May bluebells and directly at the boy. His friend was faint in the sunlight; he still wore Pa's shirt, but it was torn and dirty now.

Insects hovered; the wood was alive. It felt so good to be out of the damp Hall; it felt so good to be out with a friend.

'It is terribly tight around your neck,' said Dieter. 'I'm just not sure how to get at it properly.'

Fat bluebottles droned above the fruitcake. Dieter's hand moved from the cake knife to the hammer, then to the tin snips, finally settling on the metal file.

'I think this one first.' The bluebottles thudded into the beech trunks. 'Pop your head back then.'

The boy did.

Dieter hadn't seen him for so long. After that night at the swimming pool, he thought the boy had disappeared for good, then he thought he'd dreamt him up. But no, last week he'd found him sitting at the end of his bed.

And now there was the Plan.

Dieter slipped two fingers between the metal collar and the boy's skin; the metal of the collar was cold but the boy's skin was colder. Dieter felt the same buzzing dizziness and sickness he had whenever the boy touched him, so he talked as he filed to distract himself.

'Do you like it here, in the wood?'

The boy, head back, stared up into the new green of beech and oak leaves.

'I think there are wolves. Honest Injun. I've heard them.' Dieter thought there could be a whole pack of wolves crouching in the fern and bluebells right now. 'I think those tree trunks look like elephant feet. They look like the elephant foot umbrella stand we had in the Hall. It disappeared. I told Ma and she said that things disappear in that house and not to worry.'

Filing made Dieter's hand ache and his sickness was becoming unbearable. 'This isn't working!' he cried and he threw the file into the flowers. Dieter grabbed the fruitcake and bit because he'd found that sugar helped the sick and dizzy feeling the boy gave him, and fruitcake was the best.

His stomach settled; his vision came back.

'I hate my school,' Dieter said (because touching the boy also made him think about sad things). 'Everyone hates me.' At Dieter's village school, boys wore the red welts of ringworm on their hands and cheeks, and they couldn't say his name.

'Deeee-turrrrr?' they teased.

'Shu-guuur? After what you puts in your tea? You come from up the Hall? You posh, mind?'

'Hit-ler! Hit-ler! Hit-ler!' they yelled at him. 'Jerry! Jerry! Jerry!' and he could see the thick lines of spit between their upper and their lower teeth. It wasn't fair: Saskia was older so she went to a girls' grammar, a bus ride away in Chepstow. At his school lumpy girls held bibles while boys held sawn-off chickens' feet in their fists. They'd pull the shrivelled tendon until scaly chicken toes flexed in his face.

Dieter had forgotten he'd once been a leader.

In the fug of the bluebells Dieter thought of the Wee-Hoo gang. They had never said anything about his name. The Wee-Hoos had a Precious Palmer, a Levi Bloom and the twins Deuteronomy and Comfort Jones. These names were like cities, like countries, like whole worlds to themselves.

Deuteronomy Jones. Precious Palmer. Levi Bloom.

Dieter glanced up at the boy.

'I want to run away, back to London,' he said, 'would you like to come? You could meet Cynthia and the rest of the gang and we could ride the buses into town.' He stretched his legs out. 'You'd have to wear shoes in London, and a pair of trousers or shorts like mine. Do you have the trousers I gave to you?' Dieter felt something on his arm; it was the boy's hand.

He trembled.

The boy was nodding towards the tin snips and smiling. He had such good teeth, Dieter thought, not like Mrs Pritchard at the village shop who told Ma she was going to have all of hers pulled for her second wedding because it would be easier and brighter, her new married life, with a good set of teeth.

The boy pointed at the tin snips.

'But I tested them on a can of peaches. They cut right through and it was so sharp.'

The boy's expression, if it could be called an expression, didn't change.

'All right.' Dieter sat up. 'But don't blame me if I cut you and we have to find a doctor.'

Once again Dieter's fingers slipped in between metal and the skin of the boy's neck; he sensed the dizziness before it came and the boy's head fell back.

It was careful work, millimetre by millimetre because Dieter was fighting his faintness and thinking of the jugular vein. Cynthia had told him how some people wanted this cut before they were put in their coffins. The Jug-ew-lar. Dieter snipped with the sharp, small tool, and the thin metal of the collar began to open.

He heard the boy take a breath and he hadn't heard that before. He cut again.

'Sh!' Dieter said to the birds and the wind in the trees. His eyebrows came together with worry; his fingers shook as he snipped. He imagined the boy's head dropping off right here into the bluebells. It might roll like a hairy coconut knocked off its post at the fair. He thought about names again, and he wondered if the boy would speak and tell him his, he wondered if his name sounded as lovely as 'Precious Palmer' or 'Deuteronomy Jones'.

There wasn't any more metal to cut: Dieter let the tin snips drop in the bluebells. The wood was spinning and he grabbed the fruitcake and chewed, his mouth open with a mulch of sultanas, glacé cherries and nuts. He looked at his friend and the collar seemed to be peeling away of its own accord, like sunburnt skin. Dieter reached out and tugged its end, careful of every wobble of the boy's head. Dieter burped. 'Oh, dear,' he said and he thought of the way Ma pulled off his plasters. 'Look up at the spider!' she'd say, and by the time he'd looked to see nothing was there, the plaster was off.

Dieter yanked and the silver collar came away quick as an old scab. 'Oh,' he said.

The boy's shoulders were rising. Dieter heard a slurp.

'Did – did that hurt?' Dieter asked, and then he couldn't help it, he giggled.

There was the strangest thing – stranger than all this – because the boy giggled too. It was a light giggle, like little bells.

Dieter gasped. 'You're welcome,' he said, and then he was shy, he didn't know what to say at all. He stared at the boy's neck, at the dark mark around it, wide and blacker than the rest of the boy's now-glowing skin.

Dieter turned the cut collar in his hands. It was such a thin thing, so light for something so permanent. He held it up into the sunlight shooting past the oak leaves, and he could see the writing on it. He traced the engraved letters with his finger.

It was a 'D'.

It was a 'D-E-M'.

Dieter turned it in the light. It was a 'D-E-M-E-R-A-R-A'.

He tried to say the word, his thumb following the letters on the metal. 'Dem-er-rah-rah.'

It was an ugly name and he didn't like it.

The boy didn't react. Dieter tried again, 'Demer-rah-rah. Is that your name?' He rubbed the indentations of the letters until the silver grew warm and he cut himself on the jagged edge.

Blood swelled. It was one of those deep cuts that don't hurt at first. Dieter felt like laughing; he held out his thumb. 'Look.'

The boy took it and put it to his lips: he sucked. Dieter felt strong teeth latch on; he felt the boy's tongue, prodding the cut. It was a terribly soft tongue. Dieter thought of the calves he'd seen in the fields butting at their mother's udders. He felt so strange.

'Don't,' he tried, and he pushed the fingers of his other hand deep into the ground, and it was as easy as plunging his fingers into Ma's Cold Cream.

When Dieter opened his eyes to the bright wood, the boy had let go and he was smiling, smears of blood on his white teeth.

'Oh,' said Dieter, and he lifted his thumb into the light. It looked like it had been in hot water too long, the skin was shrivelled but there was no blood.

He looked at the boy. 'Thank you,' he said.

They were protected beneath trees when the rain came.

Around them baby oaks, no higher than houseplants, shivered. The boys were stretched out on their backs in a deep dip; the crunch of last year's dry leaves a bed beneath them.

They listened to it all: the green push above them and the brown rot beneath, the constant buzzing of flies in the bluebells. Squirrels croaked warnings from their drays while the sun tried stretching down to clear the deepest, most faraway mist.

It was like waking from the longest of sleeps. Drowsy, Dieter shifted his weight to lie on his side. He found he was facing the boy; they were almost nose-to-nose. He felt sick this close, but he could see there were flecks in the boy's eyes, like gold leaf. There was something cloudy there, too. The boy blinked – a blank blink – and Dieter saw that his friend didn't have smile-lines or creases on his skin: he seemed brand new.

Dieter made a mental list.

The boy hadn't had German Measles or the Chicken Pox.

He hadn't frowned or laughed much because his forehead was as smooth as the top of one of Ma's chilled jellies.

He felt the boy's breath on his face and it smelled of metal and of the sea. Dieter thought of moths and fireflies. He touched the boy's lips with his finger, lips that now shone like spun sugar. He wished the boy would talk.

'Do you know these woods very well?' Dieter asked.

The boy nodded.

'Do you play here?'

The boy shook his head.

'Do you have any other friends?'

The boy shook his head.

'I'm glad you…' Dieter didn't know how to put it '…found me. Is that your name, "Demerara"?'

The boy shook his head.

'It was on that collar-thing.' Dieter poked his lip out, he didn't understand. 'What is your name then?'

The boy shrugged. Dieter noticed his eyebrows moving up, then down: it was nice to see his face move.

'Have you forgotten?'

He nodded.

'Really? You've forgotten your own name?'

The boy sighed.

'That's terrible. I couldn't ever forget my name. I'm sure of it.' Dieter thought. 'We could find out if you like?' He sat up, suddenly excited. 'I'll be crafty, like Sherlock Holmes. What do you think of that?'

The boy sighed again and Dieter smelled gun smoke and metal, sea salt and rust. Dieter smelled Pa too, because Pa was still on the shirt his friend wore: strong and lemony. The boy pushed his finger against Dieter's temple and Dieter felt something drain from him. 'No,' he said, 'please don't.' He hiccupped. 'Please.'

The boy lifted his finger.

It took a moment to recover: Dieter reached for the fruitcake. 'How do you do that?' he asked. 'When you touch me it's like I'm sinking, like I'm going to be terribly ill and I can't think.'

His friend suddenly sat up and jerked his head left, then right. He sprang into a crouch, knees bent and ready.

Dieter was certain the boy was bigger.

Then Dieter thought about the Wasteland and the Wee-Hoo Gang; he thought about running. 'Do you want to play tig?' he asked.

The boy was blank.

'OK, you be "it" and you chase me, but you have to give me a head start because you're … you're…' Dieter wanted to say 'growing' but that didn't seem right.

Dieter sprang up, and then he was running through the haze of bluebells. 'Come on!' he cried as the trees blurred.

The boy didn't move, not yet. He was breathing in beech and oak and also pine from the forest nearby. He was greedy. He breathed in green and he felt green; he breathed in the sweetness of the bluebells and he felt sweet, and all this while dust-mites, dead moths and cobwebs shivered into life in the crevices of him.

He twitched to the pumping suck of a fat tick on the doe that crouched in the fern behind him. He could hear her pant; he could hear the beat of her fearful heart. He breathed in, though he didn't need the air, and his lungs turned from waterless casing to sponge; he felt fluid pump through arteries that had been black as lead. With his palms and his feet flat on the wood floor, the boy sucked up the sap from the bluebells, from their green stalks, from their buried white bulbs. He took it all until the frilled purple flowers around him were husks.

At last he stood, face up to the shafts of sun. It was easy for him to move now. He had found it so difficult at first, he had been a stiff engine, pistons dry.

A silverfish crawled from one nostril and it tickled the corner of his mouth until his tongue came out and swiped it. The boy watched Dieter disappear through the trees as he munched; he cocked his head to one side: he was waiting.

He had been waiting for such a long time.

As he walked bluebells shrivelled to brown beneath his feet.

Awakenings

13

He didn't remember.

All was grey, as grey as the moth wings that filled his mouth. That was until the child spoke to him, until that Sugar child had him appear.

It was a command, after all. The child's blood had called to his in little seductive whispers, because the child's blood was his blood. And so that day he had appeared by the window in the wooden shed. He had appeared and he had tingled and sparked and the Sugar child had fled.

After all his years, decades, almost two centuries of wandering, this time he thought he had simply stopped, disappeared, and that was an end to it. But the child had come and he'd had no choice. He knew it would be such a long and hard battle because he had fought it before. He knew he had to remember.

He didn't know what he was, not yet.

Was he born here?

He knew he had died here: for now that was enough.

In truth, he wanted to lie down, to stop and let the memories fall away like clothes in a fire. He would prefer that, to be nothing; but the child had called and now he was walking through this wood: his wood.

As he walked, nettles tickling his legs, birds stopped their song.

Foxes hid.

Squirrels spat and retreated to their holes.

The boy began to spit, too – he stopped beneath an oak, touched the rough bark and the old life thumped a fierce thump, up from the great gods of the earth – as he spat out his moths and his cobwebs, as he spat out centuries, or two at least. He spat out horsehair, twigs and bitter almonds, rat poison, cowrie shells and Indian ink. He spat and he spat until his voice came. The boy hummed first. Words were too many, too much, so the boy hummed and he walked, bluebells turning to dry crunch at his steps.

He had once hidden in this wood. That was so much time ago – because he had forgotten the trinkets that are days, months, and years.

Now he was the wood.

This boy had seen the oaks fall for Navy ships, he had seen rats crawl up from the wood floor and eat a sleeping man. He had watched a child disappear into the fern and shimmer into nothing. He had seen cats' eyes dance in the needle tips of the firs. He had seen a girl bury a living, wailing thing at the foot of a stream and he had watched a weeping willow grow there. He had heard bombs tick-tock in bottomless quarries and plump babies cry from rooks' nests. He had seen men fight with hands, with swords, with knives, with poison, with guns and with paper. This boy had seen men kiss women and men kiss men; he had seen women kiss men and women kiss women. This boy had crawled inside an acorn; he had made men dance until their legs cracked. Once, too long ago, when he was proper flesh and proper bone, when he had hidden and whimpered in the wet hollow of an ancient oak, he had seen a silver deer with the pinkest eyes dance on its hind legs.

This boy had seen men dig a grave for his mother while she still lived. He had seen her tied to an ancient yew and whipped and cut in the red garden. This boy had seen himself swinging from a rope coiled on an oak branch, his own neck snapped.

This boy had watched these woods for all of his time.

The smell of wild garlic tickled him and he walked on.

June 18th 1955
Shelley House, Churchill Gardens

Dear Dieter,

I haven't had a letter from you for ages. Did you get my letters? Are you all right? I'm scared for you, Dieter, in that big house with that strange boy. Remember what I said, don't you trust nothing you can't say is human through and through. You pray to God, Dieter, and you come back. I enclose a rabbit's foot on a key ring. Keep it safe because I'll want it back. Write to me.

Your friend,
Cynthia

Saskia's Party

14

Juniper Bledsoe was walking fast across the bright field, her liver-spotted spaniels trailing behind her, docked tails paddling the air like rudders in her wake.

'To heel, to heel,' she said every few steps. It was a soothing chant for her as well as the spaniels because Juniper was on her way to Sugar Hall and recently that ghastly place was making her remember the strangest things; recently it put her on edge. Still, she was late for the girl's party. She hadn't taken to the lumpy thing, but there was dear Lilia to consider.

Juniper didn't know what to do and this was unusual. She didn't know what to do about Lilia Sugar: poor Lilia, alone in that monstrosity. Juniper was seriously considering writing a fat cheque and telling Lilia, 'Take this and run, run away!'

She was considering running with her.

It had become worse since the boy sickened. Now the child had been taken out of school and he languished at home (this, Juniper felt, was hardly helpful). It wasn't a proper sickness; it was in the mind, and the little chap had become anaemic and accident-prone, his fingers covered in plasters, his eyes ringed with shadows. Lilia claimed the iron tablets were doing no good but Dr Portman advised patience as the best medicine.

Juniper glanced up at the barbed wire that squared her field.

She did wish her gamekeeper, Turley, wouldn't do that; hang his dead trophies from the wire fence with little orange knots of bailer twine. Country habits, she thought, as she marched past the swinging corpses of magpies, stoats and ravens.

'To heel, Bonzo, Farley! To heel!'

Perhaps the girl's birthday party will rally them all, she thought. Perhaps the Hall was filled with lightness and laughter this very second.

Juniper doubted it.

She had known the Hall and all at the Hall since she was a young bride, just seventeen. Dieter's grandfather – old Gerald Sugar had been a terrible flirt, even with her. 'See you've got yourself a young filly!' he'd said to her Brigadier once they returned from their honeymoon. 'Broken her in yet?'

He was a truly ghastly man but it had been such a decadent time, that time between the wars. She was barely out of school and hot summer evenings in daring and darling silk dresses and new jewels from her Brigadier had thrilled her. Gerald Sugar held roaring parties that would roar for days at the Hall. This was country decadence: roast swan, a fountain full of champagne and midnight ghost stories.

Juniper shivered as she stood in the long grass.

At the end of her first summer here, that terribly hot summer between the wars, Gerald's eldest boy – Richard Sugar – was dead.

Yes, Richard would have been Dieter's uncle.

It had been a night in late August, and the heat so unbearable that the chill of the Hall had been welcome. That evening hot candle wax fell from brass and copper drip pans directly onto the white linen as they feasted on a bird-within-a-bird-within-a-bird. Rather drunk on champagne, Gerald Sugar had demanded a Ouija board. Juniper had never seen one. Still, it was a nonsense-word and a nonsense-thing. She remembered laughing wildly and holding her crystal flute in the air, showing off her handsome summer-brown arms in a particularly daring sleeveless, black dress.

She knew she wasn't pretty, even then, but she had been so young.

A servant brought the board in and she was surprised to see a child's board game. Gerald told them how he had found it in a bedroom, a blue room high in the rafters of Sugar Hall. Juniper had giggled and enjoyed the cool breeze that ran down the stairwell and blew through the open door of the dining room. She even laughed when all of the candles, bar one, blew out as old Gerald placed a cut-glass tumbler upside down on the board. She played footsie with her husband as Gerald called out in a grand voice, 'Is anyone there?'

It was less of a question and more of a demand.

There was no reply.

They soon abandoned the child's game, the cut-glass tumbler lying on its side, and they turned to the brandy. A few guests seemed ruffled, but she fell deep into conversation with Peter, the younger, more delicate boy, and her age. He was going up to Cambridge that autumn and she was rather jealous. They talked the classics because she had devoured her brothers' books. This was when Richard, the eldest son, leapt up and held a carving knife to his father's throat. It was so dreadfully sudden. She remembered she'd thought it comical at first because the tall, blond Richard did so look like an efficient barber as he stood behind his father pulling the man's chin up, a greasy bone-handled carving knife at his throat. Juniper soon recognised the eldest son's feverish upper lip, the wrinkle of his papery forehead; she had seen the same look on the faces of her two brothers when they came home on leave from the great war. It was the very last time Juniper saw them.

Richard Sugar was petrified.

'Stop!' she cried from the dining table, and Richard looked at her, yelped, and threw the knife to the floor. It clattered. He ran out through the open French windows and into the garish red gardens. She remembered how a moth flew in then, and hovered so close to a candle flame at the table that its wings caught fire. Frantic, it flew about the white cloth, smoking.

Yes, Juniper remembered that: the small detail. She tossed water at the insect, and missed. The water simply drenched what was left of their bird-within-a-bird-within-a-bird. Finally, she threw her napkin over the poor thing, smothering the small flames.

'Let him stew!' the father yelled. 'It'll make a man of him, a night in the damned woods.' Gerald ordered the servants to lock the doors and windows, and for a small moment Juniper wanted to pick the knife up from the floor and finish the job herself; she knew a little of fragile young men, but a lot about bullish fathers.

She and the Brigadier left shortly afterwards. They said nothing of the ghastly evening as they undressed, as they lay together, as she wept after making love and the Brigadier called her his girl. No, they didn't mention it: that was until Peter Sugar, the youngest son, was hammering at their door and all at once they were standing out on the landing watching the servants in their dressing gowns trying to calm the young man as he begged for help to search the woods.

'Father wouldn't want the police involved, you see.'

'Does your father know Richard hasn't come back?' the Brigadier barked from their staircase.

'No, no one at the Hall does, Sir. That's why I'm begging for your assistance. Please, help me find Richard…'

'He's no doubt gone to town,' her Brigadier said. 'Why this fuss?'

But Juniper had pitter-pattered down the stairs in her silk slippers and she was telling Peter, 'yes, yes, of course we will help.'

That was the night Richard Sugar was found dead in the woods. A few weeks later Peter was lost to Cambridge and then to London; Juniper was eighteen and she doubted old Gerald

Sugar ever unlocked those doors again. The decadence of that summer was gone in an instant, decadence of that sort at least.

Yes, they were all dead now, including her darling Brigadier.

Juniper kicked her foot into the red earth of a molehill.

It was Lilia – such a sweet, pretty face – who made her think of this past. It was strange how certain people did that, unlocked something. Juniper had come to the conclusion that some people brought the past with them like so many ghosts.

'To heel, to heel,' she murmured at the spaniels, and she was glad of her tweed suit, usually so bothersome in the summer.

She rested on the top of the next stile, looking out at her land, and from here, land that belonged to Sugar Hall. It was the boy's now, she supposed, although she knew there were solicitors involved and Lilia didn't understand the half of it. She could hear the creak of diggers in the valley beyond: they were clearing council land for those houses, for 'estates' that would soon give a fresh meaning to that word. It was a pity she and the Brigadier had had only dogs; there had been no children (although Juniper preferred the term 'child-free' to 'child-less'). It was simply a pity because of all this. This damned land. She sighed at the green fields and she began to hum, for a strange sort of song had been chiming in her head all morning: a song that came from another memory in this blasted morning of recollection. Juniper just couldn't stop herself humming it as she stood, brushed her skirt down and jumped off the stile. When she marched across the next field, her hum turned to words.

'We came from way out West. We came to do our best. To fight for right, and against the might of Nazi terror-ist,' she sang and giggled, though the memory was sad.

A boy had taught her this song during the last war, a boy she had nursed, a boy who had died (and she had nursed so many, watched so many die). But this boy she remembered clearly, though his name only came to her as she'd sat on that stile:

118

Edwin. He had been an RAF pilot, and in her nurse's uniform Juniper would put her ear close to his lips as he sang, 'We have our boys in blue, in grey and khaki too, we'll sing our song and they'll fight along against the Nazi terrorist.' Edwin told her how he'd heard a man called Al Jennings sing this very song on the BBC in England, and that was why this was a great country this Mother Country of his, and it would always look after him like a beloved son. Edwin sang as she changed the dressings on his stumps; gangrene had set in and she prayed the morphine would take him. Edwin, who told her stories of his island, Jamaica, and of his parish, St Thomas; Edwin who whispered Hitler was coming to get them, so when the recruiter came calling he and his mother had taken no time in deciding. He was the man of the house and he must protect his sisters from Hitler.

He was so young, and he had sung to her.

It was Juniper's job to nurse the men who would not recover. Her superiors said she had a knack for it. It made her think of her own father and his hands, the way those hands had put his animals out of their misery: calm and swift. The horses, the many dogs, that gigantic bull; none of them saw it coming. That was the only knack you needed in death, Juniper decided: kind hands and the ability to distract. She had managed this for her many dying boys: public school boys, country boys, Londoners, Scots, Welsh, and those ones who had come from all over the world to die here, in England and for England, under her eye.

It was too unbearably sad.

Juniper took a man's white handkerchief from her sleeve and blew her nose. Sentimental old fool, she thought, and she cried out, 'to heel!' to her bolting spaniels. She was quite out of breath as she walked up Sugar Hall's long gravel drive, past the first open gate, then the second. She paused and stared up at the house. Truly, she hated the place; it made her remember the strangest things. She had to get Lilia out. She looked down at her shoes: muddy.

The Gleaner, April 1ˢᵗ, 1944
Jamaica, WI
Established 1834

The Bravery of our RAF Airmen

During the early years of the war, we started a fund to buy bombers for Britain. The money Jamaica subscribed was the foundation of the 'Bombers for Britain' Fund, to which many other Colonies and Dominions subsequently contributed. Jamaica herself contributed enough money to buy twelve Blenheims by 1941. In recognition of this service it was decided, in the words of Lord Beaverbrook, the wartime Minister of Aircraft Production, 'that Jamaica's name shall evermore be linked to the squadron of the Royal Air Force'. And so it was that No. 139 Squadron became No. 139 (Jamaica) Squadron.

In 1944 the Mosquitoes of 139 were equipped with H2S and during that year the squadron visited a long list of targets in Germany: Berlin, Hamburg, Cologne, Mannheim, Hanover, Duisburg and many others. During February to March of this year, the squadron made a series of 36 consecutive night attacks on Berlin. We salute 139 Squadron and Jamaica!

Cyllopsis pertepida dorothea Nabokov, 1942

[Nymphalidae, Satyrinae, Euptychiini]

A Trial

15

Saskia and her three school friends were crowded around the *Daily Mirror* in the Hall's boot room. Saskia was lounging on a ratty armchair, while Kit, Tina and Shirley sat on the floor around her. Saskia was a little Sultaness in one coral and one mint green glove, because the girls had rifled through a cache of mismatched evening gloves in the Ottoman. It was Saskia's Sweet Sixteenth, and although the boot room smelled of rubber, wax coats and gristle, these girls had given it a sugared note of Fruit Pastels and high spirits.

'She doesn't look like a murderer.'

'It's "murderess", Shirley.'

Shirley, the lumpiest of them, tried the word on her lisping tongue, 'Mur-der-esssss.'

The girls were decked out like wedding cakes, tiered with dresses that flared from the waist in yellow, powder blue, white, and Shirley's unfortunate brown.

'Do you think she'll hang?'

'Can't say. Probably,' Saskia told them.

'She's confessed.'

The startled and stuffed heads of glass-eyed animals stared out above the girls' demi-waved heads.

'They might find she's innocent. In the court, I mean.'

'Don't be silly, Tina.'

'Hanging sounds just awful.'

'Awful…'

'Frightful…'

The girls reached for each other's hands in solidarity; their fingers a mesh of clashing colours.

'But she did shoot that man,' Saskia told them. 'She said as much.'

There had been little else but talk of Ruth Ellis at school: the girls were bewitched. Saskia thought Ruth beautiful, and thrilling.

Kit sneered, 'My daddy said the women are like that in London. He said they shouldn't be allowed.'

'What does that mean?' Saskia snarled like the stuffed badger on the wall because she didn't like Kit's father, or Kit, that much.

'Well,' Kit, sporty and dark, tapped the newspaper with her gloved finger, 'you know what I mean, Saskia, a woman like that and in London.'

'What's the matter with London?' Saskia wanted to add, 'and what's the matter with Ruth?' Because beneath all the drama of the coming trial, beneath the hysteria; something about Ruth Ellis made her want to cry. She looked down at the newspaper picture; and yes, Ruth looked lovely, her white-blonde hair sculpted with a curl on her forehead. Ruth's black eyes shone with something Saskia didn't quite understand but Saskia knew Ruth took care of herself.

Kit was smoothing down her white tulle skirt. 'Well, Saskia,' she muttered, 'we all know what goes on in *some* parts of London.'

Saskia's head jerked up. 'Do "we"? Do "we", Kit? What's that then?' Her voice was slipping back to its Churchill Gardens twang.

'You sound funny,' Shirley whimpered.

Tina and Kit glanced across at each other, they nodded while Saskia flicked out the skirt of her new yellow Marks and Spencer dress. She stared at the rusty mole-traps, the wire snares in the corner of the room, and she tried to calm herself, to bring the new Saskia back. 'There's nothing wrong with London,' she said, glancing down at her disloyal troops. 'Anyway, you can go and watch the hangings in London. You have to put your name on a list.'

'Never!' Kit cried.

'That's simply awful!' Tina wailed.

Shirley blanched white.

'Really, you can. I haven't been yet, but my friend Flinty has...'

'Oh, I don't want to talk about this anymore,' Shirley begged. 'Poor woman. Please.' She put two gloved fingers in her ears.

Kit put her arm around Shirley. 'I think we should play some music. Shall we?'

Saskia threw the newspaper on the floor, it skidded across the red tiles and she knew that, yes, she hated Kit Goodwin.

When Saskia danced the skirt of her yellow dress flared out. She twirled in front of her new Dansette. 'Do you like it? Do you like my birthday present? Mother bought it for me.' She leant over and clicked the little lever until the stylus lifted and fell on the '45. The girls listened to a few turns of crackled air, and then Frank Sinatra sang 'Young at Heart'.

'Oh, Frank!' Shirley cried.

'I don't like him,' said Kit, 'I like Alma Cogan.'

The girls paired up, they slow-danced together: gloves clashing.

'Oh, I'm ever so glad you came to live here, Saskia, I'm so glad,' Shirley sighed as she held Saskia at the waist, her cheeks flushed bright as cherry sweets.

'I never thought your house would be so...' Kit stopped dancing '...so grand.' Her eyes sparkled because she truly was impressed.

'Well, it needs a lot of work,' Saskia told them. 'We're planning it all quite soon. A *refurbishment*.'

'How thrilling!'

Gloved hands clapped together.

'And we can have a ball! Something spectacular.'

Kit rolled her eyes. 'A ball? That's so old-fashioned, Kia.'

Saskia's lower jaw pushed out. She wasn't sure she liked her nickname, 'Kia', she'd have to sort that out later, but for now she pulled it all in and smiled: I'm not at Churchill Gardens now, she thought. 'Of course,' she said, 'we'll have a dance, not a ball. We can use my Dansette. Tina, you bring your records, what have you got?'

'"Rock Around The Clock", it's American. My mother hates it…'

'And we can invite boys…'

'Would your mother let you, Kia?'

'Of course she would, Tina! My mother trusts me. At the end of term let's have a proper summer dance here at Sugar Hall. My house. You'd like that, wouldn't you, Kit?'

Kit squirmed but nodded.

'And by then the swimming pool and the tennis court will all be put right, and we can have pool parties!'

'Oh, I'm so glad you're my friend,' Shirley sighed and laid her head on Saskia's shoulder: Saskia's mint green fingers teased Shirley's coarse curls.

I'll show you, Kit Goodwin, she thought, because Saskia had hatched a plan. Later she was going to take them up to that room Dieter and John talked about, the blue attic room with the old toys: the haunted room. Yes, she'd listened to the rumours and today she'd show Kit. She'd take her up there, make up a story and scare the bleeding life out of the stupid cow. As she hugged Shirley to her, Saskia had to swallow the bitterness down, she had to close her eyes and concentrate on being this new Saskia: the young girl of Sugar Hall, unworldly and meek.

'What shall we listen to next?' she cried, and she smiled sweetly at her school friends.

The Snoopers

16

Dieter peeked out from his den beneath the food table; the long reception room seemed greener now summer was here but no less damp. Over the past week he'd languished in here, watching Ma and Mr John redress it: paintings beneath sheets were now hanging, light bulbs were changed, furniture rearranged. He'd even seen Ma sprinkling used tealeaves on the rug, and then sweeping them off with a dustpan and brush because her friend Juniper told her this was the only way to clean old carpets. It was quite an odd thing but now the rug smelled fresh, like tea.

He bit and tugged at a plaster on his finger; this cut was deep and white from lack of air. Dieter had lots of cuts now; they were bites from the boy, bites that never had time to heal because the boy was always hungry. Ma asked him again and again how he hurt his fingers, his wrists, as she soaked his hands in a bowl of cloudy Dettol at the kitchen table, but he wouldn't tell. Ma would pinch his cheeks for colour, pull up his lips to note his pale gums; she patted Savlon into his wounds, made him eat liver, she sang to him; but still he didn't tell.

His heart thudded. Ma and Juniper were gone to collect more food and he poked his head out from beneath the tablecloth. People from the village were in the reception because Juniper had persuaded Ma to open up the house for Saskia's Sixteenth. Dieter had decided to call these people 'The Snoopers' because they sneered and prodded things, and then whispered under their breath.

'They should knock the old place down. They are knocking these empty places down, you know.'

'Sugar Hall is not empty, dear.'

'But it must be a dreadful thing to keep up, and so drafty…'

'That is exactly why only those who know how to keep our heritage, only those who share our heritage, should possess these great Halls.'

'Really, it's falling apart before our eyes. Look at the cornices, and that poor ceiling rose.'

'I heard death duties swallowed any money there was.'

'I heard things were not resolved at all.'

'It's such a strange business. Were there really no other benefactors? No other relatives?'

'Such odd circumstances, Peter Sugar was found, you know, just like his brother all those years ago…'

'Well. Tragedy has stalked this family.'

'Gossip. Vile gossip.'

'It was in the papers…'

'A tragedy. Pure and simple.'

'It is the daughter who is sixteen today? She isn't Peter's of course…'

Ma walked in and Dieter breathed at last. Juniper and John flanked her and they all carried silver plates of food. Ma had had her hair done and Dieter thought she looked beautiful, not quite glamorous yet, but so much better. When Ma smiled, the room fell silent.

'Deep breaths, deep breaths,' he heard Juniper mutter, 'they won't bite, Lilia, and if they do, bite back. Chin up, darling.' Juniper winked at his mother and then she was trailing the silent room with her plate of – he was sure it was prawn paste vol-au-vents.

'Come now, you must try one, Vicar. Lilia and I have been

working all day. Of course I'm fibbing, Ambrose. Caterers! I couldn't make these silly things!'

Dieter watched Juniper's spaniels shoot in between the guests' thick legs.

'Leave it!' she barked and the dogs froze.

He smelled the new plates of food and his stomach roared. He knew on the table above him were bowls of vegetable pieces, coronation chicken, jelly, blancmange; then countless egg sandwiches, plates of pressed tongue, those vol-au-vents stuffed with prawn paste and a glossy pork pie with a greasy bone-handled carving knife. There was Saskia's birthday cake too; it was tall and dark with cream and cherries. Dieter was so hungry, but he couldn't eat. Ma cried and told him he was skin and bone. She cooked his favourites: treacle pudding, goulash, steak and kidney pie, but he could only pick. When she tried chicken soup, sweet scrambled eggs, liver, dark greens and spoonfuls of vitamin B, Dieter gave up eating altogether.

'It's because of his imaginary friend,' Saskia said, but Ma didn't listen.

One of the Snoopers was talking loudly to his mother; he poked his head out further.

'I'm sure it is such a blessing having good help,' she said as she pointed at John, who was crouching on the floor rubbing the bellies of Juniper's spaniels. 'You are a good outdoor man! Aren't you, Phelps?' the woman cried.

John blushed and it made Dieter angry.

'Phelps here helped the Vicar and I with the garden one spring. Quite trustworthy. And it is so rare nowadays to find trustworthy help, don't you think, Mrs Sugar?' The woman coughed, 'and you yourself, my dear, were you in service when you first arrived in England?'

'Daphne!' Juniper cried. 'You are being most dreadfully rude. You do talk the most dreadful tosh.'

The woman went red in the face. 'Well, really…'

'Daphne, don't be coy. You are being rude, and rudeness is the height of bad manners.' Dieter noticed how Juniper wasn't even looking at the woman; she was walking towards John, then she crouched next to him and tickled her dogs. Dieter saw her lips move but didn't hear what she said. She stood up, 'Bonzo, down, boy! Terribly sorry, John,' she winked, 'once you give him attention he's all for you.'

Adults were so strange, Dieter thought.

Suddenly Ma was kneeling in front of the table and pulling up the tablecloth. 'Dee! Come out. You will take the sandwiches to our guests.' She reached in; ruffled his hair and he had to crawl out.

The silver plate of egg and cress triangles was heavy. Dieter walked straight to the woman called Daphne, the vicar's wife, and picked up a triangle of egg sandwich with his dirty and plastered fingers: he dropped it on her plate. 'There you are,' he smiled up at her, 'but do be careful, my Ma's egg sandwiches smell like farts.'

He moved around the room with the egg sandwiches but The Snoopers didn't care for egg, or for him. He saw Juniper standing at one of the long windows in her tweed suit, pointing out at the fields and arguing with a man who had redder cheeks than hers. They were arguing in that way that sounded like laughter. Dieter put the tray down on the groaning table of food: he was so hungry he nibbled on a loose plaster, pulling on the frayed strands with his teeth, then he walked through the Snoopers as if he were invisible.

He believed he was.

There was a new painting above the mantelpiece and he wanted to look at it. It was of Sugar Hall, but a very long time ago because the house was bright and clean, the gardens neat, and the tiny people in the foreground looked like they were made of glass. Dieter climbed up on to the seat of his grandfather's armchair, his feet creaking the old springs, until he could see the painting quite clearly.

The small figures in the foreground were so delicate, wispy and pale. Three men wore suits with short trousers and white stockings. There were ladies, three children and their mother, and they wore big puffy dresses and held parasols in their hands. They all had tall wigs, some white, some grey and they sat beneath the yew tree with Sugar Hall behind them. By the steps to the porch was a horse and a boy was holding its reins.

Dieter stopped breathing.

It was his friend, he was sure.

The boy wore a blue suit with gold buttons and white stockings. Dieter craned in closer to try and see it, the silver collar around his neck. He reached out to touch the canvas and the old paint felt hard.

'Careful, you'll fall,' a voice whispered.

Dieter felt ice at the pit of his stomach; his knees went to jelly and he crashed back into the armchair.

The adults didn't notice.

The boy was standing at the other end of the fireplace, his elbow cocked against the marble mantelpiece. He was so much bigger than before and he wasn't wearing Pa's shirt, but a blue velvet jacket with gold buttons and bright white stockings, just like in the painting.

He smiled.

'They'll see you!' Dieter glanced up at the room, expecting his ma to cry out and Juniper's dogs to howl. The Snoopers were chatting, whispering, pointing, but they hadn't noticed. 'You need to hide, they'll see you!'

Then Dieter realised something. 'You can talk,' he gasped.

His friend threw back his head and laughed, loud. Dieter shrank down in the chair, waiting for the Snoopers to react.

'Yes,' the boy said, 'I can talk,' and his voice tuned in and out; a shout in the smog, a radiogram dial turning on the airwaves. 'But they can't hear me,' and he glared at the room as if he was firing death rays from his eyes like the Mekon. 'They can't see me, either.'

The boy really was taller: his face thinner, longer. Dieter noticed he was actually wearing shoes: black with thick gold buckles on the front. He's dressed up for the party, Dieter thought.

'You…' Dieter stopped. He looked up at the painting, but the figure of the boy wearing a blue suit with gold buttons was no longer there. The horse was standing on its own.

Dieter gasped.

'Where is your sister?' the boy asked.

Dieter's teeth hurt as his friend spoke and he had to hold one side of his mouth.

Someone tugged on his arm, and Ma was craning over the armchair, 'Dee, what is it? You are so pale, Dee. You are sick?'

She held an empty tumbler in her hand; she smelled of whisky.

'Dee, my Dee, what is it?' she said. 'You are trembling!'

He looked across at the boy: he was so terribly handsome and so terribly grown that at last Dieter felt afraid.

'I'm fine, Ma. Just cold.'

The boy stepped towards Lilia. Dieter sprang up from the chair. 'Don't,' he said.

'Don't,' the boy repeated.

'Don't what, sweetheart?' Lilia asked.

Dieter tried to smile at his mother, 'I mean – don't – don't give me any more egg, Ma. I've had too much.'

'Oh, silly boy. Silly Dee,' she cried, and he knew she was a little drunk.

There was a loud droning noise outside. Lilia moved to the windows with the Snoopers to watch a small plane low in the sky.

'What's that?' the boy asked.

Dieter watched his mother go, and then replied. 'It's, it's an aeroplane, that's all.'

'Aer-o-plane?' The boy's lips stretched out in a smile. He leant his forehead against the mantlepiece. 'Do you want to leave this place, Dee-tah?'

It was the first time his friend had said his name and Dieter's ears whined.

'Do you wish to go back to London, Dee-tah? Lon-don,' the boy said it slowly, as if he were trying to see it through the smog. 'They would paint me in Lon-don.'

Dieter felt something in him give. He felt sleepy and he collapsed back in the chair. His friend walked towards him.

Yes, he was so much taller today; he was more like a man. Dieter looked up at his face and he felt dizzy. As the boy put a finger to his cheek a cold buzzing began in Dieter's belly.

'The walk was long,' the boy told him, 'they took me to a tall house, they gave me a waistcoat of gold, they had me sit in a small room, and a man, he painted me.'

'A picture?'

'A portrait.'

'Is it here?'

'No. It is gone.'

Dieter heard a strange whimpering noise and looked down to see Juniper's two spaniels crawling towards them on their bellies; their heads flat to the ground, stumpy tails jerking. The boy reached down to put a finger to each of their broad foreheads and they whined a whine of pleasure.

'Dogs,' the boy stood up. 'Dogs. Horses. I cared for them.' The boy smiled. 'And now I am hungry, Dieter Sugar.'

Dieter hid his hands behind his back.

The boy chuckled. 'No, no,' he said and Dieter thought the boy's voice was the creak of rope and he felt himself sinking. The boy was above him now, and then his hands were on his face, such cold hands, and he was leaning forward and he was kissing Dieter: first one cheek, then the other, and then gently on his lips.

The boy stayed like that for such a long time – his cold lips against Dieter's – and he breathed in Dieter's breath; he breathed in and he didn't stop.

This time it wasn't the boy's voice that was the fuzz of a tuning radio, it was Dieter himself who was tuning in and out. In this fug Dieter found himself day-dreaming. He suddenly saw himself flying away in the big balloon from the sheds. He was holding onto the sides of the wicker basket and swaying over a wide river, over fields, houses. He was waving, too, because almost at once he was gliding over the Wasteland and there were the Wee-Hoos. The twins, Deuteronomy and Comfort Jones, were running beneath him, and there, on the mound by the brick wall was Cynthia.

His dream-Cynthia was yelling up at him, she was jumping on the spot and waving. 'Dee, fight him,' she cried. 'Dee! Fight! You have to be strong. You have to run. Run away! He'll hurt you, Dieter!' And then almost at once everything was thick with smog. 'I can't see you, Dee,' his dream-Cynthia was crying. 'Where did you go? You're lost in the smog. Shout my name! Where are you, Dieter?'

'The Family of Sir William Sugar, the Grounds of Sugar Hall', Johan Zoffany, c. 1767-69

Oil on canvas, 114.3 x 167.8 cm

A Visitor

17

It was only when a strong arm tugged his waist that Dieter came to. There was high-pitched murmuring, like flies buzzing.

'Leave him be,' John was saying. 'Get that knife from him, that's all. Take the knife.'

Something was wrenched from his fingers and Dieter went limp. He opened his eyes to see Juniper standing over him and the Snoopers behind her, muttering. Ma pushed forward.

'Dee, oh, Dee, what have you done?'

He looked up at the faces. He wasn't lost in the smog on the Wasteland anymore but back in the big green armchair by the mantelpiece in the reception. He saw a carving knife in Juniper's hands: greasy with fat.

Juniper stepped closer; she stared down at him. 'Do you know what you tried to do, young man?'

He shook his head as she straightened up and pointed at the painting over the fireplace: the one with the olden-day family under the trees and Sugar Hall behind them; the one with the horse and the boy in the blue suit. Now there was a small tear in the canvas, right through the family.

'You attacked that.'

Ma was wringing her hands. 'Don't tell him…'

'Lilia,' Juniper snapped, 'he needs to know. Dieter, do you know what you did?'

He shook his head.

'You took the knife from the table and you climbed on top of the mantelpiece and you stabbed that painting with this knife.' She held it out; it was evidence. 'Why? Why did you do this, child?'

Dieter burped. 'I don't know,' he said, as calmly as he could. 'Can I go now, please?'

He saw his mother bite her lip; then she gave a nod and he slipped to the floor, he wobbled as he stood up.

'I'll take you upstairs, darling, I'll put you to bed,' she said.

'It's the girl's party, don't let him spoil it,' Juniper whispered. 'Fresh air, that's what this boy needs.'

'It is not your business, Juniper,' Ma hissed and then he saw Juniper take his mother's hand because she was the one wobbling on her feet.

When Juniper turned back to him her eyes were angry. 'Dieter,' she said, 'please could you take my dogs out; they are getting terribly restless.' She clicked her fingers and pointed to the open door. 'Outside!' she barked at the spaniels and they ran out into the passageway in a straight line. 'Now, Dieter, you too,' she commanded.

He glanced up at his mother; she looked like she might cry, so he bolted through the muttering Snoopers, and out into the passage after the dogs. He could hear Saskia's crooning music come from the boot room, but Juniper's spaniels were dashing across the big black and white tiles of the hall and he followed them. The thick front door was wide open but Dieter stopped. He watched the dogs run back and forth like crazed things on the grass; the bunches of their curly ears bouncing either side of their wide heads. Then he ducked under the chain that blocked off the staircase from those Snoopers, and he trotted up the stairs.

It was a good vantage point. He could see everything that crossed the vast hall below, he could even see the two large yellow and black butterflies that fluttered in, knocked against the pitted gilt mirror and into the arms of the chandelier hanging above. Dieter was hiding, this time behind the marble plinth that stood on the first small landing.

The space Dieter had squeezed into was tight, but he felt safe, invisible. He was a little mouse hiding. He closed his eyes and wished and wished that the boy wouldn't find him here.

A door in the passage below crashed open and he heard the gallop of Saskia and her friends as they ran across the black and white tiles of the hall, squealing. They jumped the chain across the stairs and Dieter shrank back as they thundered closer. He could smell them: fruity with new nail varnish, the scent strong as a bag of pear drops. He heard their giggling gasps, felt their heat; and then they were gone, running past him up the staircase.

'Wait for me! I'm frightened!' one of them called.

Dieter peeked out to see the girls circling each gallery, running up, up to the next and then the next floor. They were running up to the attic. The girls' footsteps were still echoing when Dieter saw a stranger walk in through the open front door.

It was a man. He stood on the threshold, stared up, and whistled through his teeth. Dieter hunched back down behind the plinth as the man took off his grey hat, walked to the table beneath the gilt mirror and placed the hat there; he ran the fingers of one hand along the edge of the table, blew on his dusty finger, and he whistled again. A grey overcoat hung over his arm, although it was summer, and Dieter watched him tap on a section of the dark wood panels that lined the hall. The two big yellow and black butterflies flitted about him, and he waved them away.

Dieter had never seen this man before.

'Well,' the stranger said out loud, and he scratched his head, pushed his glasses up his nose and whistled again.

He was standing on the bottom tread of the staircase now, straining against the chain that hung between the newel posts. This time the man tapped his fingers on the carved wooden balls of the posts; then he hung his coat on one, shook his head, and sat on the bottom step. He took out a cigarette and he lit it.

'Lily,' the man said, and Dieter felt strange: he felt like he wanted to run down these stairs and shoo the stranger out and far away.

There were footsteps coming from the passageway and all at once Ma and Juniper were standing in front of the stranger with empty silver salvers in their hands. Dieter saw his mother's face fall, and as it did the big silver plate fell too, and by the time that had landed with a crash so loud Dieter had to put his fingers in his ears, Ma was also on the black and white floor; a small and crumpled thing.

Ma had fainted. If Tommy Perrot were here he'd say she'd gone down like a ton of bricks.

The stranger sprung up, he cried, 'Liliana!'

Dieter didn't move.

A black shoe – Ma's nice high heel, thick and suede – was lying on its side a few inches from her stocking foot. Dieter thought that both the foot and the shoe looked so sad, so helpless, parted like that.

How to Treat Shock

1) Treat any obvious injuries
2) Lay the person down with a blanket or a rug.
   Keep the person warm
3) Reassure them
4) Loosen any tight clothing
5) Hot, sweet tea can revive a person

Strong Black Coffee

18

Juniper admired the way Lilia's forthright nature revealed itself once she came to. Lilia had demanded they take her into the library and close the door, that Dieter should go outside and the guests be asked to leave, she demanded that Saskia and the girls were left to play – they must all keep to the birthday plan, she said, the girls would catch the 4.38 bus into Cheltenham and the girls would see *Richard III*. Lilia was adamant. Lilia had demanded strong, black coffee.

Juniper took great pleasure in asking everyone in the reception to go, and with no explanation. She loitered on the threshold of the green room as the guests shuffled past.

'What has happened, Juniper?'

'This is disgraceful.'

'I've never been so…'

'Well, really…'

In truth, Juniper's enjoyment was rather tempered by her concern for Lilia, and now, as she stood over the black range in the basement kitchen, she hurried with the bitter coffee. She had opened the back door and fresh summer air wafted down the outside steps; she could hear her dogs tumble in the garden and it calmed her. Juniper cut the dark, heady fruitcake, laid out cups, saucers and small plates. She placed the silver pot of steaming coffee on the tray and added more cake; it seemed these fainting Sugars needed something sweet.

As she managed the kitchen steps, Juniper considered what sort of scene was being acted out above her in the library: Lilia on the red chaise longue with that strange man at her feet, and outside poor love-struck John Phelps gnashing his teeth at the library window. No, this was rather too *Wuthering Heights* in tone. The stranger had declared himself to be one 'Alex'. He had informed them all he was a childhood friend from Germany. Although he didn't sound overly German to Juniper, his voice was American, like one of her GIs. Still, once Lilia came to, she'd kissed the stranger all over his face, so Juniper suspected he was a long-lost sweetheart and concluded he was telling the truth.

She stepped into the dark passageway and stopped. Her arms were strong and the tray didn't wobble but in the damp darkness she shivered, the hairs standing up at the back of her neck. She breathed deep just as her mother had taught her whenever she fell badly from her horse. Juniper steadied herself, and then walked on. In the hall she placed the tray on the table by the gilt mirror, next to the stranger's grey hat, and walked to the foot of the staircase.

Juniper needed a pause.

Sugar Hall had always done this to her, she supposed it was because of the dead. She glanced up at the gallery of the landing, at the portraits of dead Sugars lined up there like so many ducks. Most faces were centuries old, but at the head of the stairs there was the old man Gerald and there was Richard, his eldest boy, to his right. Both had been painted in uniform. There had been a portrait of Peter Sugar there, too; but it made sense that Lilia had taken that down.

They were all dead. Dead, dead, dead.

Who knew, Juniper thought as she stretched her legs out, easing the tightness of her morning walk, perhaps Richard would have come a cropper in any case. Perhaps if they hadn't found him that terrible summer night strung up like gamekeeper's quarry from the arm of that ancient oak, perhaps he would have simply been shot down in the next war. Perhaps he would have bought it on these country lanes in his new motorcar, toot-tooting like Toad of Toad Hall; perhaps he would have taken a swim in Cannop Ponds one night with too much brandy and too much verve. There were so many possibilities.

Juniper looked up because something kept tickling the back of her neck, something up there was setting her teeth on edge. She shook her head, there was nothing but shadow. Juniper stood and marched back to the tray; she popped a sugarcube into her mouth because she needed the strength, too. She knew she would be walking into a scene in the library, and how Juniper detested scenes.

She paused as girlish laughter came from the high landings above. Juniper began to whistle, and she was soothed by the sharp clip of her sensible brown shoes as she strode towards the gaudy red library, the tray in one hand.

Inside, she poured the strong coffee and they were oblivious to her. The stranger and Lilia were speaking in a language that she could only part understand, she had studied German at school but this was a strange, mangled German. Juniper picked up words, phrases, but then she gave up and picked up the silver tongs to grasp at the sugar cubes; she stirred and the black coffee became thick. She walked to the red chaise longue where Lilia was sitting; the stranger perched on a small pouf at her feet. He was rather like a faithful dog, Juniper thought, a French bulldog perhaps. Lilia truly was a flame, a honeypot, all of those phrases Juniper disliked. For a moment she wondered if she too were simply orbiting around the sweetness of Lilia Sugar.

'Here, Lilia,' she said, holding out a rose and gold lacquer cup and saucer. 'Drink.'

When the stranger took his cup she saw that he was much younger than he seemed, and apart from the way he sat on that pouf he was quite handsome in a darkish way. Juniper liked the way he was solidly built: his black hair was so admirably thick, though in need of a trim. She was wondering if she should stay when Lilia looked up at her, took her hand and squeezed it.

'Thank you,' she said, 'please sit, Juniper.'

Lilia didn't introduce the man or offer the space next to her, and Juniper was glad. She wanted to distance herself from their shocked faces, their odd muttering, and the cloying atmosphere that hugged them.

Juniper settled in a rather pleasing Queen Anne chair by the bay windows. The chair was slightly turned away from the pair and Juniper stared out at the lawns as she sipped her sweet coffee. She hated sweet coffee. She also hated the garish red of this room. A library should relax a person but here the frighteningly red carpet, the thick sponge-like wallpaper (embossed with the black silhouettes of butterflies in an attempt – Juniper could only fathom – at relief) made it a Maharaja's Palace and not conducive to reading at all. Butterflies and moths: mad Gerald had been obsessed. He'd once shown her his collection in some locked room upstairs. 'My husks', he called them.

Sunlight hit her sensibly shoed foot and she felt its warmth penetrate the leather. She took the teaspoon from the saucer and used its end to clean under her nails, and by the time she noticed the voices were talking in English, Juniper was drenched in sun.

'So many years I have been writing, writing,' the man was saying. He sounded a little more German now beneath the American twang.

There were heavy beats of silence.

'Do you know…' the man asked.

'No,' Lilia said.

Another beat of silence.

Juniper wanted to block her ears, instead she gazed out at the mangled red gardens and tried not to listen.

'America is a long way to come.'

'I have business here. In London.'

'That's a long way to come. London to here.'

'It is nothing, Lily, nothing!'

'How did you find me here?'

'I went to Churchill Gardens. What a name, Lily! Your neighbour she gave me the forwarding address.'

'But how did you find me…'

'Lily…'

'I thought. Alex, I thought…'

There was silence again, and then Lilia's voice was less than a whisper. 'Tell me where in America, Alex? What do you do? Oh, Alex, you are here…'

Juniper began to tap the small teaspoon on the arm of the chair because she hated to hear these intimacies, these silences heavy with things she had already guessed at. She knew what Lilia's story must be, and how the poor girl got out of Germany in time was a miracle. She obviously had nobody left, but now this stranger had appeared: it was too, too much for Juniper. To stop herself eavesdropping, she found herself humming Edwin's song, the poor dead RAF pilot's song, until the words came to her in whispers. 'We came from way out West, we came to do our best … to fight for right and against the might of the Nazi terrorist.'

Edwin had been so unbearably young.

'We have our boys in blue, in grey and khaki too, we'll sing our song and they'll fight along against Nazi terrorist,' she trilled.

Juniper wiped her cheeks with the back of her hand, and then she had to smile at her ridiculous show; the cloying atmosphere in here was catching. Sentimental fool. She stretched her foot out further and noticed two moths with wings patterned like bark on the bright panes of the windows; they were completely still, stunned by the light. It took a few moments for her to notice a heavier silence and then to look across to find Lilia and the stranger, Alex, staring at her with shocked faces.

'Oh, please don't mind me, I was…' but Juniper didn't know what she was doing; it was too much sherry and too much sweet black coffee. It was too much drama and this room really was too red. 'Do forgive me. I was daydreaming.' She cleared her throat and stood.

She was sick of indolence; she should be out with her spaniels.

The teaspoon dropped to the floor and she smoothed down her tweed skirt. 'Lilia, dear, please, don't take offence,' she said because Lilia's face was quite a picture. Strong, robust, she marched over to her. 'And now that you are recovered I must be going. Thank you for such a marvellous afternoon.' She suddenly whispered because she was afraid words might damage her friend in some way. 'My dear, I will come over with the vitamins we talked of, and brewer's yeast, you do look a fright.'

Juniper took Lilia's hand from her lap and tried to squeeze it. She leant over and pecked her on the cheek, but it was like kissing a hung and plucked bird. There's no life in it, Juniper thought, and there should be, there should be! For a moment she was angry. As for the stranger, Alex, he didn't move from the leather pouf, he simply blinked. When Juniper opened the door, Dieter walked in looking as pale and bereft as his mother.

'There's fruitcake on the tray, you should eat a little,' she told him, 'you don't want to faint again. Make sure your mother takes some, too.'

Juniper left the room.

Outside, as she strode down the potholed drive, relieved to be in the fresh air, she called her dogs to heel. She hated to see them so skittish but they always were up here at the Hall. Next time she would leave them at home. She stopped suddenly and glanced back at the grand facade of the ugly place, at the dark stone; at

147

the great pillars, bigger than they needed to be. She noticed that raven of John's on the peak of the porch. It was cawing, over and over, caw-caw-caw.

Ravens were omens, weren't they?

Juniper heard girlish screams from inside and the hair rose once again at the back of her neck, then she remembered Saskia's party. Of course, Saskia and her friends were still playing in there, causing havoc.

'To heel! To heel!' she cried at her spaniels.

As Juniper straddled the first stile, she looked back at the Hall. Juniper knew what haunted meant; she had known since she first walked into Sugar Hall that hot summer between the wars. She knew about the ghost too, though she had never seen him. The fact of 'the Slave Boy' – as they called him in the village – was common knowledge and had been for years. The ghost simply was, like the apple trees along the tennis courts here, like the forest plantation behind this monstrous eyesore of a house. Juniper wasn't quite sure if she believed in this ghost or not but she knew this didn't matter. She had never mentioned it to Lilia and Lilia had never mentioned anything to her.

It was the living that concerned Juniper.

Yes, as she straddled the stile, Juniper decided to help Lilia more than she had because Juniper realised how much she liked Lilia – she couldn't fathom the reason but she knew it was tied to her strong spirit rather than her weak body. After all, the poor thing had survived in this ghastly hall with two children for over five months, and Juniper could hardly survive the day in there.

She would write that cheque. She would get them all out of the ghastly place.

She jumped to the spongy ground. It was a strange and very small world, Juniper thought, and she snuck her hands in the sleeves of her tweed jacket and marched on.

Thunder

19

Once Juniper left, Lilia didn't *think* of pinching herself – she pinched, and hard. Now red welts patterned her arms.

Alex was here: Alex Behr.

The last time she saw Alex Behr she was fifteen years old.

He had found her here, in the mausoleum of Sugar Hall. It wasn't what she had expected today, it was enough that the Nosey Parkers from the village had come, it was enough that Saskia's friends were to be entertained, it was enough that Dieter wasn't strong like he should be, it was all enough. And now here Alex was.

He held her hands so tight her ring pinched, but she wouldn't move. They were done with talking. There was too much and too little to say. She gazed at him. She was sure her Alex Behr was hidden somewhere in this man's face: the bright brown eyes, the freckles on the bridge of the nose, the thick hair. She'd let her fingers rest in that hair when she was nothing but a child. They would swim in the river with her brothers, she and Alex. He would tease her, splash her, tell her she was skinny Lily. Then they were older and he had teased her but it was different. She had known – even then – that he loved her.

Alex Behr, four years older and her brothers' friend: her brothers, she wanted to block their names out, but now Alex's voice had broken her because it was a voice that belonged to another life, it was a voice loved by another girl – Lily Fisch.

She felt her skin prick with panic. Suddenly she wanted to scream but she didn't. She noticed Dieter standing by the door.

'Lily,' Alex was speaking, 'I said, why here, Lily? Why are you here, alone?'

'I am not alone, I told you.'

'Yes, yes…' Alex looked over at Dieter and smiled.

'I am not alone,' she repeated.

'What is this place?'

She shook her head because she hardly knew.

'I do not think this is for you, Liliana, not for you.'

She tried to laugh because Alex Behr hadn't changed, here he was after sixteen years telling her what she should do, telling her what was right and what was wrong: what was right for her.

'Sh, Alex, sh…' she whispered. 'Please. I need to hear about your life. Tell me now. I want to know your life.'

He grinned; his teeth were better than they'd ever been as a child. He reached out and he touched her hair.

'You're blonde, Lily?'

She felt like blushing and she couldn't fathom why. 'It suits me,' she said chin out.

'You think?'

'Alex, stop it,' she smiled. 'You cannot be right about everything. Tell me about your life. Please.'

He sighed. 'I live in Brooklyn. I like Brooklyn, just next to the park.'

'Brooklyn,' she said, and it sounded strange.

He was stroking her cheek, 'Lily, my Lily, where have you been? I have written, written so many times…'

'Please, no. You tell me about your life…'

It was a strange feeling when she heard the scream, it came from beyond the closed library door and it was as if someone was screaming for her. A silence followed that seemed louder, as if the house was holding its breath, preparing itself for the next outburst.

Alex started. 'Lily, what is…?'

More screams followed, and they came at different pitches. Alex stood and rushed to the door. He looked back. 'Lily?'

She didn't move. Whatever was coming, she didn't want it. Lilia Sugar, Lily Fisch, or whoever she was now, was tired; she was exhausted. She wouldn't move. Let whatever was out there stay out there. She wanted this moment with Alex, the flurry of this surprise hello, the tenderness of it; she wanted to tease it out. But now she knew it was over because something dreadful was happening out there.

Lilia considered the English word, 'dread'.

She swallowed air like she was drowning. Yes, she had thought it before and she thought it again; she was drowning.

That was when she heard the thunder.

For a moment she thought how refreshing a summer storm might be, but at the same time she knew it wasn't that sort of thunder, this noise was coming from inside the house.

This was it then: at last Sugar Hall was falling to the ground.

The thunder rumbled above them: louder, louder.

'Lily!' Alex cried, and finally she sprang up.

She pushed past him, past Dieter, she pushed the door and marched into the passage and out onto the hall.

She would put a stop to this.

The thunder was coming from upstairs.

Lilia was sick of being scared in this house, she was sick of panic. She walked across those silly black and white tiles to the foot of the stairs, she put her fists on her hips and she looked up.

High up on one of the dark landings she saw shapes blur with movement as they turned in wide circles from one landing down to the next. That was the thunder and it came with squeals and whimpers. The shapes began to come into focus and all at once

Lilia knew she was staring up at legs: the flash of girls' legs through the barley twist rails. She saw flashes of white underwear, too; she saw skirts swishing, ballooning up in white, brown, yellow and blue.

As the legs tumbled the thunder grew louder.

Saskia and her friends must have been up in the attic and now they were gathering momentum as they ran down in one great rush.

Lilia tried to spot Saskia in the jumble of limbs because she suddenly thought how she would love to slap her daughter's legs, like her own mother had slapped hers; her mother whom she had loved more than ice cream. How Lilia would love to put Saskia over her knee and slap her pink thighs until they scalded red: Saskia who was ruining her peace now, Saskia who had always ruined her peace.

The girls yelped as they stumbled. Lilia held onto the newel post and wondered if they'd trip over each other and fall all this way down. She wondered if there would be blood and, if so, how much. She wondered if the other girls would stumble and land on top of Saskia, crushing her. Lilia noticed a flash of colours now as the girls grasped hold of the banisters at each turn: she noticed the bright colours of their evening gloves; the whiteness of their bobby socks.

Suddenly Lilia was jealous of Saskia, this fat-hipped girl of hers, so spoilt, so unwanted. She felt it rise up in her as she stared up at her clumsy child running down the stairs. Lilia reached out and held onto the thin brass chain she'd looped across the staircase. She shook her head, for by God she didn't want to remember all that. Still, she couldn't stop staring up at those ugly girls and their ugly dresses with their ugly spoilt and fat legs as they thundered down these ugly stairs. No, Lilia didn't want to remember: she had to stop herself remembering. But it was here, right here, she could taste it: Berlin and the boy who had done that to her (she had the urge to point up at Saskia and yell 'that!') She didn't want

153

to remember the boy's eyes and his wet lips as he spat at her and grunted over her like the pig he was. She didn't want to remember his breath, strangely sweet like he'd just eaten a toffee, as he growled ugly words in her ear. She didn't want to remember how he pulled her in from the street and into a stairwell of a building on Mülhauser Strasse. When Lilia saw the light brown uniform she knew what it meant. Then she couldn't think because his breath was so close as he spat his words at her, *'Nimm dies, nimm dies, nimm dies!'* He'd laughed then, *'Mein Geschenk für Dich, mein Geschenk für Dich!'*

He'd told her: have this, have this, my gift to you.

Lilia stared up at her daughter and she wanted to laugh. It was his gift thundering down these dusty steps: her girl with heavenly hips and that boy's eyes. Lilia had woken up the next morning in the stairwell in Mülhauser Strasse and a woman had stepped over her, like this happened every day. It did, of course.

The four girls turned on the first landing and they rushed down the last set of stairs in a pack towards her.

They were a strange sight, their demi-waved hair matted with sweat, their faces white and their mouths drawn tight, teeth showing like frightened cats. The one she knew as Tina had a torn sleeve and Saskia had lost a shoe somewhere on her journey down; her neck was terribly scratched, too. Another had spots of blood on the front of her dress, and the short fat one had a small cut below her eye. The thunder kept up and Lilia stepped away. Saskia was the first because she was pushing the other girls back as she leapt, four steps before the hard floor of the hall. Saskia snapped the thin brass chain with her heavenly hips and landed with a great thud on the black and white tiles. Lilia noticed her wince; she watched her daughter stand up, shake herself, and then run to the open front door.

The other three girls tumbled past, and then Lilia felt inclined to look up once again.

Far up, on one of the upper floors, she was sure she saw something shimmer. It was almost gold: it sparked. She couldn't see anything clearly but she heard a boy's giggle. The sound made her swallow her breath, because Dieter was over there standing next to Alex, and anyway this wasn't the sort of giggle to warm your heart, it was the sort of sound that froze it sure as the North wind.

Alex watched all this from the middle of the hall and he thought of nothing because Alex knew how to blank his mind. He had become expert at it.

'Beruhigt Euch, Mädchen!' he said as the girls ran past him.

As for the girls, they ran out into the bright garden, out onto the lawn, then past the sprouting tennis courts and the vegetable patch, on and on until suddenly, out of breath and stunned as rabbits, they couldn't run any more and each girl dropped as if touched on the shoulder by a hypnotist and told to sleep. Each girl fell to the lush green ground and each girl slept where she lay: a tangle of flushed coltish limbs, a mess of flared skirts and bobby socks.

Saskia snored immediately.

TO:
Liliana Fisch
c/o
German Jewish Aid Committee
Woburn House
Bloomsbury
London, WC1
April 17th 1955

Dear Lily,

I have written this letter so many times
over the years but I've heard nothing.
Still, I will write to you. I hope you
are there. I pray you are.

I'm coming to London on a business trip
in a few months and I want to find you.

I'm doing well. America has treated me
well. I am divorced. I have a daughter.

I hope this letter finds you.

Alex Behr

p.s. I should ask, do you remember me?

Alex Behr
149 Crown St,
Brooklyn, NY, 11225

The Lepidopterist

20

It had been a disaster of a birthday party, that much was clear to the vicar, Ambrose Hetherington. His housekeeper had brought in tea and Madeira cake while parents were called. The whimpering girls from Sugar Hall had been given blankets, and for now they shared the flower-patterned sofa that dominated his living room (part of the garish three-piece suite his wife, Daphne, had insisted on).

'It felt like bees, like a swarm of bees,' one of the hefty girls had told him when they'd first tried to settle them. 'It was suddenly black and I couldn't see and I couldn't breathe,' she'd sobbed. Ambrose had attempted to engage. 'Where were you, child?' he'd asked.

'In that blue room. I trod on Shirley.'

'I beg your pardon?'

'We all trod on Shirley, didn't we?'

The lumpiest, clearly Shirley, had moaned and Ambrose had stepped back. It was the Sugar girl who'd continued. 'It was day outside and I'm sure the curtains were open, but suddenly it was dark in that room and when we ran, Shirley fell, and we trod on her. Poor Shirley.'

Since the Madeira cake, the girls had thankfully fallen silent. They nibbled on the sweet sponge and stared – rather lifeless – at

Daphne's samplers that adorned one wall. Ambrose didn't care for Daphne's samplers, they told him, 'Bless This House', 'A Man's Heart is His Home' and 'A Woman's Work is Never Done'. Ambrose turned to the small animal figurines that crowded shelves in the corner of the room. These were also Daphne's: minute, shiny and badly made, they reminded Ambrose a little of her.

One of the girls kept pulling the top of her ripped sleeve up towards her shoulder; another held a hand to her cut cheek and swollen eye, the hair on the head of that lumpiest girl buzzed with something like static and her foot was set up on a stool, tightly bandaged. The daughter, Saskia, was rubbing her fingers over her scratched neck and cheek. She wore one shoe.

Female hysteria, the vicar thought, and he shuddered from his toes up.

The thing that irked him most about these girls was their awful mismatched gloves: long evening gloves in mint green, coral, siren red, cobalt blue, ivory and black. He attempted to calm himself with the thought that parents would be here soon.

Daphne had switched on the four-bar heater even though it was summer, because these girls *would* shiver. She sat adjacent to the fire, smiling at the children, while he stood in front of the red-hot tubes, his knees bending like a policeman. He hated to be alone with women, and this was more than uncomfortable. The other men, Phelps and a strange man with an accent, had left for the Hall (the vicar still couldn't believe Phelps had been standing in his drawing room in his boots because Daphne was too slow with the newspaper). The men had driven back to the Hall, the vicar's shooting sticks under their arms to check for robbers, gypsies, or both, these were the usual culprits. Ambrose knew that anyone could sneak into that big place and hide for weeks if they chose. It was a vast and foolish place for a widow and her children. Daphne had even told him how this little family had crammed themselves into one room –and he supposed the Sugar woman, Lilia, was used to that sort of living. He had hoped to see more of the house today, but it had all ended so mysteriously, Juniper Bledsoe barging in and telling – not asking – them all to leave when they hadn't even cut the girl's birthday cake. And now he and Daphne had only been home an hour or so when the odd – but he had to confess, pretty – little Sugar woman was knocking on his door with a gaggle of hysterical girls who had refused to walk back into the Hall.

'I won't go back in there, I won't!' one had sobbed.

'A boy, I saw a boy,' the fat daughter said.

Ambrose felt as if he had been let into a secret then, but so far no amount of subtle prods or blatant questions had illuminated much beyond this statement.

Yes, heaven knows what had happened up at Sugar Hall, although Ambrose had an inkling.

He glanced at Lilia Sugar sitting in the armchair with her son; they were squashed in together and it was unseemly. There was no denying that she was a pretty thing, but Ambrose did wonder what sort of life she had come from. He knew she was German, but the children seemed English enough. Still, the world was different now and people were forever telling him all that shouldn't matter.

Of course, it did.

He watched Lilia lean over and kiss the son and heir, Dieter, on the crown of his head; it was a loud kiss and Lilia came to rest her cheek on the boy's fair hair. Ambrose didn't care for the way the boy's red legs stuck out of grey shorts; it looked ridiculous for the child must have been ten at least. The boy reminded Ambrose of the drooling blond Labrador pup Daphne had once taken in. Still, as he bent his knees while standing in front of the electric fire, he felt the pricking of guilt. After a first brief visit back in January, he and Daphne had ignored this family because – he reasoned – they had made themselves easy to ignore. He had felt it best to leave well alone. It was the battered air of this Sugar woman that irked him; it was as unseemly as this show of affection between mother and son. The vicar saw this family as barnacles, foreign barnacles because the rock they clung to wasn't even theirs. They were tenants, squatters.

Ambrose bit hard into his soft Madeira cake as the bars of the fire grew hot on the back of his dress trousers. He watched the lumpy Sugar daughter stand up, place her blanket on the arm of the sofa, and in a loud voice ask where the toilet might be. Ambrose shuddered as he wiped crumbs from his cuffs.

Toilet: yes, it really was unseemly.

Later, when his house was quiet, the children gone, Ambrose Hetherington stood in front of his thick-legged writing desk, the ironing board out and pointing its nose towards the drawn curtains. His study door was locked. Daphne would never come in here unannounced, but Ambrose preferred the security of a lock as he stood, trouserless, his tight sock suspenders digging in below the knees and just the way he liked it.

He folded the pair of ironed white underpants, placed them on the pile, and picked out the next: only he could ever iron these intimate things of his, it was bad enough the help dealing with the washing and boiling of his smalls, let alone spending time pushing a hot iron into their creases; perhaps looking a little too close, perhaps allowing drops of sweat to fall on the cotton. Ambrose turned his underpants, pressed the iron down, and coughed.

Not long after those parents came to pick up their charges, faces white with worry – and who could blame them – the drawing-room door had opened and Phelps and that foreign man had walked in. Ambrose thought how strange that was, his own doors being pushed open roughly while the maid, Gladys, squawked from the hall.

'It is empty up there, Lilia, we've been through all the rooms,' Phelps said to the Sugar woman. 'Just a lot of mess in the old blue room in the attics.' Again, Phelps hadn't taken off his boots.

'It's as if the girls had been playing, Lily,' the foreign man added, and he'd knelt in front of Mrs Sugar like a suitor, holding her small hand and rubbing it. 'I think those girls spooked themselves,' he nodded at the daughter who had fallen asleep on the sofa next to the rag-tag boy.

'We can go back, then?' she'd asked, but her voice was wavering. Ambrose would term it frightened. He'd looked at his wife, trying to communicate, but that had always been a chore.

Then Mrs Sugar was standing in front of him, offering him a weak hand to shake and saying, 'Thank you for your hospitality. We will go. Come now, Dieter, wake, wake up. Saskia. Come now, we go home.'

'Are you sure, Mrs Sugar?' he'd asked out of politeness.

'Of course, girls' silliness, that is all. Nothing, there is nothing.'

For a moment Ambrose thought the fat daughter would plead to stay because she wouldn't move from Daphne's rose-pattern sofa, and she kept muttering about, 'the boy upstairs, the horrid boy, he'll hurt us.' Then something in her seemed to switch off and she stood. She thanked him for having her.

They were such strange children.

After they left, Daphne had insisted Gladys dust down the sitting room because their visitors had left a strange smell. It was a scent akin to fearful animals, Ambrose thought: musty, vinegary, though at the same time creamily sweet, like hard toffees warmed by the sun. The shivering teenagers had left that scent on the fabrics, and Gladys had to open the windows. Now that Daphne had sent Gladys home, she was dealing with the supper alone. This was never good, and Ambrose was glad to be locked away in his study; he was also glad of his hidden box of chocolate liqueurs on the top shelf of his bookcase.

He pressed down onto the white cotton with the hot iron and a thrill ran up from the soles of his feet to the tops of his thighs; he touched the iron and winced, giggling, because he loved the sharp heat that an iron brought. As a child he'd wait at the foot of his bed every night, while his mother ironed sheets that were already tucked into the mattress. It had been such a glorious feeling crawling into that warmth.

His bare legs were cold, the suspenders cutting in tight below the knee. He picked up a white vest and thought of the fat daughter's words: 'the boy upstairs, the horrid boy'. Ambrose let the steam rise to his face, and breathed it in.

Ambrose knew whom she meant.

He had, for his first and rather long winter here, researched even embraced local stories. After all as vicar he had to know exactly what his congregation feared (apart from God). He had to know what he was up against. Sugar Hall had one peculiar story, and it was a story the whole village claimed. It seemed there were many ghosts at the Hall; Cavaliers, Roundheads, jilted brides, headless knights, but the one ghost that lived present in the imagination of his parishioners was 'the Slave Boy'. That was the name they gave him, plain and simple. Ambrose had listened to the stories of a slave child come back to haunt his masters, a tale of revenge. The gossips in the village said the boy had been hanged in the woods behind Sugar Hall for some crime almost two centuries ago, and a curse had fallen on the Sugars ever since. There were so many stories. They said the slave boy was a Sugar himself, born at the hall to a lascivious master; they said he had attacked this master when the master killed the boy's mother out in the Hall's graveyard. They also said the boy had killed the master's son because this son had forced himself on a sister, and there was a child; they said the boy had fallen in love with someone he shouldn't and the old master had taken his revenge. Love seemed unlikely, but Ambrose had listened as former staff from the Hall told him tales of plates smashing, shoes and hats disappearing (they were very definite about the shoes), figures walking out of paintings, and a cold blue room in the attic. It was too ridiculous and Ambrose knew this first-hand because as hard as he had researched he had found no firm record of this particular boy in parish records. Slaves in the English country home were signs of great wealth, he'd discovered, but still they were commodities. At any one time – back in those days – Sugar Hall seemed to have between one to three slaves, yet they changed hands so fast, they were sold on so frequently, it was impossible to tell one apart from the other in the parish books.

Ambrose guffawed and bent at the knee as he thought of the names he had stumbled upon, so ill-fitting: 'Caius', 'Scipio', 'Romulus', 'Remus', 'Caesar', even a 'Pompey'. One note in the records told him, 'Julius Caesar, a black drummer was buried, 15th February, 1795, out of hallowed ground'. Another told him, 'Ino Caesar Hinton, a lusty black fellow…' and something in the vicar thrilled to the word 'lusty' '…ran away the 16th from the service of Mr Viney of the city of _____ with a blue Livery lined with yellow and a dark brown wig.' Ambrose wondered how far the fellow had reached dressed like that.

There was nothing of a hanging in the woods: nothing about a slave boy and a crime.

In his research he had noted that the women were given plainer names – 'Sarah', 'Susannah', 'Hannah', 'Charlotte', 'Betsy' – though he did recall a 'Dido'. Their place of origin was sometimes local, it seems some of these slaves were actually born here; slaves begat slaves, Ambrose supposed, and indeed masters begat slaves. He shuddered and pressed down on the iron until the hairs on his legs stood to attention. Yes, he had found some were born here and some weren't slaves at all, but servants, indeed some were perfectly free and always had been (to his surprise he'd discovered records in Bristol of four businessmen, two violinists, a circus owner, and a gentlewoman). In fact Ambrose had spent a most vexing afternoon when he'd discovered baptismal and burial records going back to 1583. He'd become dreadfully confused because he was almost sure most *had* arrived on slave ships – though whether from the West Indies, the Americas, or directly from West Africa itself, he couldn't always tell. But one thing he was certain of, many of those dreaded vessels had sailed to Bristol port, and some up the Severn River itself, barely a mile away. The Middle Passage, Ambrose had read, was a dreadful endurance, and as the abolitionists told him in their pamphlets (he'd been very happy to find two in the local library) many did not endure. Then if the West Indies or the Americas beckoned it seemed plantation life was another dreadful existence. Ambrose was proud of his careful study of the workings of sugar plantations in Barbados, in Antigua, in Jamaica (he found he understood the English colonies far better). He'd learned new words: 'overseer', 'field hand', 'absentee landlord', and it seemed that sugar had been quite the modern industry. How he imagined himself the missionary out there, saving poor lost souls!

Yes, the Slave Trade, the Trade Route – like a triangle across the Atlantic – was all tied up with sugar, coffee, cotton and rum, and slaves of course. Also, from what the vicar could tell, little white shells that made necklaces were dreadfully important.

He pressed down hard with the iron.

That first winter he had taken copious notes; the research had quite possessed him. Daphne called him a 'busy bee' and he hadn't stopped with parish and library records, no. He had read around his subject until this small story of the Slave Boy of Sugar Hall, the slave who came back to haunt his masters descendants, was forgotten. This figure was merely the trigger, and Ambrose had even indulged in a little Abolitionist literature, in Equiano himself. He had noted the rebellion in Haiti and a tremendous man called Toussaint L'Ouverture. He had read about Obeah and Voudum (such superstitious nonsense) while the runaway slaves called 'maroons' fascinated him and he discovered the Gullah people in South Carolina had their very own language. Ingenious! It really was all quite stimulating. One evening, though, he had seen a photograph of a fearful-looking man in a great trailing mask; he was, the book said, 'an egungun', and Ambrose had had to snap the book shut.

This was the end of the vicar's interest in the Slave Boy of Sugar Hall.

'Damn!' he spat through the steam. Ambrose saw the browning of the iron on his underpants; he had left it on the cloth too long, a schoolboy error. He set the iron down, admired his successful pile of pressed and folded white underwear, and made himself ignore the mistake. Ambrose shook himself and walked to the high desk that stood against the far wall. It was raised but tilted, ideal for his work. He sat, trouserless, and switched on the anglepoise lamp. He reached for his magnifying glasses.

During the peak of his research, Ambrose had purchased a map of Africa, one that charted the ancient kingdoms. The names had pleased him so: 'Dahomey' was such a strange word. He had read that the kings of Dahomey dressed in leopard skins and would bury their wives, alive. A smile tickled on Ambrose's lips because he recalled the very moment he had read this – sitting across from Daphne in front of the four-bar fire – he remembered that his fingers had twitched on the page. In fact, as he'd watched her swollen hands twist around her crochet needle he'd given her a lingering look from the crown of her flat-haired head down to her thick ankles, and at that moment Ambrose had greatly admired those Kings of Dahomey. Burying your wife alive suddenly seemed like an awfully good idea, and he imagined himself in the skin of a leopard, standing over her open grave. He imagined it all, dust to dust, ashes to ashes, and the knock of her fists on the coffin.

Now, as he settled down on his stool, fine tweezers in his hand, his magnifying glasses on, Ambrose made himself think of nothing. He poured the acetone in a small Petri dish and on to the abdomen of the creature, and slowly, carefully, he began removing the tiny hairs.

Acherontia atropos

His display case, oak, was half full but there had been such a glut of moths in his traps these past months that Ambrose was behind with his local collection. Angle-Striped Sallow, Common Fanfoot, the Great Oak Beauty; they would all have to wait. The butterflies, too: the Small Pearl-bordered Fritillary, Wood White, Green Hairstreak, Purple Hairstreak; they were all delayed. The stunning and the killing were done, and thankfully before wings were shredded in fright, but now Ambrose had to set and pin: the most delicate of jobs. He was particularly proud of a stunning Pale Bridled Beauty and he thrilled at the thought of it. And then of course there was his exotic collection. Ambrose thrilled a little more, because tomorrow he expected a delivery; he had a particularly beautiful Large Blue – Maculinea Arion – arriving from London, and he had to prepare.

Ambrose was soon lost in the intricacies of his work and any thoughts of Sugar Hall, the Slave Boy or the strange Lilia Sugar and her stranger children were forgotten. He tapped his shoes on the strut of his stool and he listed his collection out loud.

'Garden Tiger, Alder Kitten, Pale Bridled Beauty, Scalloped Oak, Pearl-bordered Fritillary, Angle-Striped Sallow, Silver-Washed Fritillary, Lunar Hornet, Ghost Moth, Diamond Back, Map-Winged Swift, Bird-Cherry Ermine.'

The words spilled from his lips as sacred as the Lord's Prayer. Ambrose bit his lip and he said the last words once more, 'Bird-Cherry Ermine'.

Later that evening as Ambrose, now fully clothed, and Mrs Daphne Hetherington cut their pork luncheon meat and lettuce into small, manageable piles, both were thinking of the goings on up at the Hall that day and how the fabric of society was simply failing. And then, as the clocks ticked and her figurines on the display shelves gathered dust, both Ambrose and Daphne considered how much they disliked each other. Though this wasn't in a clear tangible way, rather it came in small pulses of disgust: as Daphne passed the salt and Ambrose said, 'very nice, dear,' and pushed his half-eaten plate away.

A Manual of Instructions for the amateur
lepidopterist

Doctor Portman's Orders

21

Lilia was singing and it was a new song: '*Hänschen klein ging allein in die weite Welt hinein. Stock und Hut steht ihm gut, ist gar wohlgemut.*' She was sitting out in the sun because Alex had cleaned down the old stone benches and he'd found an iron table that was quite secure. '*Doch die Mutter weinet sehr, hat ja nun kein Hänschen mehr! "Wünsch dir Glück!" sagt ihr Blick, "Kehr' nur bald zurück!"*'

She stopped the song, shaking her head.

The lawn was now Lilia's place and the sun was out and it was as if nothing strange had happened at all. She had made herself forget the chaos at the Hall that day; it had been two weeks since Saskia became a Sweet Sixteen and this passage of time had calmed Lilia.

Dieter was eating again; his fingers were healing, and they had slotted together: her family and Alex. They took their meals in the kitchen and when Alex said 'please pass the butter' to Dieter at breakfast, Lilia didn't even look up from her paper. It was as if it had always been. She and Alex stuck to English now because in truth they had felt so awkward, like children, in their old language (also Dieter hated it, he'd asked her what secrets she was keeping).

So, it was almost July and Alex was still here. He'd driven off that morning with Saskia in his hire car. They were shopping and Alex was treating the girl. Lilia appreciated his kindness. She stared down at Dieter and John as they worked on that old air balloon and basket at the edge of the ha-ha.

It was doctor's orders.

Doctor Portman told her that a project was the best idea for her boy. Doctor Portman had said keeping Dieter out of school but keeping him occupied was a grand plan. 'He simply needs feeding up, Mrs Sugar. No rations now, there's no need to scrimp.'

'What is this "scrimp"?' she'd asked, because there were still times when English words tripped her up.

John was pulling the big wicker basket across the lawn and dust clouded up in the breeze. Lilia thought that for a slight man John was terribly strong and she liked the way his rolled-up sleeves showed his brown arms. She sipped her coffee and listened.

'Best we lay it out, lad, see what we've got,' John said. 'You grab that end and I'll get this!'

She watched Dieter run to the other side of the balloon's flat skin: eager, laughing. It pleased her so, that sound. She thought about the good cut of beef in the larder and a generous dose of horseradish (because Juniper had visited with her usual gifts). John was walking around the balloon like a policeman inspecting the scene of a crime. Lilia hid a giggle with her hand.

'Reckon that bit of old material was tied to this basket, do you?' he asked Dieter.

'Of course, it's called a flying balloon! Dr Samuel Ferguson flew one with his servant Joe, and his friend Dick Kennedy in *Five Weeks in a Balloon*.'

'What's that?'

'It's my favourite book by Jules Verne. They fly across Timbuktu and all over Africa! No! Not there, John, here!'

Lilia loved to hear Dieter light up like this. She watched the chaffinches nibble seed at the bird table as red admirals and cabbage whites fed on the flowering lines of purple and red buddleia. Lilia lifted her face to the sun.

'I don't have time for your nonsense now, lad,' John laughed, 'just tell me how we put these two together because it's not a puzzle I can fathom.'

'Well, it needs all sorts of gases to fly. Like camping stove gases or something. I'll have to look in my book. I think Dr Ferguson used hydrogen, like the bombs. Pa said they used balloons in the war.'

Lilia shifted in her seat, she had a cushion but the stone was hard. She shielded her eyes and frowned. Could John truly get the thing to fly? No, he couldn't, surely. She imagined standing in that ratty basket, and the feeling of it taking off, just inches above the lawn.

At least she would feel free, weightless, for the tiniest of seconds.

'Let's shake it out,' John said, 'you hold it that end, tight now it's heavy, mind.'

Lilia half stood, on the verge of helping as Dieter and John lifted an end each; she watched the balloon sag in the middle with the weight.

'Now hold it, lad, hold it while I shake!'

John shook the thing and Dieter fell. Lilia was on her feet as decades of insects and dust puffed up and into the breeze. She watched the wind carry the cloud over the ha-ha and into the field beyond: it danced, and now Dieter was coughing and laughing and on his feet and the skin of the balloon was almost bright.

She sat back down.

'Let's wash the rest off, lad, let's see those pretty patterns,' John said, and then he was striding past her to the back of the Hall. John didn't look down at her but she enjoyed the firm crunch of his boots on the gravel. John hadn't spoken to her much since Alex arrived. She knew he was jealous, but what could she do? She turned back to see Dieter jumping around the balloon and the basket, hollering and waving his palm over his mouth. 'Weeee-hooo-hooo! Weee-eeee-hooo-hooo!' he cried. Lilia reached for a shortbread biscuit.

Lilia thought of Alex as she crunched. She had set up a camp bed in the boot room for him, simply because it was the only other warm room in the Hall and the toilet there worked. She sighed. Alex Behr was sleeping in her home. It was strange but she didn't want him to leave, not yet. She poured herself more coffee from the pot and watched John walk back across the lawn with a bucket of soapy water, it steamed in the sun. This time he did look down at her as he passed; he nodded but he didn't smile.

Yes, John was sulking.

So much had changed in these weeks, and one thing had been decided Saskia was leaving them for a holiday. Saskia was going to London to see her friend Flinty. Letters had been written. Phone calls had been made. Lilia tried not to think about it, because what she didn't want to think about was her relief. She knew she should be with her daughter now, out in town, picking out a new dress, a handbag, but she had sent Alex instead. Saskia would catch the 8:08 next Thursday morning, and Flinty promised faithfully to meet her at Paddington. 'She doesn't have to, Mother! I know my way around London!' Saskia had cried, 'I don't need meeting!'

Lilia didn't let Thursday worry her. Today she would sit in the sun and watch Dieter laugh; she would drink an entire pot of coffee and relish the quake it gave her. In fact the coffee was starting to make her feel as if she wasn't here at all; as if she was floating up in this summer's day; as if she was grasping the edges of that wicker basket while the old balloon carried her high above the Hall, above the tops of the oaks, the forest beyond, and away from here.

She lifted her sandals off the ground, almost happy.

Alex drove past the first gate. Lily's house had two gates and that sure was something. In fact Lily's house was something. As he turned up the driveway lined with ancient trees he couldn't name, Alex wondered at the size of the place. At this distance the falling gutters, the missing roof tiles, the strangling ivy, were blurred; it seemed like the grandest of houses and not somewhere he'd expect to find Lily Fisch. He thought of Flatbush Avenue and the way it ran through Prospect Park; it wasn't a touch on the wildness of Lily's home.

Alex changed gear a little late; it had been so long since he had driven shift.

The daughter, Saskia, was sitting in the front seat and he couldn't wait to get her out of the car.

'Thank you so much, Mr Behr.'

'I've told you, kid, call me Alex.'

She giggled and he pressed down on the accelerator.

'All these things you bought for me. It was so kind.'

'Not at all.'

She giggled again and Alex was glad to spot Lily on the lawn, a dot in the distance, but Lily nonetheless.

'Are you sure?' Saskia said, her voice suddenly serious.

'Of course, you call me Alex, sweetheart.'

He felt her turn to him, almost climbing across the seat. 'No, not that. The other question.'

They jogged into a pothole and Alex shifted gears: the clutch stuck. 'God damn it.' He tried again.

'Are you sure…?'

'I told you, there is no way, honey.' He said this as firmly as he could, staring forwards, praying the car would get them to the front door soon and he wouldn't have to listen to this girl anymore.

'I think you must be.'

'I've told you…'

173

'We have the same look.'

'And what look is that?'

'You are my father, I know you are.'

Alex slammed on the brakes. Saskia tumbled forward.

He winced because she bumped her head on the dashboard. When she looked up at him, half-crumpled, she was close to tears.

'Honey, you've got to understand, your mother and me…' he coughed. 'We were kids. I can't be your father, sweetheart. It's just not possible. Do you understand what I'm saying?'

Tears popped from her big blue eyes but Alex could see little comprehension in them.

'It's just not possible,' he repeated, but he knew he'd have to speak to Lily, it was ridiculous but there you were. English girls were so unworldly, backwards. It both pleased, and in this instance, annoyed him to hell.

'Hey, don't spoil the day. OK?' Alex patted Saskia on the arm, but she was hysterical now, little gulps of sobs came from her so he put the car in neutral and handed her his white handkerchief. He stared through the windscreen at the big house and he wondered how Lily had got herself into this fix, all alone in an English palace with two kids and no husband. He wondered how he could get her out of it.

His Lily.

Alex Behr thought of his simple apartment in Park Slope. He'd bought it after his divorce. South facing, the light came right into his living room. At weekends he'd lie back in his recliner and let that sun heat him up. It was a luxury. Then there was the kitchen: clean white, a dishwasher, washing machine, and him standing over the counter watching cars zoom up to Prospect Park. And here Lily was, in this forgotten place tucked away like a mouldy book when Alex wanted her to be lying in a recliner next to him, the blind a quarter down. Alex wanted them to hold hands as the business of a Brooklyn weekend roared outside.

He was a romantic fool; he knew that.

Alex chewed the inside of his mouth, a habit he'd not lost. Lily: his Lily. He thought of yesterday and how he'd found her down in that crypt of a kitchen, a big wooden spoon in her hands, stirring clothes in a pot like some peasant.

He'd tip-toed up behind her and whispered, 'You know you live in a modern world, right?'

She had straightened up, arching her back against him.

'In America we've got machines, Lily.'

'Mm…'

'We got the atomic bomb, too…'

She turned to him, wiped the sweat from her face. 'What?'

'Checking you were listening…'

'I am busy, Alex, can't you see that?'

'You need someone to do this for you.'

'You think I am made of money?' She was getting angry, and he hadn't meant for that to happen.

He'd changed tack. 'You know in America you can go for a hamburger in the middle of the night. You can have a coffee at 3am.'

'I can have a coffee at 3am here, Alex.'

'Not like this coffee.' He smiled, touching her wet arm.

'A hamburger?' she smiled back. 'What do I want with food in the middle of the night. I am greedy?'

'No,' he laughed.

'In the middle of the night I am sleeping. So when do you sleep, Alex?'

'I sleep.'

For a moment he lost his playfulness. He watched the scummy suds rise in that copper pot, and Lilia went back to stirring. 'Patience, Alex,' she told him, 'you must have patience.'

They'd looked at each other then, and in that small moment Alex Behr allowed memory through. All at once he was reading over Lilia's shoulder at her mother's dining room table, he was

175

laughing with her middle brother – Ari – down by the river. Alex had fallen in love with Lilia Fisch the first time he saw her, when she was nine and he was, what, thirteen, fourteen? He had come home from his new school with Ari and Leon, and there Lily was, sitting like a madam in a high-backed chair by the open window reading a book. She glanced up at him only once when Ari said, 'and that's my sister, don't mind her.' She'd shrugged and Alex felt his flesh pulse: he'd never recovered. 'Don't you want to come out and play?' he asked her once, and she hadn't even looked up at him; she'd turned the page of her book. Always so contrary, in her own world, cut off, that was Lily Fisch.

As he stood in the basement kitchen of Sugar Hall, Alex tugged the rope of the wooden Jenny; he had to put these thoughts out of his mind, because of course these thoughts led to others that Alex Behr knew it was unwise to touch.

'Lily, I'm not kidding,' he told her.

She was back to stirring the dirty washing.

'Lily, listen to me!' Exasperated, Alex slumped into a hard kitchen chair. 'OK, then, but what if this place eats you up, Lily? What if you can't do it?'

She stopped and turned to him, wiping her top lip. 'You think I can't?'

Alex knew he had said the wrong thing. Never challenge Lily Fisch, he'd learnt that the year she left for Berlin. He leant back in the kitchen chair. 'You can't stay here, you must protect yourself and your family, Lilia,' he told her, using her proper name.

'You silly man,' she said as the steam from the pot covered her face, 'what do you think I'm doing?'

English cars were like tanks, Alex thought. He gripped the wheel of the hire car and longed to sink into his Lincoln Continental. Saskia seemed to have calmed, he could only hear the tiniest of gulps from her now in the passenger seat.

'You better?'

She nodded at him. Alex sighed. He could tell she wouldn't let go, that she didn't believe his denial. Well, I'll be her goddamned father, he thought, miracles do happen! Alex pressed on the gas, released the handbrake, and continued up the drive.

'You know your name, "Behr"?' Saskia asked with a parched whisper.

He couldn't fathom where the girl was going with this, but he doubted it would be good. 'Sure.'

'Mr Behr is the man Jo March marries in *Little Women*.'

Alex had to think. 'Right.'

'Oh! You know the book?'

'My daughter's favourite. Read it to her, now she reads it herself,' he tried to remember the book, it was hazy.

'You have another daughter?'

'I have *a* daughter, yes.'

'How old is she?'

Alex had to count. The divorce had been unpleasant and – he believed – a truly American experience. 'She's eight. Peggy's eight.' Alex considered this: his little girl was growing up.

It seemed that Saskia wasn't giving him his handkerchief back, and Alex drove on, past the waterless fountain, past those shattered greenhouses; happy to see the dot of Lily grow bigger as she stood up to greet them.

He had a few more weeks, tops, then he'd have to fly home. Business was business and right now Alex Behr's was entirely neglected. This was the longest break he'd taken his entire life and he wanted it to mean something. To get what he wanted he would have to work faster. There was his Lily, he just had to grab her while she was still flesh and bone, before this place entombed her.

'Will you come up to see me in London?' the girl asked.

Alex lied, 'Of course, sweetheart. Of course.'

He made a vow then: in two weeks he'd be gone from this God-awful place and Lily with him, however she came and whoever came with her.

July 1st 1955

Dear Sugar Girl,

I heard about what happened at the hall. I am writing to you as you are still here. Theres badness up at the hall and now you seen it it will hurt you. It will always hurt the Sugars and it will frighten the living daylights out of us. I worked at the hall for a long time and I know the boy that haunts there. If you don't look after him he gets angry. You're not safe, girl. You should leave, fast as you can. You keep this to yourself. Don't tell my son John that I'm writing.

Mrs Annie Phelps

A Midnight Feast

22

When Dieter woke to see the boy sitting on the end of his bed, a pudding bowl of jelly at his chest, he wanted to scream. Instead he sat up, pulled his sheet to his neck and whispered, 'You've come back.'

'You've come back,' the boy copied.

'But where have you been?'

'Where have you been?' the boy said.

The lights were on. Dieter panicked and looked for Ma and Saskia: there they were in their beds, sleeping soundly.

The boy seemed smaller again, the velvet blue suit he wore was baggy: he had bare feet; his bright buckled shoes and the white tights were gone. He pushed a silver spoon into the bowl of red jelly and it made a thock noise. He shoved a wobbling spoonful into his mouth but he didn't chew, he sat there; cheeks puffed out, eyes blank. Jelly fell on the bed.

'You have to chew,' Dieter whispered and his breath was white in the cold. He watched the boy's cheeks deflate as he smacked his lips. 'Sh!' Dieter hissed and he looked over at his mother: her face was to one side, the sheet was down by her waist and she had one milky arm up above her head and hanging over the side of the bed.

Saskia snored.

The boy put the bowl on Dieter's bed. 'They won't wake up.'

Dieter felt that rising tide of panic come back, 'Why?'

'Trust me.'

Dieter kept his eyes on his mother. 'Is she just sleeping? What have you done to her?'

'Shhhhhhhh!' the boy said and the long sound cut Dieter in half, the breath went out of him and he fell back onto his pillows, slack. He watched: how long had it been since Saskia's party, since he last saw him?

The boy let his head drop to one shoulder, his eyebrows raised, 'You want to ask me a question?'

Dieter nodded. The boy ate jelly.

'What did you do to my sister that day?' Dieter tried to steady his voice. 'At her birthday, you scared those girls. What did you do?' Dieter thought about the things that would scare him. 'Did you play Murder in the Dark?'

The boy smiled, bits of red jelly pressing through his teeth. 'I appeared,' he said.

'What else?'

'I appeared.'

Dieter's chin trembled. 'Is that all?'

His friend laughed and Ma flinched in her sleep. Dieter tried to get his breath. 'Why did you go away?' he whispered.

'I didn't.'

'You did! You've been gone for ages, you didn't even say goodbye.'

'But I am always here, Dee—tah.' The boy reached out and touched Dieter's cheek. 'I am hungry,' he said.

Dieter felt a sick shudder and groaned, 'No,' he whimpered.

The boy grinned.

Dieter glanced down at the healed white scars of nips and bites on his fingers. He thought they were like little ghosts. He wondered if it would hurt as much when the boy bit into him.

Then he felt the bed move, and he looked up to see the boy climbing over his mother.

'No!' he cried.

'Sh! Dee-tah Sugar,' the boy said and Dieter fell back again.

It looked so horrible; the boy was now sitting on his mother's chest and gazing down at her, his face moved closer to hers. Dieter could hear him suck the air, suck in his mother's breath.

'No,' he cried. 'Please don't hurt her!'

But the boy was so close now it looked like he was kissing her. 'Please!'

Saskia snorted in her sleep and the boy jerked his head up. He laughed.

'Please,' Dieter said again. His mother's breath was white in the freezing air; he saw the boy's small toes flex and press in her flesh and her nightie. Dieter wanted to jump out of bed and hit him away but he couldn't move. He started to cry.

'You smell of your mother,' the boy said.

'What?'

'You smell of her.'

For a reason he couldn't quite fathom, Dieter blushed. Then he felt angry. He wiped his cheeks, 'What does your mother smell like, then?'

The boy stretched his chin up and Dieter saw the dark mark around his neck. 'My mother,' he hacked a cough. Something flew out of his mouth; it hit the hanging bulb in the room, and fell to the floor: a moth.

'Maybe...' the boy paused as he gazed down at Lilia. 'Maybe she smells of sweat and metal. She smells of stone.'

Dieter wanted to say that his ma smelled of Rose Laird face powder and sweet coffee. Dieter wanted to shout at the boy and tell him to get off his mother, to stop sitting on her like that, his feet on her chest as if she were a doormat, but the boy was shaking his head. 'No, Dee-tah, I smell nothing of my mother. I see nothing of her. Just touch. Scars, there are scars on her neck, her back, like…' the boy shook his head as he stared down at Lilia. 'I do not remember. I was born here. She was not. I lived and she did not want me to live.'

He licked his lips, leant forward and kissed Lilia on the forehead. He stared down at her. 'They took her to the islands in the oak ship. They brought her to this island. I am born at Sugar Hall. She speaks in another tongue, my mother, but she tells me I am the toubab's. I am his. This is my house.'

Dieter's head swam, his vision blurred. 'But…'

'They tied her to the yew tree,' he motioned at the window, 'out in these gardens. She hurt the toubab. They buried her but she was not dead.' The boy closed his eyes; he was trying to capture something. 'I do not remember.'

Dieter heard his springs creak before he saw the boy move, but there he was at the end of his bed again, the jelly bowl in his arms. Dieter looked back at his mother: her face was so white, her lips shivering, her breath laboured, but the boy wasn't on her any more. Dieter heard the thoc! as the boy spooned red jelly from the bowl.

'Why are you here!' Dieter spat. 'It's the middle of the night.'

'I want to play.'

Dieter stared at his mother's breath coming in puffs like a steam train, *shuu-tuuu*. 'I don't want to play now.'

'You should be happy to see me.' The boy threw the bowl on the bed. 'We can't play tomorrow. Tomorrow I may be gone,' he said.

Dieter looked up, 'Tomorrow?'

'Yes.'

All Dieter felt was relief. 'Oh,' he said.

The boy slipped off the bed and shot beneath it: he came back up with a book. It was *Alice's Adventures in Wonderland*. He opened it and turned the foxed pages, a white spider crawled across his hand.

'What are you doing?' Dieter asked.

When the boy looked up Dieter saw something in his face, something animated he hadn't seen before: golden flecks in his eyes sparkled.

'I am saying goodbye.'

The boy pointed his finger and the pages of the book turned, fast, faster.

It's magic, Dieter thought, and then his friend's finger stopped and landed on the picture of the Mock Turtle sitting on a rock, crying. The Mock Turtle had always made Dieter feel strange because it was such a mournful creature; so soft inside that hard shell of his.

'He wants to be a real turtle,' Dieter murmured.

The boy flicked through more pages with that magic finger until he stopped at the drawing of the Queen of Hearts. 'Off with her head!' she was screaming, and the boy laughed.

'I must say goodbye to your mother, Dee-tah,' he said, and he traced the face of the Queen. 'I must kiss her properly.'

'No!' Dieter grabbed the boy's arm. 'She'll wake up this time.'

'She won't. I have promised.' He left the book on Dieter's bed, next to the bowl of jelly.

Dieter's breathing quickened as the boy stood above his mother, 'Watch,' he said. He leant over until Dieter couldn't see her face or the rise and fall of her chest, all he saw was her milky arm above her head and he wanted to scream the biggest scream he could find. He hit his chest with his fist. 'No,' he moaned.

The boy straightened up. Dieter heard his mother sigh.

'Dee-tah, you must kiss her, too.'

He was trembling all over now – he drew his knees up to his chest. Somehow he knew a simple kiss on Ma's creamy cheek would mean something. It would mean something big and grand and unstoppable, it would mean something he could never take back.

'Come here and kiss her,' the boy commanded.

Dieter saw the book again: 'Off with her head!' he read. Clammy sweat covered his forehead and he wanted to be sick.

'Kiss her.'

Dieter thought the boy's eyes weren't black or brown or blue or green or bright with gold anymore, they weren't even eyes, they were things that Dieter couldn't put a name to. He felt a tug and he pulled back his bedding and let his feet drop to the side of the bed, then he stumbled towards his mother's bed and he kissed her roughly on the cheek, hoping she'd wake.

But the boy was right, she didn't.

'Now, let's play,' and the boy was already standing at the bedroom door. 'Hurry up, Deee-tah. Follow me.'

A History of the Hot Air Balloon.

On the 19th September 1783 Pilatre De Rozier, a scientist, launched the first hot air balloon called 'Aerostat Reveillon'. The passengers were a sheep, a duck and a rooster and the balloon stayed in the air for a grand total of 15 minutes before crashing back to the ground.

The first manned attempt came about 2 months later on 21st November, with a balloon made by 2 French brothers, Joseph and Etienne Montgolfier. The balloon was launched from the centre of Paris and flew for a period of 20 minutes. The birth of hot air ballooning.

Just 2 years later in 1785 a French balloonist, Jean Pierre Blanchard, and his American co pilot, John Jefferies, became the first to fly across the English Channel. In these early days of ballooning, the English Channel was considered the first step to long-distance ballooning so this was a large benchmark in ballooning history.

Unfortunately, this same year Pilatre De Rozier was killed in his attempt at crossing the channel. His balloon exploded half an hour after take-off due to the experimental design of using a hydrogen balloon and hot-air balloon tied together.

Fire Lantern

23

Lilia watched the fire lanterns go up into the night.

Alex was sitting next to her out on the metal bench by the overgrown tennis courts and they sipped a little of John's home—made Damson wine. The wine was so sweet and syrupy she thought of cough medicine.

'He is a good man,' Alex said.

'Who?' Lilia turned to face Alex, and smiled. The late and golden sun caught her and she squinted.

Alex took her hand; she felt how her chilblains pressed her flesh out around her wedding ring and she tried to snatch it away. 'Don't,' she said.

'Don't what?'

'My hands are so ugly.'

'Silly girl.'

'But it's true, Alex.' She held both hands up, splayed. Swollen, they looked at odds with her thin wrists.

'You should take the ring off. It might hurt you.'

Lilia didn't react. She accepted the truth of this. 'It is so strange. I remember in London I worked so hard. I scrub, I clean, but always, always I am losing this ring. It just falls off. I would sit and listen to the wireless, and I would turn and turn that ring on my finger. I would turn it when I waited for Peter to come home. I would turn it when Peter was alive. I would turn it when he was dead. Now I can no longer turn it.'

'It's the cold.'

'The damp. English damp.'

They both stared at Lilia's pitifully swollen hands, golden sunlight shafting through the fat fingers.

'Chill-blains,' Lilia said. 'Juniper, she told me the name. Chill-blains. For so long I thought it was "chill-blades". That made more sense, because the pain, you see?'

'*Frostbeule.*'

'Chilblain.'

Lilia took a deep breath of the golden air: night jasmine, she thought. There was humming and singing coming from the gardens, from Dieter and John, and everything seemed alive now: birds, insects, trees, plants; the air itself. Butterflies still fed on the buddleia and robins fought. She breathed deeper. It was lovely to be out of the house. It was another world. A ladybird landed on her thumb and she stared as it twitched its back, trying to get the very tip of its wings folded in. It tickled. What was that rhyme? She tried it.

'Ladybird, ladybird, fly away home. Your house is on fire and your children are gone.'

Miraculously the insect opened its back, and thin wings took it off, quick, into the sunlight.

Lilia laughed, shocked.

'Ladybird, ladybird, fly away home. Your house is on fire and your children are gone,' she repeated, and felt her heart drop. The words were terrible. She was sorry for the poor insect, as if her saying those words had made it true, her chest heaved, a little sore. Alex moved along the bench, and put his arm around her.

'Silly Lily,' he said and sighed. 'Liliana, you know I must go soon. I have work waiting for me.'

She straightened up. 'Then you must go.'

'Will you come back with me?'

She looked at him and she laughed. It wasn't a cruel laugh; it was because his question came too easily. She watched his forehead crush into a frown and immediately she wanted to rub it away.

'Think, Lily. Think about it. You have one life.'

'One life.' She laughed again, and her laugh was joined by the laughter of Dieter and John beyond the ha-ha.

'If you came to America, you could have everything, Lily.'

'And what would I do with everything? Where would I keep "everything"?'

'I've told you, you can get a coffee at 3am.' He smiled.

'And I've told you I can have my own coffee at 3am, here, Alex.'

'Not like this coffee.'

She folded her hands on her lap. 'I cannot.'

'Why?'

'I cannot.'

'Lily…'

'Sh, Alex. Don't spoil tonight. It's so pretty.'

She could feel him stare at her as she gazed up at the rising fire lanterns: Dieter and John had been making them all day.

'But, Alex,' she suddenly turned to him, 'do not go yet. Saskia is leaving tomorrow. Dieter has John. You and I, we could…'

'We could what, Lily?'

She smiled, 'We could have a picnic.'

'Ha!'

'Don't you laugh at me!'

'Oh, Lily.' He sat back; she thought he looked rather crumpled. 'I never forgot you.'

She raised an eyebrow. 'But you married, you had a family…'

'And you married, you had a family…'

'You have a divorce. That's terrible, Alex…'

'Lily!'

She giggled.

189

'You always teased me, always. I'm the older one, I am meant to tease.'

Suddenly Lilia was serious again. 'Is your daughter very pretty?'

'Peggy's cute, sure.'

'I think she would be very pretty.' Lilia pointed as another lantern rose.

They both watched it shuffle up on the wind in front of the large oak.

'They are like wishes,' she said.

'They are lanterns, Lily, just lanterns.'

It stopped rising.

'Look,' she said, 'it's stuck.' And it was, in the highest branch of the oak. The flame pulsed and the branch caught a little.

'Oh,' Lilia cried, 'it will burn the tree.'

'No…'

'But look.'

The lantern was flaming now, the paper puffing smoke and fire. The dead branch of the oak flickered, too, and Lilia held her breath: *one-two-three*.

There was something about it that was so pretty to Lilia; she wanted to cry. She thought of *Jane Eyre*, that novel that stayed with her. She thought of Alex Behr reading to her when she was nine years old, even though she could read herself. Yes, fire could come, it could swallow them all up, purge them, and there'd only be the ruins of this horrid old house. Ladybird, Ladybird, fly away home…. Lilia watched the fire in the tree heighten and then just as suddenly die: it was over.

She looked up past Alex's face to the other lanterns her son was lighting; the orange glow of fire through the paper, the little trails of black smoke coming from their tails in the evening light. One or two caught alight high up in the air, and she watched the flames, so pretty in the sky, and the slow drip-drip of scorched paper falling back down to the ground.

'She is leaving tomorrow, my girl,' she said. In fact Saskia was inside packing. Lilia had never seen her so focused on a task and in truth she couldn't blame her.

'She will be back in two weeks, Lilia.'

'I know, but she is still my girl.'

'She thinks I am her father, you know.'

Lilia froze.

'This is what she thinks, Lily. Ridiculous. Miraculous.'

'She asked you this?'

'Constantly.'

'Oh.' She went to stand.

'Don't Lily, stay. She's packing. She's trying on her new clothes. Let her come down when she wants.'

Lilia settled.

'Is her father English?'

'I don't think of it. Neither should you.'

She felt Alex fidget on the bench. 'I'm sorry, Lily, I don't mean to make you angry.'

'You don't.'

Alex had her hand again. He was turned towards her, one knee pointing out as if he might kneel and for a terrible moment Lilia thought he might propose. She put a swollen hand on Alex's cheek. It looked so strange, his white cheek and her awful red hand. He had such a pretty face for a full-grown man, and his hair; so thick and dark.

'Lily, I…'

'Sh, Alex.'

'You make me feel like a boy again. A stupid, stumbling boy. It's crazy.'

'Sh,' she repeated, soothing him, 'sh.'

'I'm a man, Lily, and you will listen to me.' Alex leant into her hand. He was quiet.

191

John lit the rag stuck on the wire, he marvelled as the hot air made the big paper bag float, higher, then higher, black soot coming out. He liked standing in the Hall's garden, his fingers a little burnt and his matches nearly gone. It was a grand evening, the sky red and a little pink like the ploughed earth here.

'Look at that one,' Dieter said, pointing into the dusk. The lantern rose above a far tree and made it glisten. 'And another, John, and another!'

John thought how it was good they'd become proper friends.

'And another!' Dieter jumped up and down, pointing.

He's a boy at last, John thought, a proper boy jumping and laughing like that; he can't keep his legs still. It was good to see, though the lad did look tired in the half-light. Still, he was jumping on the spot and John couldn't help but laugh.

'I've got a plan, John!' he said.

'And what's that then?'

'I have to get away. I do, I really do.'

The boy was wild-eyed for a moment, feverish as a cornered rabbit.

'I'm going back to London, John. I'm going in the air balloon!'

John relaxed a little; the boy was just playing. He smiled though he knew not to laugh. 'Is that right?'

'Yes. Don't breath a word to anyone, don't tell…' he looked back at the house, it seemed like he was checking the attic windows, but John couldn't tell exactly.

John decided to humour him. 'Better take provisions then. A good pork pie. A flask of tea. You'll need it.'

'Will you come with me? You can help with all the flying.'

John coughed in the damp summer air. 'Always wanted to go to London, I have.'

'There's smog. Smog will be bad for your lungs.'

'I've had worse.'

'My friend Jim Foley was killed by the smog. He's Billy's brother. That was three years ago now.'

John looked down at him. 'Sorry to hear that, lad.'

'Jim was a Wee-Hoo.'

'What's that?'

'I told you, my gang. We're the Wee-Hoos, we're the best gang on the Wasteland and I'm the leader. If you came to London, John, I'd let you join the Wee-Hoos. We'd have to take a vote, but I bet they'd like you as much as I do.'

'Well,' John laughed, 'I might be a bit old.' He coughed and it cut into him.

John had to sit on the stone bench. He wiped his brow and felt his chest tighten. It would pass. He watched the last fire lantern rise up into the red sky and then he looked back up at the house, at the high, black windows of Sugar Hall. They were blank in the growing darkness and John was glad. Then he looked down at Lilia and that man, Alex. John's fingers picked at the dead lichen on the stone bench as he wished for something he knew he'd never have, but it was nice to wish all the same.

Acherontia Atropos — Death's Hawk Moth

Set Them Free

24

The dark panels that lined the crowded walls in this upstairs room were cold as ice sheets. The oak floor creaked beneath Dieter's footsteps as the boy switched on the overhead chandeliers. Dieter shivered in his dressing gown. He didn't want to be here in the middle of the night, but like every night this week the boy had woken him.

This was the room Ma had locked all those months ago, the room filled with animal heads, animal skins, wooden masks, moths and butterflies. On the wall Dieter saw a lion's face creased into a roar, above him a rhino was dusty, and opposite him frightening wooden masks made his lips shiver some more. He glanced at the floor; it was patterned with animal skins and he stepped between them on the oak floorboards.

Dieter was so tired he thought he might be dreaming; he thought he might be going mad.

More lights flashed awake above glass cases of specimens, and the room was suddenly bright.

'Please…'

'Shhhh!' said the boy.

All Dieter wanted to know was, why were they in here? He knew there was little point in asking why was he awake, why did the boy want to play in the middle of these awful nights, or why had he come back. Dieter walked between the pinned displays of moths and butterflies, animal skins dry and crunchy under his feet.

This room smelled like the Natural History Museum in London. He wiped the dust from the glass of one case to see four huge butterflies in sparkling blues and purples and greens.

Blue Morphia. Black Swallowtail. Appalachian Azure, the labels said.

He wiped the dust from the next case; these were moths and they had hairy heads and antenna that looked tickly. They were as big as small dogs, or big cats.

Giant Leopard Moth, Atlas Moth.

He imagined his Grandpa Sugar up in that balloon above Africa, China, India and Sumatra. He imagined him with a telescope and a big net, scouring these lands for giant butterflies in the daytime, and giant moths at night. When he glanced up at the animal heads he imagined Grandpa Sugar with a huge blunderbuss gun, shooting and chopping off the heads of all these animals, dragging the heads back home on the ropes of the balloon.

'Grandfather Sugar is dead and this house is mine because I am the last Sugar left,' Dieter murmured.

The boy was standing by the tall sash windows. Dieter noticed the windows were all open now. Out above the cedar, Dieter saw a red moon.

When he looked back down into the next glass case and saw skulls on the backs of a line of moths, he jumped back.

Death's Head Hawksmoth, the label said.

'Please,' Dieter cried, 'can I go back to bed?'

'Watch me, Dee-tah,' the boy was saying and then another sound tickled Dieter's ears. The boy was stretching his arms out at his sides by those open windows. 'You must lie down now, Dee-tah,' he said, 'be quick.'

The boy began to hum. It was quiet at first, a low murmur, but the sound grew, climbing higher, then higher in seconds. The boy opened his mouth wide and suddenly the sound hurt so much Dieter had to put his hands over his ears. Then the sound got to Dieter's bones and he didn't have any choice: he felt his knees give and he fell on a zebra skin.

The boy's cry grew even higher in pitch: the air in the room seemed to tremble then boil. The boy pushed out more sound until Dieter felt his eyes turn back in their sockets and the glass in the room smashed. It was an explosion, like a bomb. The display cases, the windows, the glass panes, the cut-glass crystal droppers and the arms of the grimy chandeliers: they all cracked then shattered. Dieter cried out and crawled beneath a display case as glass shards fell around him.

The boy went back to a lower register then, and that was when the insects twitched.

If Dieter could have seen them, he would have seen their veins grow fat, their thin wings shiver; the tiny hairs on their legs stand on end, the silver heads of the small pins begin to tremble. He would have soon seen them wriggling in their pinned positions, working themselves free.

The giant butterflies were the first to detach – the Swallowtails, Blue Morphos, the Monarchs – their large abdomens pulsed and pulled away from the pins in one tug: their wings shuddered, ready to fly. Slowly – the Helliconians and Fritillaries, Hairstreaks and Coppers – they were all wriggling and crawling up over the broken glass.

The moths were slower; their fat bodies took a few seconds more to twitch into hairy life; it took a few more tugs to pull away from their pins.

Most fell to the floor, and when they did they crawled over Dieter's feet, over his body, his face, in his hair. 'Make him stop,' Dieter gasped as the insects crawled up his pyjama legs, tickling his skin with their thrumming legs, some scratching him with the silver pins still stuck through their bodies. They felt his warmth and they tried to burrow into the warm corners of his eyes, his mouth, into his ears.

The boy laughed as the butterflies and moths animated: crashing against the cracked chandeliers and the black panels of the room.

'Make him stop,' Dieter repeated but as he opened his mouth again moths flew in until he spat and screamed.

The boy clapped his hands and suddenly the swarm of insects moved with one jerk towards him. They poured around him, wings purring, greeting him, and he smiled. Then they flew out of the gaping windows, and out into the summer night.

Dieter felt a hand on his; he yelped.

'Come along now, Deee-tah. We're going to play more games tonight.'

Thursday morning

Dear Cynthia,

You were right. Ghosts that are duppies are dangerous. I'm sorry I didn't listen. I miss you.

Your friend,

Dieter

Saskia Says Goodbye

25

'You look tired.'

'I am.'

'Well you should get some rest.'

Dieter yawned.

Brother and sister stood on the tiny station platform: it was open to the air, pitted with yellow-headed weeds and bouncing crows. They could hear the forest plantation whisper around them and they tried not to listen.

'Are you sure you feel OK, Dee?' she asked, surprised at her concern: the black rings beneath his eyes had returned. He seemed thin again. He looked up at her, hands in his pockets; he truly did look ill and something pulsed in her.

He shrugged, 'I'm OK.'

Saskia turned away; she didn't like that feeling scratching at her belly, this melting concern for her baby brother, and he really was a baby, Ma still had him in short trousers. Saskia wondered when he would ever grow up: she wondered if he'd be Lord of the Manor when they were older and if she would visit. She pulled up the netting on her new hat and as the white handle of her handbag swung on her wrist, Saskia knew she was ready for London: she knew this creeping concern for Dieter would soon evaporate.

'You're not coming back, are you, Sas?' he said.

She froze; Saskia smoothed down her new skirt and tugged at her kidskin gloves. 'Don't talk nonsense, Dee…'

'It's OK, if I was going I wouldn't come back. Sas?'

'Yes.'

'Give this to Cynthia Nurse will you?'

She risked a look at him, his cheeks were so white and hollow. He was holding out a letter and suddenly she couldn't say no. She unclasped her new white bag. 'Of course, Dee. She's number 43, right?'

He nodded.

'You'll look after Ma, won't you?' she said, her voice odd. She coughed and Dieter shrugged. He really was a pest. 'I mean it. You're the man of the house now, don't forget.'

He looked down at his sandals. 'Ma doesn't care, Ma's too busy with *Mr Behr*…'

'Don't say it like that Dieter, he's very nice.'

'He's leaving soon, I heard him. He lives in America. He has to work. He wants Ma to go with him…'

Saskia felt a hard twist in her stomach. 'Don't talk silly.'

'He does.'

She glanced over at the ticket office: she scratched her arm. 'I said, don't talk stupid, Dee. Mr Behr isn't going anywhere, and if he is he'll take us all.'

'Did you ask him?'

'Ask him what?'

'If he's your father…'

'Sh!'

'Well, did you?'

Saskia tugged at her gloves. 'It's a delicate subject.'

'I'd ask him,' Dieter hopped, arms out, 'if it was me, and before he leaves.'

Saskia noticed her brother's hands, his fingers; they were

201

plastered again; the nicks and cuts had come back. 'Dee, you will look after yourself, won't you?'

He looked up at her and she suddenly felt scared for him.

'I mean, I know things have been just awful, but we've got to grow up, haven't we?' She noticed how much taller than him she was in her new high heels.

'I think they'll hung her,' he said.

'What?'

'That lady, in the papers.'

'What lady?'

'The one with the blonde hair.'

Saskia shook her head.

'The one who shot her boyfriend in the street, you told me all about it.'

Saskia opened her mouth, 'Ruth Ellis.'

'That's her. They'll hung her.'

'Hang, Dieter. They'll hang her...'

'They'll hang her, then,' he mumbled.

'Yes, it's decided. They will.' Saskia bit her bottom lip and tasted waxy lipstick. 'Dee, please be careful.'

'What of?'

She didn't know how to say it so her brother did it for her. 'Don't worry about me, Sas. He's promised, he's my friend.'

'Dieter, don't...'

'I know you saw him, Sas, on your birthday up in that blue room, I know because he told me...'

All at once Saskia was on her knees on the rough platform, damn her stockings, and she was hugging him to her, 'Dee, come with me, come to London. Come with me now, why not? Flinty wouldn't mind...'

He felt limp in her arms. Then she felt him chuckle against her. He brushed her hair behind her ear, leant in and whispered. 'He doesn't mean to scare you, Saskia. He only wants to play.'

She jerked back.

Dieter's voice sounded strange, his face was the same, though, pale and blank.

'Stay away from it, Dieter,' she said.

'He's my friend…'

'Stay away from it…'

He smiled.

Saskia stood and she brushed the scree from her knees; she could feel her heart thunder. She glanced at the train tracks and tried not to think.

Her mother and Alex were walking towards them now; they looked like a perfect couple, and together they could be her Ma *and* her Pa. A train hooted in the distance, and Saskia thought it was a little like the sound the nights here made, all those hissing and hooting owls.

She gave her mother and Alex Behr a beaming smile. 'Goodbye Ma. Goodbye…' Saskia smiled her best smile, 'Goodbye, Mr Behr.'

He walked to her, 'Call me Alex, kid.'

With a lot of noise and fuss and steam, the train pushed into the small station.

'Oh, my girl! Come here!' Lilia cried.

Saskia felt her mother kiss her on each cheek and then Alex hugged her and she thought he smelled of fine cologne and fathers.

The steam settled; the train shrieked.

'Bye, Sas.' Dieter was still there though she couldn't see him in the fog.

She stepped back, 'Bye, Dee.'

Alex opened the carriage door.

When the whistle blew and they all waved Saskia off, it was terribly grown up and terribly sad in a way that wasn't sad at all.

'You will be home two weeks Sunday evening!' Lilia cried from the platform and Saskia felt her skin prick: she couldn't think of coming back here. She settled into her carriage as the train said *shu-tu, shu-tu*, and she felt the two letters crackle in her summer jacket pocket: the one from Dieter to his old friend, Cynthia Nurse, and the other she'd received just the other morning. It had told them all to leave Sugar Hall and Saskia had found it on the hall table. She'd meant to give it to Ma, she'd meant to laugh at it because it was from John Phelps' mother and she had sounded quite mad.

In the end, Saskia hid the letter; she hadn't wanted to cause a fuss. She wouldn't let anything change this, she simply had to leave.

Half a day later, by the time Saskia stepped out of her damp train carriage and into the warm roar of Paddington, she had forgotten these two letters all together. In fact as the sound of London brought something back to life in her, Saskia Sugar felt she could forget it all: cold, old Sugar Hall; her mother and brother and her potential father, Mr Alex Behr.

'Exhibits from the Plantation'

Exhibit. 1 - The practice of freed female slaves was to make effigies (or dolls) of themselves using their own hair and clothes. These objects would be stuffed with paper, tree moss, or strange objects, and would be gifted and handed to their former masters as signifiers of their freedom (see also Exhibit 7 and 23, Voudum, Obeah and the Plantation).

A Gift

26

Up in the attics of the Hall, through the thin glass of the blue-room window, the boy watched the car leave. They were taking the sister away, she was leaving for London; he knew that.

It was almost warm in this room and sun lit the blue to a brightness that made him rub his eyes. He glanced back at the twin beds, they were neatly made with patchwork quilt covers, but only one had an indent in the pillow. The bars across the outside of the window threw lines of shadows on the sunlit, cluttered floor.

It is a prison, he thought.

No one had been into this room since that day he had crouched in the corner over there and watched those girls.

He gazed down at the scattered toys – teddy bears, spinning tops, board games, wooden animals, the alphabet blocks he'd taken to, the strange clown with a key in its back – all of the bright things that had been tipped on the floor once the chaos began that day. The boy noted shattered glass and the rug turned over.

He smiled. He could still taste those girls in the air and their taste was so sweet and pulpy it made his teeth ache. Those girls had been afraid; they had scratched at each other to get out, they had torn each other's arms and cheeks when he'd brought darkness to this room.

The boy breathed deep, and as dead insects twitched into life on the windowsill, he walked to the bed and picked up the pillow.

Beneath it was a doll stuck with a needle and thread.

He retreated to a sunny corner and he began to sew.

'I am making,' he said out loud. He was sewing what looked like hair onto the head of the doll: it was his hair.

'This is for you, Dee-tah,' he said.

The doll wore the same velvet blue uniform with gold buttons that he had to wear, it wore the whitest of stockings too. He touched its coat: it was expertly done. As he threaded the needle through the doll's head over and over with tiny, perfect stitches, he began to think about the child, about the last Sugar: Dieter.

He wondered what he had learned from Dieter. It wasn't much but perhaps it was enough. He had learnt that in London there were red machines called buses. (Dieter said these were two storeys high and had a bell that rang every time you wanted to stop.) He knew that Dieter came from London but his mother had come from somewhere else because another war had begun.

More wars.

Dieter had told him that if there were a war now, everything would be gone, even the birds, because this war would be fought with bombs that ate the air, bombs called HYDROGEN and ATOM. Dieter had told him there was a man called DAN DARE who would save them all from this, from all the bombs that ate the air.

It was strange how Dieter kept asking him where had he been and why had he gone away, because he had only been sitting here in this blue room. He had been here all along.

Then he thought about the doll he was making: he would leave it on Dieter's bed. He smoothed its hair then turned the doll, pulling up the small blue velvet jacket and teasing open the small gap in its back. The boy felt in his pocket, he brought out a handful of dead moths and he began to stuff them into the half-filled body of the doll: they crunched. 'This,' he said, 'this is for you, Dee-tah.'

It was the boy's mother who had taught him this, she hadn't taught him his name, his proper name, because she refused to give him one, but she had taught him this when his hands were too young and soft to hold a needle. She had told him this before they killed her.

She taught him how to make and how to curse.

The boy closed up the hole and finally cut the cotton with his teeth. 'This is for you, Dee-tah,' he said again as he held the doll up into the sunlight then he dropped it on the floor and he walked to the window.

The boy was impatient.

The boy was hungry.

Butterflies, two Red Admirals, two Painted Ladies and a single Purple Emperor were crashing at the panes, thud, thud, thud. The boy gazed out at the gardens.

'I saw. They tied her to the yew tree,' the boy nodded at the window. 'In these gardens, they buried her. She was not dead, my mother. I heard her scream and it was the scream of a knife.'

The boy's head was unsteady on his shoulders; it was his turn to feel dizzy now. The lawns were untidy – not flat and clipped as they once had been. Buttercups and clover had taken over and the thistle was tall – some yellow, some purple. The boy supposed it was thistle, he was always learning, you see, with each new generation here at his Hall he was learning. He didn't like to think of his mother's scream, he didn't like to think of touching the scars on her neck, her back. The boy had too much past and so he turned from it. He wanted to suck up the present and the future. He wanted to learn. The boy felt himself shimmer in the sunlight.

Beyond the ha-ha, in the field with the big tree, he saw the man. The man was dragging a large basket across the field. The boy watched him struggle as he tried to hang the skin of an air balloon from the branches of that big tree.

He knew this man: he knew he had eyes as blue as this room because he had known him when he was a child. The boy thought: yes, he was called John and he would hide in the scullery with his mother.

The boy burped: yes, he was hungry.

Metamorphosis

Lily,   Tuesday

Ari has promised me he will give this to you. Can you meet
me after school? Tell your mother you have to work at
the Library, or tell her you are going to Hannah's. I'll be
down at the river in our place, I will wait.
Alex.

The River

27

In the cold kitchen Lilia poured her coffee into the cracked cup she was growing fond of. She had been sleeping so soundly, as deep as the ocean her mother would say, it had been hard to wake. She sipped the black drink, one hand around the hot porcelain as she thought of fire lanterns. They had been so beautiful the other week: little golden wishes rising into the sky. Lilia knew she was becoming sentimental and it was Alex's fault.

She placed the greaseproof paper on top of the damson jam and she swilled the bread knife. Dieter had made such a mess getting his own breakfast; the loaf had been hacked at, she had even found a slice in the porch, jam everywhere. He was working his way through the jellies, the blancmange she had made: half-empty bowls were on the table. She couldn't be angry with him because it was such a relief to know he was eating. John had mentioned he was looking sick again, but Lilia refused to see it: her boy was eating her out of house and home! He was out there playing in the summer morning! He was getting better and she had cancelled the doctor!

Dieter had a project, the balloon, and it was a comfort to know he was out in the bright morning, planning the balloon repairs with John. She wouldn't hear from them today. She reached over the Belfast sink to wipe the windowsill down with a cloth; it was covered with small white and dead moths, they'd been trapped in this underground kitchen overnight, she supposed.

Lilia dragged a kitchen chair from the damp shadows and sat in the light shafting down the back-door steps. She smoothed her dress and wondered if the little red patterns on it were strawberries or cherries. She peered up at the beginnings of the busy garden. Summer was deafening there: the chirruping insects and birds that made her ears ring. She thought of her tomatoes and cucumbers, her potato plants and her mint and she inhaled it all. She was glad the damp chill of the house was at her back because Lilia wouldn't think of winter, not yet. She would only think about today because today was beautiful, today was alive, and Lilia Sugar felt that life pulse back into her.

When Dieter didn't appear for lunch, she didn't worry; he had had breakfast and it meant the doctor was right, it meant things were back to normal. In London Dieter would be lost for the whole day on the Wasteland with his friends; he'd come back when he was hungry. She and Alex had decided to bring their lunch out into the garden and they sat on the very edge of the ha-ha, staring out at the fields. Bramble curled up from the drop. Alex looked up from his plate. 'You are happy today,' he said to her, and it didn't sound like a question.

She smiled and ripped at the bread.

'You're hungry today,' Alex laughed. 'You look very beautiful, Lily,' he told her, and she blushed. It was as if she was fourteen again and they were sitting at the Fisch's dining-room table with her mother fussing over them all. It was almost like that, but of course it was nothing like that.

He took out a white handkerchief and wiped his face. 'We should do something, Lily.'

'What?'

'You promised me a swim, remember?'

She laughed, 'Are you saying I'm getting fat?' Butter shone on her lips. She put one hand on her waist and one arm up in the air, twisting in her seat.

He smiled. 'No, no, my Lily, I am not saying that. What I am saying – I am saying "let's go swimming".'

Lilia took another big bite from her bread, golden with butter, and she nodded, showing her teeth as she ate. Lilia Sugar was very, very hungry.

She had left a note on the kitchen table.

Dieter darling and John, We are out to the river, we are swimming. There are sandwiches and drink in the larder. Ma xx

She and Alex had parked the car and were walking down through the woods to the River Wye. It was nothing like that brown churn of mud, the Severn, over the fields from Sugar Hall: the Wye had her thinking of childhood summers. She turned to Alex on the path. 'It is such a waste that car, only sitting there,' she told him.

'We're using it today, Lily.'

'We should use it more.'

'Well, I'll drive you across the sea in it, Liliana, all the way to Brooklyn,' he laughed as a branch hit him on the cheek and Lilia was surprised to feel a girlish flutter.

The cover of the trees was welcome; the thin beech leaves were cool shadows of green. Lilia focused on every nettle, every hoop of bramble that stuck out from the verges; she twisted and jumped and giggled as her bare legs were brushed by stings, by thorns.

'If you run, Lily, they don't hurt.'

'I can't run!'

'Sure you can!'

Lilia held her towel and bolted into a sprint, leaping over the green nettles, careful of her footing on the damp path. Alex wrapped his towel around his neck and admired her as her laughter echoed in the woods, blackbirds shrieking and scattering.

'Hurry!' she cried.

The sudden brightness of the meadow stunned them for a moment: it was a golden blur of buttercups. The red earth of molehills dotted the ground while black and white cows grazed. This close the cows scared Lilia, she had never liked cows; their doleful eyes seemed a lie. She remembered dissection class at school, the bull's eye; it burst under her scalpel.

Dizzy with nerves, they giggled like children.

'Run!' he yelled.

And they did.

They were out of breath by the time they reached the riverbank; they stood, silent, as whirlpools spun in the flowing current. It was silly; they had no costumes and suddenly they were shy. Alex listened to the angry hum of brown horse flies. Lilia bent down and unclasped her blue scandals.

She was so quick; her dress was over her head, and in an instant she was walking down the incline in her slip, to the little piece of shore splattered with cowpats and deep hoof prints.

'It is not cold, Alex!' she cried, 'at least only a little!'

She watched him as he gazed down at her dress in the thick grass; she wondered if he saw the strawberries on it, or perhaps they were cherries. A milk cow lowed behind him, he jumped and Lilia laughed, splashing. It really was so silly, she thought: they'd swum together as children, as teenagers, and now they were adults they could do as they pleased, but she knew Alex was shy as he unbuckled his belt, folded his glasses and placed them in his brown shoe.

Lilia watched him strip to his underwear, his vest. He had been a slight boy but she had always loved the darkness of his skin. It was far browner than hers, even without sun, and it seemed to shine. She skimmed the surface of the water with her cupped hands as Alex stood on the shore, fists to his hips; elbows out like a bird. The top of his chest was dark with hair.

He waded towards her in his vest and underpants. He was such a neat man that it almost made her laugh.

'Do you swim here often?' he asked, eyes squinting in the sun.

Lilia decided to make him smile. 'No, Alex, I come here only with you.'

He walked against the current.

'Swim, Alex, why don't you swim?'

'Why don't you?'

They were bashful again, and then they heard rumbling coming from the bank. They turned to see the cows tumbling down the incline, over their clothes; one after the other, clumsy and dangerous and heavy with milk.

'No!' Lilia cried.

'I'll go back,' he turned in the water.

'No. Stay.' She reached out for him.

The cows lurched towards the water and Lilia bent her knees until her shoulders were under and suddenly, this close to him, she didn't care about clothes or shoes or glasses or cows: Lilia's hands moved around his hips.

'Our clothes are ruined,' he said, smiling down at her. 'My glasses will be crushed.'

'I hate cows,' she murmured.

He stroked her hair, her cheek, 'You live in the countryside.'

'But I don't like cows.'

He bent his knees, too, and she felt his arms around her waist. With their feet pushing from rock to rock they floated together in the weak summer current of the river. Lilia rested her head on his shoulder, and at last she thought of nothing.

Alex was thinking. He was thinking of that day at the river in Demmin, even now. The memory was fresh as new paint and it was a clean memory because here she was, his Lily, not dead, not dead at all. That day Lily had been wearing a summer dress in pale blue, he was sure, and she had dangled her legs from the bank. She had blushed and smiled and then he'd crawled out of the water, knelt down and kissed her. It was a daring thing to do. He was a friend of Ari's, but still. That day Alex couldn't help himself. That day young Lily Fisch pushed him in the river, and that moment was the moment he knew he'd love her for as long as he could. He'd love her because she had laughed.

Now, floating with her in his arms, Alex remembered it all perfectly: holding Lily Fisch, kissing Lily Fisch with simple teenage kisses down by their river back home.

Alex felt young and he had felt so old for so long.

'I'm going to swim,' Lilia murmured at his ear, and she untangled herself from him. He stared across at her – wet in her slip – but before he could reach for her she had pushed off into the current. Alex sighed and fell back into floating, content: there was no rushing with Lily Fisch.

Beneath the water, he listened to the run of the River Wye and the rush of his own blood. He could hear Lilia's splashing from a distance but beneath the water everything seemed so fantastically cut off; there was the thud-thud-thud of his heart, his breath and the trickle of water. Alex squeezed his eyes shut and breathed through his nose. He was trying to think of good things; he was trying so hard to think of good things and with the smell of Lilia on the tip of his nose it should have been easy.

The feeling was creeping up on him, though, like a fever. It was the river's fault. When he'd stood on the shore and saw the low hanging branches of a willow dragged out like tugged hair he'd felt it shiver into life. Now, he couldn't stop it.

Alex had returned once after the war. There was no one to go back to, but the fact that he was driving to his town a grown man when he had run away from it a scared boy, pleased him. By his second day there, he realised the trip was mistake. That morning an old, spitting man at the bus stop had told him a story he didn't want to hear. (Of course the trip had been filled with these stories, but this one was different: it had been a shock.) The man's teeth had been worn to stubs and the smoke in his mouth seemed black as he'd spoken of the river.

'OK, maybe it wasn't a thousand, maybe there were nine hundred. Nine hundred killed themselves. Out there in the water,' the old man said.

The 'nine hundred' had been men, women and children. The war was over and these men, women and children were defeated, and though Alex couldn't be sorry about that, he'd baulked at the old man's tale. The Red Army was advancing and so these nine hundred men, women and children of the town – once his town – had walked to the river and drowned themselves (though in the case of the children, Alex thought, they had *been* drowned). At the time he'd been in America, he'd heard nothing of this: nothing of these German civilians and their final act. Later that morning as he'd stared down at his childhood river (because he'd had to go back to it, he'd had to see how a town could drown) all he could think was – it was such a small river for nine hundred – maybe a thousand – to drown in; it was too shallow. Drowning in it must have taken all the will, all the effort in the world.

Alex sat up; he couldn't see Lilia, the cows were drinking at the shore and the current had taken him too far. He stood and the water rushed from him; the river reached his hips.

She was floating beneath the shadows of the weeping willow – the dangling, light branches tickling her legs. She was holding onto one branch to stay put, to stop the current taking her. She heard splashing and when she saw Alex wading towards her she closed her eyes as little waves pushed up against her: she tasted little trickles of river in her mouth.

His hands were underneath her body; he held her as she listened to the rush of her own blood in her ears, to the current of the bright river.

When he guided her to the bank beneath the willow, when he kissed her and she felt herself being pushed into the silty mud, Lilia pulled off that silly white vest of his and she kissed him back. For so long now Lilia had thought of nothing but old songs, she had been singing nothing but old songs. But as Alex Behr kissed her, as he tugged off her slip, Lilia thought of Saskia's Dansette record player and that one song 'Dreamboat' by Alma Cogan.

Lilia began to hum.

By the time they were chasing each other through the beech and oak wood, they felt like tiny children. They shrieked with pleasure as nettles snapped at them along the pathway. Alex was laughing from the bones in his legs up to the crown of his head. He felt weak with it; he felt weak with Lilia.

'Come on!' she cried.

And they ran; their clothes tight with damp.

Lilia was sunburnt and she relished the rough sting of it on her shoulders, her forehead and cheeks. She felt the damp and the slime and the mildew of Sugar Hall pass through her. This morning she had woken up a toad but now she was a bright, sun-warmed bird: a freed canary, or a finch – clear and colourful with a beak of steel. Lilia felt strong and suddenly she knew, as she ran and her new breath cut her, that she was leaving Sugar Hall. She would simply go. She would pack up and sell every knick-knack and oak table in that place and she would take the money and she would buy a washing machine, a Frigidaire, a few months rent on a new flat in London. Perhaps she'd buy a ticket to New York. She would send Saskia to secretarial college and Dieter to a good school, not the best, but a school close to home wherever they lived and she would forget all this and she would let her shoulders brown in the sun and her laughter come out, and there would be no past, only their futures.

Against the Clock

28

Once a little darkness fell Lilia forgot happiness. Once Dieter's supper plate had cooled at the kitchen table and she and Alex had searched Sugar Hall from top to bottom, she couldn't remember what happiness was. She jumped onto Saskia's old bike. She refused the car.

'Don't be crazy, Lily, he's out there somewhere, playing. He'll be with John.'

'You take the car and find Juniper. Alex, you find her. You remember her house?'

'Yes, Lily, yes, but…'

Lilia was already pedalling down the gravel drive. At the second gate and past the grand sycamores she turned left onto the black lane, brambles biting at her bare legs and arms; she knew the way without seeing much.

It seemed endless, this dreadful lane: endless and black.

At last she rumbled to the bottom of the hill. Here at the crossroads she turned right and soon she was passing the church and the vicarage. There in the distance was the village shop, the pub and the green. Lilia's dress stuck to her back, she battled to catch her breath but she kept on, skidding into another sharp right and on, on up to the line of cottages that backed the village.

There were still people out; it wasn't so late. He is just playing, he is out playing like he used to play in London on the Wasteland, she thought, when she and the other mothers had to shout and beg for their wayward children to come home. Lilia pushed her whole weight down on the pedals. John's home was the semi-detached on the end. The cottages were brick but painted white. Here she would find Dieter: here she would laugh at her silliness and take him home.

She threw the Raleigh into the nettles, ran up the path and pounded on the door. 'John! John? It is Lilia, Lilia Sugar. John!'

When he finally stood there, blocking the light from inside, a surprised look on his face, Lilia wanted to scream. His mother was pulling at his elbow. 'Let her in, John, let her in.' Lilia hadn't seen the mother before.

She shot under John's arm and into the house. 'He is here, yes? Dieter, he is here?' she said this though she knew the answer. Lilia began to wring her hands. Her legs felt wet; she glanced down to see long and deep scratches pearled with blood.

'Dieter, he is…?'

'What happened?'

'He is here?' she shouted.

John's raven flew off the edge of the draining board and onto the kitchen table. There she saw the pink bodies of three skinned rabbits. At last Lilia screamed.

'Lilia! Sh! Sh, now.' John went to her but she stepped back. 'Let me see to those scratches then,' he said, and he went to the sink for a cloth. As he passed the skinned rabbits he laid a white cloth over them, then knelt at her feet and wiped her legs with another. Lilia felt soothed. Gaslight threw shadows on the walls and for a very small moment she felt as calm and clouded as a petted dog; this tiny home was warm, and she envied John and his mother. His hands were on the back of her calf now, holding her, and then he was standing, dabbing her arms, and she saw there were streaks of blood on the off-white cloth.

'When did you last see him, John?'

He was holding her arm, blowing on the bramble scratches.

'John, when did you leave the Hall?'

He walked back to the sink and dropped the cloth on the draining board. 'I haven't been up to the Hall today,' he muttered.

'What?'

'I'm sorry…'

John looked guilty and she wondered what for.

'I haven't seen him; I haven't seen the lad today. Not at all.'

She felt her knees go. 'John, please…'

'I was shooting, see…' he nodded at the rabbits.

'Yes he was,' the mother barked, 'and a few rabbits is nothing to write home about.'

Lilia turned to see the old woman glaring at her from the foot of the stairs. She found herself wanting to laugh; his mother was worrying about the rabbits. What did she care for rabbits!

Lilia held her hands together; it steadied the shaking. 'John, you will come back with me.'

'Don't get messed up in things that don't concern you,' the mother growled.

John picked up his coat. 'I'm going to help, Mam,' he said. 'I'll be back soon as I can.'

With her chin out and elbows to the west and the east, Mrs Phelps shook her head, but they were already out of the door.

There was a small crowd on the grey steps beyond the open porch. The light from the old glass chandelier in the grand hall poured out. John was guiding her on the bike, his hands on the bars. 'We'll find him and in no time,' he was saying.

Lilia jumped off the bike and stared at the gathering. She was thinking of deep wells and quarries, of locked and forgotten rooms that could swallow her boy up, of those priest holes, that dumb waiter, of the black sheds at the end of the red gardens, of treetops,

223

bulls' horns, horses' hooves, train tracks, guttering, dark lanes, snares in the wood, and, oh, the black water of that old swimming pool.

She was thinking of hunger and thirst and rusty farm machinery. The more hands the better, the more eyes the better, she told herself.

Juniper walked forward and hugged her. 'He is not with John, then,' Juniper said. 'Now, I've brought three of my men, don't fret, darling, we'll find the boy.'

'Where is Alex?'

'Inside, on the telephone.'

As Juniper released her, Lilia looked over at the men. She recognised one as Juniper's gamekeeper. She supposed the other two – younger, but with the gamekeeper's eyes – were his sons. They were staring in at the hall, mouths open. She noticed their guns: thick black twelve-bores cocked over the crooks of their arms. 'No guns,' she said in a whisper: and then louder. 'No guns, Juniper. Tell them.'

Juniper nodded and the men pulled out the red cartridges with their thumbs and forefingers, delicate as ladies picking up dainties. They put the cartridges in their pockets and laid the empty guns against the wall.

Alex walked down the steps to Lilia. He hugged her and she felt rather crushed. 'The police will be here when they can,' he whispered into her ear.

She wriggled from him, 'They are not coming now?'

'They are waiting until the morning.'

'No…'

'Lilia, they are right, a boy sleeping in the woods, that is all, a boy off with his friends…'

'Dieter doesn't have any friends here!'

The gamekeeper and his lads looked away. Alex pressed her arms as if he was trying to push her back together again. 'Trust me, Lily, he is having boy's fun, mischief, I am sure.'

'How can you be?'

Juniper clapped her hands together: Juniper was taking control and Lilia was glad. 'I've brought my horse and one other, will you ride, Lilia?' she asked.

Lilia shook her head; she was scared to death of Juniper's huge horses, their thighs wide as fat dogs.

'Then, John, you are to take Lilia. Turley, you sweep the woods in the opposite direction with your boys.'

The gamekeeper nodded.

'And I'll take Hispid out on Black Boy Hill. Would you join me, vicar?'

Lilia hadn't noticed the vicar beneath the porch.

'I'll wait here,' Alex said, 'someone should be here when Dieter comes back.'

'First we search this house,' Juniper told them.

'But we've looked,' Lilia whispered.

Juniper ignored her. 'First the house, and then the buildings out there, the sheds for a start.'

'The swimming pool,' Lilia whispered again.

'Turley, you start with the outbuildings. Then on to Sugar's woods.'

The men nodded and marched off, cigarettes red dots in the half-darkness.

'The rest of us crack to it, one floor each to start with, and here's chalk…' Juniper handed a nub of white chalk to each one of them. She knew this from her stint driving ambulances: if a building was empty, if a room was clear and checked, you marked it.

'Every room you check, mark a cross on it, and then we know where we are. You don't mind do you, Lilia? The marks, I mean. It's a pretty foolproof system.'

Lilia was staring into space.

'The marks. You don't mind, the marks on the doors, darling?'

Lilia snatched a piece of chalk; she shook her head. No. No.

No, she thought, mark everything; mark it all in this damned and awful place. Mark it all and we can burn it later. Lilia ran up the steps. 'I will start!' she cried, and she sprinted across the hall, along the cold passageway, and down the hard and stone steps to her basement kitchen: Lilia would check and chalk the meat safe, the cupboards, and the small hatches of the black range.

The west wood was dark and loud and John held her hand. They each had a torch. The Hall hadn't given up her boy, but now each door was patterned with a white cross.

John walked a step ahead as they followed the path. Lilia's throat was cracked from crying, 'Deeeeee-taaaaaaaaaah! Deeeeeee-taaaaaah!' She was quiet now; a few murmurs of 'Deee, Deeee, Deeeee,' was all she could manage as she walked: exhausted.

John led her through the wide, wet fronds of bracken. He switched off his torch: hers, too. 'We're better in the dark. Just follow me,' he pulled back the fern, grasped bramble stalks with thumb and finger. Soon there was little scrub on the ground and John was pushing away the sweeping brush-tail branches of Douglas firs as he led her deeper into the forest itself.

It was made up of darkness and echo in here, Lilia thought. The spongy ground made her footsteps nothing. All seemed dead to the eye as John's grip grew firmer with each step. Damp and bog filled her nostrils, she cringed at the howling sound the fir trees made above, and she thought of those who had hidden in a forest, for years and years and years. She had read about them; men, women and children hiding in the thick trees, the dead trunks, the moss and the excrement; hiding from guns and from soldiers and from war and from death.

John kept the pace up.

She suddenly covered her nose. 'Oh God, John, the smell!'

A tawny owl shrieked.

There was a creaking noise, different from the creak of the

branches in the wind. John switched on his torch and she saw them.

Foxes.

'Ah,' she cried and she covered her mouth, her sandals dug into the soft ground.

'Only vermin,' John said.

The foxes were hanging in a circle. Four were fresh, bright and red, but one had clearly been there for so long it was black bone.

John pulled her to him. In the folds of his jacket, his arms around her, she felt the wave come and Lilia gave in: she sobbed. She pressed her face into his chest and open-mouthed soundless sobs cut into her.

'Lilia,' he whispered.

When she raised her head she knew John was going to kiss her and she didn't care. He lifted her chin, wiped her cheeks with his rough thumbs, and very gently, he kissed her on the lips: it was a child's kiss, really. Lilia didn't want a child's kiss, and she fought against it by opening her mouth and pushing into him with her tongue. He pulled away but then he came back and he kissed her hard on the mouth. His stubble hurt, but not enough, Lilia wanted something to bring her back to life: anything. She had to breathe through her nose and the terrible smell of those foxes filled her as John kissed her with sucking swallows. Lilia pressed into him and he groaned, she guided his big paddle of a hand between her legs; she felt for him. His mouth pulled away again, he gasped, but then he buried himself in her neck, his other hand moving up her body, yanking her little dress decorated with strawberries or cherries away from her chest. Lilia felt her back rub against the bark of the fir tree as she held onto him, and helped him push into her.

She stared up at the trees, she saw nothing; she felt nothing. There was only blackness and the smell of the dead foxes and the sound of John's breath, deep and sharp, as if he were running, running, running, as if it was all happening too soon. He whined.

Poor John, she thought. She felt his hand pinch at her breast and she cried out, 'Deeeeee-taaaahhhh!'

Her shout came back, an echo.

John was leaning against her now. His muscles had gone, his strings had been cut and he fought for air.

'Sh…' she said, a hand patting his back.

She continued to stare up at nothing. The owl hooted in time with John's gulps.

'Sh,' she told him, and then he was stepping away from her, rubbing his chest. He sounded like the bellows she would use for the fire at the Hall. He crouched on the forest floor, wheezing.

'Lil…' he tried.

She was still staring up at the angry tops of the Douglas firs that howled like wolves in the wind.

'Lil-ia.'

She didn't look down at him.

'Lilia,' he gulped. 'Are you…?'

'The foxes smell,' she said.

'Then, here. Come here,' he took a deep gasp, and stood, unsteady. He led her to the other side of the trunk. 'No wind here. Lilia, my Lilia, listen, will you wait a moment? I need to check something, see.'

'What?'

'Nothing. But promise me you won't move.'

'Why?'

'Promise me. Lilia.'

'Yes.'

He kissed her, it was a delicate kiss and she hated it.

'Five minutes. That's all I'm asking, my love.'

'I won't move for five minutes, John. I promise. I'll listen to the owl.'

She heard him walk up the hill, his whining breath cutting the quiet of the night. She sank to her knees, back against the fir, and she hummed for company.

The old oak was up here at the brow of the hill.

Thing was, you'd never play here, you'd never hang a swing from that tree. You'd never carve a sweetheart's name on this trunk. You'd never sit beneath it for shade or a nap. Sheep wouldn't shelter under it either; they'd shiver over by the fence there, the wool on their backs catching on the wire.

This was a tree you might stand under to curse someone who'd done you wrong.

That's what John knew. He also knew he loved her; his Lilia.

He climbed over the deer fence.

He made himself think of the ghost as he strode through the misty grass towards the old tree, he made himself think of the ghost because his mind and his body were so full of Lilia he could hardly see.

The little Slave Boy – so the story went – had hidden in this tree; John's mam and every other Mam in the forest had told this tale. The child had hidden in the little hollow in the east side of the trunk when he was still flesh and blood: just a scared little lad. This was where his masters had found him and hanged him, and for what John didn't know.

That was centuries ago, John thought.

'You get lost in that forest and the boy'll have you, sure as eggs is eggs,' his mam had told him when he was a bab. 'He'll have you and he'll drag you down the roots of that old tree and take you straight to hell, so you stick with your mam, you stick with her and you'll be all right, John.'

He gazed up at the branches. The moon shone through them, making them silver. It was true that he was frightened for himself, but most of all he was frightened for Lilia. He shone the beam of his torch up into the great twisted thing.

229

It took a good while, searching out every lichen-covered limb, listening for a creak that wasn't the creak of old wood in the wind. This tree was where they hanged the boy and it was where they'd found Richard Sugar, too. John knew that story.

He breathed at last; there was nothing here but the branches.

But of course there were the roots, and he walked around the trunk, lighting up every hole, every crevice at the base of the ancient tree.

Nothing.

John switched off his torch and waited for his eyes to adjust back to darkness. He had no idea what he would have said to her, to Lilia, if he had found her boy here. It was foolish, childish, a silly superstition, an old wives tale: all of it. He turned and ran back towards the fence, glad it was all nonsense. Her boy would be fine. Dieter wasn't cursed like his mam had said.

He jogged down the slope and into the thick forest, his footsteps hollow on the spongy floor. He had to get back to Lilia and tell her how much he loved her, and how her boy wasn't dead at all.

Juniper had left the vicar behind, she couldn't wait about for the silly man; he would have to find his own way. The bare hill felt so open, so fresh, and a bright westerly blew into her. In truth it was keeping her awake. Hispid jangled beneath her and she gripped him, heels in, as he trotted up the hills snorting and rattling his bridle.

Her eyes were accustomed now, though she could feel the coming of dawn in her bones. She stopped at the brow of the hill and gazed out into the grey light. It was quite beautiful: the low mist sucking at the ground, the peep-peep-peep of early robins, the shriek of waking blackbirds, and curlews moaning from the estuary below, from the wide brown mud of the Severn river. It was quite the view here; there was Wales to the right, the

230

Cotswolds straight ahead, and here she was in the place she had always been. Above the mud of the river she was sure she could see the dot of an air balloon. It was all charming, quite charming: Juniper felt her big horse shiver with it.

The land – even in this half-darkness – looked so simple. There, far behind and to her left, was Sugar Hall nestling at the foot of the forest, grey in the morning mist. She wondered how many years ago it had been the only place in a sea of trees. Many of the oaks had been cut years, decades, centuries ago for ships. It was a simple landscape but still it had been cut and hacked at; it had histories written on it and this was something Juniper appreciated. Yet at the same time, she felt uneasy with the whole thing. Still, there was new writing on this land: in the far distance across the Severn and nearer to the flatness of the larger towns would be the new builds, the post-war boom of baby bungalows, and to her far right lay a field of prefabs. She had walked among them as they were constructed; to Juniper they seemed rather neat and pleasing. She doubted they would ever be cold.

Juniper was a practical woman and she believed Dieter had hopped on the milk train to London. She hadn't been able to say this at the Hall in the darkness of Lilia's panic, and so she had to put this effort in. In any case, these dark hours had been quite glorious, Hispid quivering beneath her and a new day dawning. What other opportunity would there have been to gallivant across the county like she did as a girl? Juniper sighed; she remembered how she had disappeared for days on that old horse of hers, and no one had noticed, not even her father. It had been bliss.

Hispid shook his head, the bridle creaked and clattered, and she let the reins go. As the horse munched cool meadow grass, Juniper glanced about, and then she lay back on his rump and waited for the rising sun.

TIDAL TIMETABLE
Weds 13 July, 1955
Sunrise 4:59 AM BST
Low tide 2:50 AM BST

The Cow

29

Dieter was so tired but the boy wouldn't let him sleep. He had woken him in the early hours, and they had been playing all day and now it was night again, and he had eaten all the damson sandwiches he'd made and he was still in his pyjamas. He shivered in the cowshed as the animals made sounds like old men, coughing. He was so tired and so hungry he couldn't remember how to get home, even if the boy allowed him.

'Where are you?' Dieter whispered.

There was the slam of a hoof on the concrete floor, the ghostly brush of a tail and the wet, lippy grind of cows' jaws. A dog barked from somewhere but it sounded muffled.

'Please,' he whispered, 'come back. I have to get home to Ma.'

Moonlight shone through the open side of the shed and Dieter saw the milking herd shuffle and chew; they licked the cow cake and peed yellow as disinfectant while their calves shivered in the stalls. Dieter saw their clouds of breath in the bright moonlight as they jostled in one direction. It looked like they were trying to let something through.

'Is that you?' Dieter asked, and the black and white cows were suddenly still. Dieter walked forwards, trying not to think of the cowpats or the puddles of pee beneath his thin slippers.

This close he could see how huge they were. Their eyes were

luminous green in the milky light and when they lowered their square heads and shook their necks Dieter saw steam rise. He felt warmer this close to them. He crouched; he was looking for the boy's legs among the hooves.

'Where did you go?'

A cow made an awful noise at the far end of the shed. The herd shuffled again.

Dieter tiptoed across the straw and muck, his slippers sliding in pockets of softness.

He could just make out one cow pressed against the shed's far wall. She was alone and as Dieter walked to her he saw she was dazed, her big eyes bulging. Dieter heard a strange noise in between the cow's moans. He stepped closer, as close as he dared, and there he was – the boy. He was sitting on the ground, his back to Dieter: his face pushing against the cow's udder.

The boy was bigger again.

Dieter felt the hot movement of the herd behind him; they were panting and steaming in the moonlight; they were pacing, afraid, and so was he.

The single cow opened her mouth and bellowed.

'Don't hurt it,' Dieter said, because the boy's head was jerking back and forth so hard, and at each jerk the cow shook her head.

'We have to…' Dieter started to say, but the pulsing of the boy's head had him dazed too, and then there was the sound: the deep suck-suck-suck-suck like the boy was sucking up the world; the earth, the sea, the sky, not just that cow.

As he watched, Dieter felt something nuzzle against his arm, and then something warm and wet was snuffling against his hand. Before he could move, that something tugged hard at his fingers. It was a calf the size of a very large dog, and it had his hand in its mouth. The calf's suck was strong, its rough tongue curled around his fingers, and Dieter thought maybe his skin would come off. He tried to pull away but the calf had such a firm hold.

Suddenly, the big cow in front of him slumped forward: he heard the air go out of it with a sigh. That's how I feel when he touches me, Dieter thought.

The calf kept its hold on his fingers.

He was light-headed. Behind him the herd was restless, skittish. He felt their warmth step closer. Dieter closed his eyes and when he did this all he could hear was sucking, the sucking of the calf on his fingers and the sucking of the boy on the fading milk-cow.

The boy had told Dieter that after he fed they were going down to the big, wide river. He told Dieter he had a surprise for him and they were going to the river that led to the sea, the river where tall ships once sailed, and from there they were going to fly away across oceans in the balloon Dieter loved so much: they were going to have such adventures.

Dieter would have loved that game if he weren't so tired, if he wasn't so faint and so hungry. Tonight he was cold and he was scared and these cows smelled so, and he wanted to go home. Tonight he hated the thought of that big muddy river that he saw every day from Sugar Hall, because his slippers were dirty enough. In any case, Dieter reasoned, it would be impossible to drag the balloon and the basket down there; it was at least a mile away. Dieter wanted to go home, no matter where it was; he wanted the warmth of his own bed, maybe the warmth of his mother.

Dieter didn't want to play with the boy: not anymore.

July 13th, 1955, 7:00 BST

30

A new day called the searchers back to the Hall.

Lilia walked across the sodden grass, led by John; they held hands and their faces were blotched with night-cold. Juniper stood at the stone trough as her horse drank. She patted Hispid's haunches and cooed, admiring how he steamed in the growing sunlight; flies teased his ears, and his glossy skin twitched, back legs kicking out with irritation.

The vicar had left his borrowed horse at the Hall and he'd walked home hours ago. He was tucked up safe in his bed now, across from Daphne's single bed. The vicar had no trouble sleeping. The keeper, Turley, and his sons were leaning up against the sun-side of the grey stone Hall, one knee bent and feet flat to the stone. They were smoking, rolled fags hanging like tree moss from their lips. Turley had retrieved his twelve bore and it stood open across the crook of his arm; he held it as delicately as a lady would a pretty night shawl. Inside Sugar Hall, Alex was walking up from the kitchen a silver tray in his hands; he had made coffee, he had cut bread and found a second large pot of damson jam.

When Juniper turned, her back to the warmth of her horse, and she saw Lilia and John, she wasn't surprised they had taken comfort in one another, but she was surprised at Lilia's face. There was no light in it, no hope. The girl wasn't bouncing across the lawn to them, demanding, 'Is he upstairs? Have you found him?'

Juniper shook her head. It was true that the boy had been gone all night, it was true that they couldn't find him, but she wondered why Alex hadn't thought to telephone the boy's sister in London; Dieter was with Saskia, there was little doubt. Juniper would have to choose the right time to mention this and act on it, and meanwhile she imagined taking Dieter over her knee and giving him the hiding of his life: she doubted anyone ever had.

Alex stopped at the top step by one of the grand grey pillars, a tea towel over one shoulder, the tray in his hands.

'Have you,' he asked Juniper and the men, but he didn't finish because the faces told him, 'no'.

Lilia and John's steps crunched the gravel. Turley and his boys peered round the house at the missus. Alex tried not to notice Lilia's hand, tied up with John's, and Lilia kept her face down until she saw Juniper's strong, brown riding boots.

She looked up.

It was then the whole group heard a strange noise, not quite like the ringing of the telephone – although at first Alex moved back into the Hall as if to answer it.

Juniper secured both horses as Alex put the tray down on the top step. John and Lilia turned towards the sound.

Turley threw his fag onto the wet grass, his sons copied him, straightening their backs and squaring their shoulders just like their father because they knew this sound: they knew it well and they were ready for it.

It was the police car. Turley and his sons called her 'Jenny' they were so familiar with her. Black and shiny, her chrome bumpers had grills like teeth, her wing mirrors were silver capon wings stuck to her bulging black sides. The youngest Turley, George, had always thought their local police car looked like a mustachioed general, and it put the fear of God into him: George stood to attention.

Jenny's silver bells rang louder.

When the police car took the bend of the drive, pushing fast, Lilia was simply glad that they had finally come to help while Juniper thought of the grand cars that had regularly travelled up this drive once upon a time: the Rolls Royces, the Bentleys. It took what felt like an age for the car to make the final rise to the front of the Hall.

At last, it ground to a stop, gravel spitting from the wheels. When the two policemen and the one policewoman stepped out of the car, pausing for a moment, and then – very slowly – removed their hats, it was Alex who sprinted first. He ran down the wide stone steps towards Lilia; he ran, but he was too late.

John Phelps had her hand, but he was too busy staring at the policemen and the policewoman. He was so busy staring that he had simply felt a tug on his fingers and then on his wrist as Lilia fainted, collapsing face first to the gravel.

As soon as she saw those uniforms and those hatless heads, Lilia Sugar had thought of her pearls and how they sprayed from her neck when she pulled at them that winter morning at Churchill Gardens. She had torn at her pearls because another policeman and another policewoman had stood on her threshold, hats in their hands too, and they had told her that her husband was dead. And that morning when Lilia had scratched at her throat, her cheeks; pulled her hair and her necklace, some of those pearls – which were the real thing – had rolled between the polished black shoes of that policeman and the policewoman. The pearls had bounced back and forth; back and forth between their shoes like the silver ball in a game of pinball.

And when Lilia heard the ringing bells of this police car, 'Jenny', when she'd looked up at these two new policemen and the policewoman taking off their hats and walking towards her in front of Sugar Hall, she thought of those rolling pearls and of Peter; and she heard nothing but the rush of blood in her ears and felt nothing but the stone on her teeth and the turn of her insides. It was such a hard turn, as if she was inside out and all was wrong and all was different: which of course, it was.

July 13th, 8:50 BST

31

Saskia stood on the edge of the curb. Next to her a mother jogged her pram up and down and the baby wailed. The mother grinned at Saskia. 'Bless her bones, she can feel it, she can,' the woman said.

Saskia hugged herself and looked into the blackness of the pram. Hood up it looked like a great cave; gurgles came from inside with the smell of sour milk.

'Bless her,' the mother repeated, 'she's praying with us all. In her own way. Little lamb. Ain't you?' The woman looked up. 'Have you got a watch, love?'

Saskia turned to the woman, 'Sorry?'

'A watch? You got one? I ain't, you see. And I want to count down. You here last night?'

'Me?'

'Well who else am I talking to?'

'No. I came here early this morning.'

'Well, last night my sister was here, and she said there was crowds that deep,' the woman pointed to end of the street. 'She said they was all crying and banging on the doors there,' the woman made the same motion at the great prison doors in the distance. 'And they was crying out for Ruth to pray with them, to pray to be saved. And they was singing, blowing the roof off, my sister said. But d'you know what happened?'

Saskia shook her head. She was wishing she were back with Flinty and her mother at Churchill Gardens: Flinty, who had refused to come.

'Well, they send the guards out, don't they. Then they send the police.'

Saskia didn't like the way this woman, small and bottle-blonde, said 'pow-leece'.

'Yes, they sends out the pow-leece, with women and children here, and the pow-leece gets nasty, and tells them all to bugger off home.' The woman was jogging the ugly pram now as if she wanted the child to cry out. 'Terrible,' she muttered.

Saskia nodded.

'And he come yesterday, the hangman. My sister said she seen him. We all know him here. Albert…' the woman crossed herself.

'Oh.' Saskia felt cold. The people around her were suddenly quiet, most of them staring down at their watches. Then the mumbling came, turning to a slow chant. They were counting: 'Twenty, nineteen, eighteen.' Saskia looked down at her own wristwatch, a tiny little gold thing that Peter had bought her. He had laced it around her wrist. It was tight now; she should drop it off at the menders for a bigger strap.

'Seventeen, sixteen,' the girl in front of her said.

Saskia was sure it didn't work like that. They couldn't hang someone to time. What if something went wrong? What if Ruth took longer lacing her shoes? Having her breakfast?

Saskia jogged from foot to foot as the sun caught the crowd.

She would write to Ma and Dieter tonight, she would tell them she was coming home. She wasn't enjoying staying with Flinty as much as she had hoped. Flinty wasn't a bad girl, but she wasn't a good girl either. Flinty had her day job, and then she had another as a cigarette girl at the Palais on Friday and Saturday nights. She had told them she was eighteen.

The crowd, mostly women and children, were chanting the numbers loudly now. Saskia stepped off the curb and she turned and she pushed through them, away from the prison doors.

'Watch it, love…'

'Hey look where you're going…'

'Steady!'

'Eight-seven-six…'

When she could, when she was free of the push of summer coats, crying women and mewling children, Saskia began to run. She ran all the way down the Holloway Road; she ran beyond her bus stop, beyond the tube station. Saskia ran until her blouse was wet with sweat and the sick feeling that tickled her skin was almost gone.

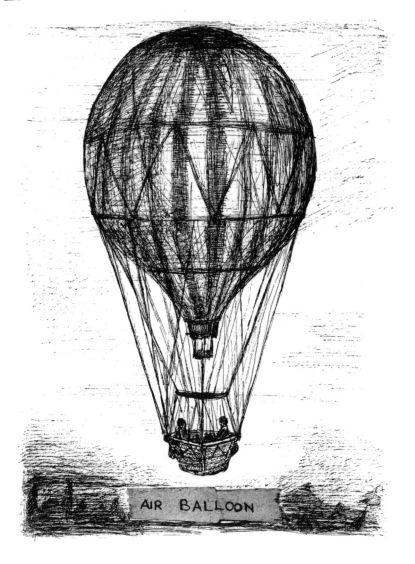

AIR BALLOON

Up, Up, in Our Air Balloon!

32

Dieter felt terribly odd when at last he opened his eyes. He found himself sitting in a corner of the big wicker basket, and it smelled of the sea. Above him was the big balloon and it was filled with air.

He remembered the river, but he didn't remember the balloon. He remembered the boy pulling him across the flat fields in the dark; he remembered the sting of thistles on his ankles and the milky light of the moon. He remembered the high-pitched trills of those long-beaked birds once he reached the mud of the shore, and he remembered the roar of the tidal river, though it was far away. He remembered the boy dragging him into the mud and then dragging him further, but there had been no water, only the slick suck of that mud. Dieter remembered the suck of it at his feet, at his ankles. He remembered losing his slippers and then losing his feet altogether because suddenly he couldn't lift or feel them anymore and he fell backwards with a splat! and lost the boy's hand. He'd stared up at the stars. All that time, the boy hadn't sunk at all: he hadn't even left footprints. As Dieter lay there in the oily mud he thought of John Phelps' story of the ponies struggling and sinking here each summer, and Dieter remembered how he'd asked John why the ponies were foolish enough to do this *every* summer, and of course John had replied that they weren't the same ponies at all because sinking in the mud of the Severn wasn't something a horse could be saved from, ropes and chains or what.

Dieter had struggled and sunk a little more then. He had been very cold and very wet and he remembered the taste of mud in his mouth and the sting of it in his eyes and the sound of it pushing into his ears; and he remembered crying as the sky disappeared, and then he remembered sleeping, and it was such a relief.

Yes, Dieter remembered all this but he didn't remember climbing into this wicker basket and firing up the balloon.

It was daylight and he was shocked to see that he was clean; there was no mud stuck to his pyjamas, though here was blood; just a few drops on his lapels. He spat on his fingers because he wanted to rub the stains away but there was blood in his spit, too. Dieter felt his mouth; it was sticky.

He felt a jolt as the basket shook.

'Is this fun?' the boy asked because he was standing right there in his bright blue uniform, in his clean white tights, almost a grown boy again, and he was looking out beyond the lip of the basket. Dieter heard a great pouring rush like a waterfall or that crashing noise you hear just before you faint.

He tried to stand up, but it was so difficult, it felt like someone was pressing on his shoulders *and* pulling him down by the ankles. He reached up to grip one of the balloon's ropes and his stomach lurched as the whooshing sound grew louder and the rattan rubbed against his legs. Then Dieter heard a voice he recognised. 'Here! Over here!' it said.

He knew that voice was Tommy Perrot. But what was Tommy doing here?

If only he could stand up and look.

That was when Dieter heard the Wee-Hoo Gang. Different voices yelled his name and they made a sound like Indian Braves. 'Wooo-woooo-wooo-woo!'

He fought against the push on his shoulders and he stood and peered into the mist, crunching his eyes up, until finally he swore he could see them. They were running on the hard flat ground of the Wasteland and the balloon was so low it was almost in reach.

'Where have you bin? You've bin gone ages, son,' Tommy said and he was walking towards him through the mist, a rolled cigarette behind his ear. Tommy was a grown up. He had shiny grease in his hair and it was piled up, sculpted.

'I've come back,' Dieter said.

'Yeah, we can see that, moron. You ain't changed, not a bit.'

'Oh.'

Dieter could see other figures now, like they were coming out of thick London smog. He searched and searched for her, but he couldn't see Cynthia. He called her name but she didn't come running in her pa's cardigan, crying, 'Dee, Dee!'

There was Jim, though. Jim Foley who had died in the big smog three years ago. Jim threw something at him. 'Come on, son, catch!'

It was a hard ball and it hit his arm, he saw Jim had a big brown leather glove like some alien hand. Jim ran backwards, the glove raised above his head. 'Come on, chuck it!'

Dieter picked up the hard white ball and he wished Jim would stop running backwards; he grimaced, leant back and threw it. It was a good throw and he watched the ball arc; he listened to the skylarks, to the grumble of London beyond, and then, suddenly, he felt another jolt. Something slammed into his chest and he felt a terrible, almighty tug.

'Jim! Tommy!' Dieter cried.

The tug kept up, it was as if he was leaving his stomach on the floor; his legs were more jelly-ish than the jelly in Ma's pudding bowls. The feeling kept on, it wouldn't stop, because the balloon's basket was swaying and rocking and rising so quickly. Dieter knew he couldn't stand up much longer, he knew the force of that something he should have learned about in school would pull him down again, crush him onto the floor like an angry headmaster. He looked above him: he could just make out the tangle of ropes. Dieter wondered if he could climb up them, if he could use them to escape. Then there was a roar and a hiss so loud he thought of giant snakes. His throat tightened and he began to cry.

He felt a hand. It slipped over his.

'Don't be afraid,' the boy said, 'it's an adventure.'

When the whole of the sun twitched above the lie of the land Dieter's jelly-legs were solid once more. In fact he was standing next to the boy, gripping the edge of the balloon's basket, and staring out at the brightening view. It wasn't London, it wasn't the Wasteland anymore; Dieter pointed at a river, at cows, at a horse gone mad at the sight of a hot-air balloon. The horse kicked and the boy laughed and shouted, 'boo!'

Dieter looked up at the balloon's inflated skin. He did wonder how the boy had made the ancient thing fly, but he didn't want to ask, he suspected the spell would be broken if he did and they'd come crashing down to the earth. Dieter tried to enjoy the view because that was what you were meant to do in air balloons. As the sun brightened everything, he was glad to be having an adventure; he was glad to be with his friend up here at the top of the world. He suddenly ran, though it was just four steps, to the opposite side of the basket. He held onto the rope. The sun was behind him now and it gradually lit the way like a stage light. It touched the tops of the fir trees, and then it made the fluttering leaves of the oak and beech woods sparkle. The light reached beyond a town and a train station – Dieter could just see the black lines of tracks.

'London is the place for me,' he murmured, 'London, this lovely city.'

They rose higher, until all Dieter could see were squares of land, squares in different shades and colours. They rose higher, higher and there were lakes and mountains, and Dieter felt terribly cold. His knees softened and his lungs sighed. His hand slipped down the rough rope and he slumped in a corner, back against the creaking wicker, humming Cynthia's song.

'London, hmm-hmm-hmm-hmm-hmm-hmm-hmm.'

Dieter wondered if he was dying. 'I want to go back,' he murmured.

The boy sat next to him. He took off his blue jacket and draped it across Dieter's shoulders. Dieter's lips were as blue as the coat and so the boy kissed them, gently. When Dieter's head fell onto the boy's lap, the boy decided to let him snuggle down and he smoothed his bright blond hair. The boy didn't mind at all when Dieter curled up, tight. In fact his other hand touched Dieter's shoulder and rubbed it with a flat palm to ease his shivering.

The boy closed his eyes. He breathed in breath he didn't need, and he saw the darkness come as the balloon rose and he smelled the sea and he listened to the creaking ropes above them. He hugged his friend close.

He was no longer the child who was born in the red gardens of Sugar Hall. He was no longer the toubab's, the slave in the blue velvet uniform watching his mother scream her knife-scream and knowing that she would kill or be killed. He was no longer the Slave Boy, Demerara, born to the Sugars, who stood in the corner of that first master's nursery in a silver collar. He was no longer the slave with the horse's bridle in his hands, the slave with the cockatiel, the spaniel, the salver of fruit. He was no longer the boy who was hanged by his father, his master, in the woods. He was no longer the ghost of Sugar Hall, the duppy: the succubus.

He had sucked up his past and the pasts of those around him and he felt his edges fizz and spark with them and he wondered if the sparks were golden or bright green, like a firework: like a bright fire lantern in the night. The boy began to sing, and he sang Dieter's song. 'London is the place for me,' he trilled, 'London, this lovely city…'

The boy stared ahead of him and sparked, his head unsteady on his shoulders, as his friend Dieter Sugar trembled in his lap.

A Late Autumn Auction

33

Once the solicitors agreed to the sale it had been organised quickly, and it was Juniper who had done most; down to labels so fiddly her fingers could hardly manage. Every object needed to be labelled and entered into the inventory. The solicitors had sent help and the auctioneers were at the Hall to fulfill their duty, but still Juniper knew that if you wanted a job doing well invariably you had to do it yourself.

She was sitting in the Queen Anne chair by the large windows in the red library, enjoying the last of the day's sun. She listened to the flurry of activity coming from the main hall. It was so strange to hear the clatter of many footfalls, the clanging of objects being moved. The auctioneers were an army of red ants; they had poured over the Hall and stripped it. They had had a viewing today. It had been quite ghastly, strangers and nosy acquaintances poking about in boxes, tables, drawers, in chests and cases, billing and cooing. The auction was tomorrow, and the space out in the hall was so expansive they had decided proceedings would take place out there: the auctioneer was to sit on a platform attached to the staircase while his helpers (including herself) carried labelled objects from each room in strict order. Juniper supposed the crowds would spill out of the front doors: people eager for a knick-knack, a souvenir of Sugar Hall before they closed it up for good.

'Stay, Bonzo,' she muttered. She could feel the spaniel twitch at the noises in the passageway. 'Good boy.'

Juniper had received letters: many from the daughter, Saskia, and one from Lilia. Mother and daughter were in separate cities now, and it seemed rather sad, though a little sadness among tragedy was, Juniper knew, laughable. Saskia had remained in London, and her last letter had said, 'Thank you, Mrs Bledsoe, for your kindness. I am sharing a flat in Pimlico with three other girls which suits me quite well, and your kindness with the fees for my secretarial school helps no end. Of course it is difficult to be on my own so suddenly.' Juniper knew the girl was asking for more money and somehow, she didn't mind one bit. In fact Juniper rather admired her gumption and she had sent two five-pound notes. Lilia had practically abandoned her daughter and Juniper felt Saskia was right to grasp at any help she was offered, Lord knows there was little else for her.

Juniper crossed her ankles. Bonzo sighed.

Lilia hadn't gone to America with that man, Alex, as they all expected: Lilia wasn't an American housewife with a neat pinny and a Frigidaire.

No, Lilia had gone back to Germany. She was in a place called Schlasgsdof now; it was a mouthful and Juniper had to look it up on the map. It seemed to be on the border between the new East and the West.

'I am existing,' Lilia wrote, 'I am working and I like the work. Simple work, I do not think about it. It is strange to be here, but at the same moment it is not.'

She was punishing herself, of course. Juniper had yet to reply. It was difficult to know what to say, and she knew her words had to be right; Lilia was worth that. Juniper's chilblains pained at the thought of lovely Lilia and what fun they had had; she slipped off her shoe and rubbed her calf.

The last time Juniper saw her friend was the night they viewed the body at that ghastly hospital mortuary in Gloucester. The child had been dragged from the mud just hours before, they hadn't cleaned him off, and that had made Juniper so angry. It had been chance that had found him before the tide came in: chance and a man with a dog.

Thank heavens Alex was there that night; they'd had to sedate Lilia, Alex had come back to Sugar Hall to pack her things and by the following day they had left for London. The child had been buried but it had been done so quickly that Juniper hadn't had the chance to attend.

It was a dreadful accident: somehow the boy had wandered down to the River Severn, he had been sleepwalking, or … Juniper had turned it round and around in her mind because why would he walk more than a mile to play in mud? He hadn't drowned, because the tide never reached him, the poor child had simply died of cold and exhaustion. Hypothermia. Death by Misadventure, the hospital doctor declared. There would be no inquest.

Lilia left and it was over: until Juniper received that letter late in September.

'We buried him, Alex and I, next to his father,' she wrote. 'I have not seen Alex since.'

Juniper fidgeted in the Queen Anne chair.

She did miss Lilia so. Lovely Lilia. She would reply to her letter: she would brave it tonight at home.

There was someone else Juniper truly regretted: John Phelps. He was still suffering.

Only last week she had been down in the kitchen sorting through what could be given away and what the solicitors termed 'valuable' (she doubted the white bowls and the butter churner could be that, still it was her duty to write the inventory).

John had given her such a fright when he charged down those outside steps and stormed in. 'Sorting through her possessions are you, Mrs Bledsoe?' he'd said and his voice was clogged.

She wanted to say, 'How are you, John? I haven't seen you in so long!' but his ridiculous raven had hopped onto the long kitchen table and she'd almost dropped a bowl. 'John! For God sakes, get that damned bird out!'

'Why are you going through her things?' he'd half-yelled back.

She had been quite surprised by his tone. 'It's something I have to do. Solicitors orders. Everything to be sold. Death duties, John.'

'Why are *you* doing it?'

'Because I was her friend.'

He started to cry then, and Juniper had to bundle him into a chair next to the range. She stroked and patted his back.

'It's a dreadful thing, John, dreadful, but we must be strong.'

'She'll not come back.'

She drew a chair next to him and sat. 'No, she won't.' Juniper sighed. 'Would you?'

He looked at her, his bright blue eyes blurred.

'You were close to the boy, weren't you, John?'

'He was a good lad.'

'It is such a terrible thing.'

'We didn't find him, why didn't we find him?'

'Sh…'

'I never took him down to that river. I wouldn't do that, so why would he go all that way on his own? How did he get down there? Who took him…?'

'Sh…'

'It's my fault, I know it is!'

'John, don't talk nonsense. It was a terrible accident.'

John sobbed, louder, and Juniper didn't know where to look.

'She was too good for me,' he said at last, 'she was…' but he couldn't speak any more and all Juniper could do was stand and place the black kettle on the hob.

'That's enough now, John,' she told him.

Now, as she settled deeper into the Queen Anne chair and

began thinking of a well-earned snooze, Juniper was glad it would soon be done with. Sugar Hall and all its contents would go under the hammer and that would be that. It was true that Lilia was the one to pity in all this, but still Juniper couldn't help thinking Lilia had left them all, and in her leaving irreparable ruptures had been made. It was a ridiculous, selfish thought: but there it was. The sooner this place was closed up, the sooner it was razed to the ground or sold on, the better. Let the Sugar curse or the plain bad luck this family had be razed with it.

There was a knock at the door.

Bonzo growled.

'Mrs Bledsoe?'

Juniper shook herself. The girl standing at the open door was Hannah, one of the auctioneer staff; a sweet and pretty thing with charming glasses who insisted on wearing a ponytail. Still so young, Juniper thought.

'Mrs Bledsoe, I am terribly sorry, but we're locking up soon.'

Juniper smiled; it amused her how these auctioneers felt they owned the place already. She patted the arms of the Queen Anne chair. 'This chair, Hannah, what lot number is this old thing?'

'Is there a ticket?'

'No, it doesn't seem so.'

'I'd have to check, Mrs Bledsoe.'

'Could you, dear?' Juniper smiled.

'We are locking up. I'm not sure if…'

'That is so kind.' Juniper's tone was final: she wanted to be left for a while longer. Then she noticed something in Hannah's hand: Bonzo whined.

'What is that dreadful thing?'

Hannah giggled, 'Oh, this? We found it under a pillow in the…' her smile disappeared. 'In the, the little boy's room.'

'Bring it here,' Juniper said and Hannah – a good girl – did what she was told.

It was a cloth doll, quite delicately made but rather startling. It looked ancient and it wore the blue livery of a servant. Juniper touched the life like hair on its head and a shudder went through her. As she held its body it seemed to crunch beneath her fingers. Bonzo trembled at her ankles.

'Take it away, Hannah, there's a good girl. If I were you I'd burn it.'

'Oh, I can't do that, Mrs. Bledsoe, it's in the inventory now.'

Juniper stared at the face of the doll: the eyes, nose and lips were made with terribly precise white, red and brown stitches. 'You go on now, Hannah,' she said, 'take it.'

'But…'

'Ten minutes, dear. You will give me ten minutes.'

Hannah took back the doll and when she closed the door Bonzo settled.

Juniper thought of the room above her: Lilia's room, Saskia's room, Dieter's room. The worst thing had been packing the clothes, the personal items up there. She had had to see to those. She'd steeled herself and spent a whole morning packing the boy's things up in a leather suitcase, folding Lilia's pretty dresses, her framed photographs, and she'd stacked Saskia's books. Juniper had been glad to be alone because she had made the most dreadful fuss. Not since the Brigadier died had she made such a scene: she'd had to bathe her eyes with cucumber and cold teabags when she returned home. It was the smell of the family in those clothes; it was the comfort of that smell. Juniper had her man take the three leather cases and the trunk of Peter's possessions to her house and they now sat in one of the locked rooms she never used. It wasn't until Saskia had written to her that she could ask what to do with them. 'I don't care,' Saskia replied. 'I don't want anything from that place.'

The library door opened again, but it wasn't Hannah.

'Mrs Bledsoe, there you are!'

Juniper straightened her back as the vicar, Ambrose, and his tepid wife, Daphne, walked into the library. Juniper didn't stand up.

'We have come for a private view,' he smiled.

Bonzo barked.

'Steady,' Juniper muttered. 'Wait.'

'It is such a pity about the collection, such a pity,' Ambrose was walking towards her, 'who would have done such a thing? I mean, who, Mrs Bledsoe?'

'What are you talking about, Ambrose?'

'Why the collection of course. Old Sugar's magnificent lepidoptera collection. The butterflies and moths, dear…'

'I am aware of the term "lepidoptera", Vicar…'

'Well, did you not know the old man had a whole room here? I had hoped to see it this summer, at the girl's party. But now the auctioneers tell me it was completely ruined, smashed, vandalised. Nothing left.'

'Terrible,' Daphne said.

'Every last specimen taken, who could have done such a thing, Mrs Bledsoe? Who?'

Juniper suddenly found the fight in her was gone: all at once she couldn't care less what this foolish man was implying. If he wanted to believe that Lilia had left Sugar Hall to bury her young son with a suitcase full of dead moths and butterflies, then so be it.

Bonzo growled at her feet.

The vicar twitched. 'In a strange way I hope they *were* stolen, I do hope that poor troubled child didn't simply smash the whole room, or…'

Juniper pressed her finger and thumb to the bridge of her nose; she wanted to block the vicar out.

Something had caught his eye and Ambrose was striding over to a painting up against a red wall. 'But this,' he said, and he knelt to tap the gilt frame. 'This once hung in the reception, did it not?'

'Perhaps,' Juniper sighed.

'Yes, this would do very well, very well for my study.'

He picked it up, and held it above him. Juniper watched Daphne pick up a big silver cake knife from the collection of cutlery on the main table. The vicar walked to the window with the painting.

'Hmm,' he said. 'Yes. Quite. Of course there is damage. Right through the figures here. I remember now. The boy, that poor, odd boy, he attacked it, didn't he? With a knife. Do you remember, Mrs Bledsoe? Daphne?'

'Yes,' Daphne said, her eyes still on the silver. She put the cake knife down.

Juniper gazed at the painting and the small slash through it, because she did remember. Perhaps that had been the beginning of it all. Dieter had behaved so strangely, a carving knife in his hand and his eyes glazed as if he was in a trance; and all she had done was dismiss him. She'd told him to go outside and play with her dogs. She felt the nausea of guilt as she stared at the painting.

It wasn't much to report: a family portrait. Eighteenth century, she'd written up the note for the catalogue. Ancient Sugars were arranged beneath a large oak tree, the Hall behind them. The women wore delicate gowns and tall wigs but of course they were rather damaged now. To the left of the picture there was a beautiful bay horse and a servant boy in blue livery holding its reins.

Juniper frowned.

'Yes, this will do quite well,' the vicar said. He looked down at her. 'Perhaps I can purchase it direct, Juniper? An auction is such a public thing.'

Juniper tapped her foot on the ground. Bonzo snarled.

'Wait,' Juniper muttered to her dog, 'good boy. Wait.'

Epilogue, September 12th, 1965

34

Her hands had suffered most and Lilia was glad she'd been forced to wear gloves. They were huge gloves, thick, red and plastic, but she hardly noticed in her uniform (if it could be called that: a green, faded overall she had to darn every few months).

The noise of the milking factory was worse than the gloves or the uniform, but she'd been here so long she believed she'd gone a little deaf. The constant chug of the machines, the roar of the lorries and the awful yell of those cows had seen to that.

Lilia had been here for six years; she'd spent four years before this trying to get back to her old home but there were new borders. Always borders were in her way, and so Lilia had settled for the first thing she'd found: the milking factory.

Lilia had always hated cows: now she pitied them.

It was truly mind numbing and this was a blessing; through the long days she didn't have to think, and so the nights were her own.

At four o'clock the buzzers blasted and Lilia could pack up, fold her overall into a plastic bag, and leave. It was the same every day. She waited at the bus stop outside the factory with the other women (they ignored her now; at first they had tried with pleasantries but nothing had come of it). They thought she was strange, English and strange, and something about this made Lilia want to laugh. Or cry. She hardly knew anymore. Lilia would settle into the back seat of the bus, next to the window.

This morning she had received a brief letter from Saskia, who wrote a few times a year to say, 'Look after yourself, Mother. The children send their regards to their grandmother and they wish they could see her again.'

Of course when Saskia married and when she started with those many, many children, Lilia had saved and she had taken the train and the boat back to England. But in the end it had been too much. She had visited four times over the last ten years, once for the wedding and three times for each of the earlier children; for the last two she had sent cards and fruit cake.

Lilia climbed the stairs to her flat, she had been lucky to get it, and for what it was, it pleased her. There were four flights to walk and though it kept her fit, it didn't keep her from feeling old.

Forty-one, I am only forty-one, she thought, but recently Lilia had had to catch her breath.

As she stood inside her hallway and locked and bolted her door, she placed the plastic bag with her dirty overall on the small hall table and cried, 'Hello, hello!'

A big tortoiseshell cat trotted from behind the bathroom door: he liked to sleep in the bidet and she didn't begrudge him. Too many years in England had Lilia confused by the bidet; and so it was the cat's bed.

'Hello,' she said, 'hello, my boy.'

The lazy cat purred a lazy purr and dropped to the floor, belly up. They would share supper tonight, he and she. Lilia had bought chicken legs and she was going to roast them with thyme and honey.

It was time to soak her hands and her feet in salt water, to listen to her radio and to treat herself to the last of the whisky.

It was going to be a feast tonight.

It would be quiet too, not that Lilia minded the noise in these flats. At times her neighbours' lives were a comfort but the four young girls next door were gone for three days. 'We're off to the big city, Ma,' they told her because they thought she was so much older (Lilia had long forgotten about colouring her hair and when she first grew the blonde out she'd been shocked to find her roots were white: quite white. She was used to it now).

'There's a big concert and we're going East!' the skinniest of the girls told her.

'Yeah,' another said.

'And they'll be there, The Rolling Stones!' and the skinny girl had screamed as loud as murder down their stairwell. Lilia had laughed. She tried to remember her name, was it Petra or Patrina?

'Be careful,' she told them, 'you have to be careful out there, don't forget your papers.'

'Don't worry, Ma.'

'Do you want me to watch your flat?'

'No, Ma…'

'Where will you stay?' Lilia held onto her door handle, her cheek against the edge of the wood; she liked these girls, they were bright and silly but she wouldn't let them in.

'Oh, Ma, we'll sleep in the park, at the train station, Berlin's safe!'

They laughed.

'And if it's not, they'll have us to battle with!'

'You have fun. Please be careful.'

'I'm going to kiss Mick Jagger!'

'I'm sure,' Lilia smiled.

'I'm going to screw Brian Jones!'

'Sh! Girls, be quiet, you know Mr Steingräber will be out any moment yelling at you.' Lilia laughed, but she had to close her door: these modern girls were priceless.

The chicken legs were crisping and Lilia settled into her armchair by the window. Once she stopped visiting Saskia in

England, this chair had been her treat. She drank the whisky from her cut-glass tumbler as she watched her nameless and lazy cat think about jumping on her lap.

'Come on, you can do it,' she coaxed.

It flicked the tip of its tail but didn't move.

The evening September sun was still warm and Lilia relished the last of it on her face. She closed her eyes, listened to the silence, and tried to get the pulsing chug of those milking machines out of her mind, out of her bones – though her foot still tapped to their rhythm. That pulse was in her blood now.

Lilia sighed and wondered if all her hard work would ever be over, her days at the factory, her nights at the University and the buses in between. She did wonder what she had done it for, that study. Did she think she could work as a translator? Did she think she could find a proper job in Paris, London, in New York? Was she going to call up Alex Behr out of the blue after all these years?

'Hello, Alex?' she would say and he would cry, 'Lily! Oh, my Lily!'

She opened her eyes.

No: this was too much. Lilia sighed and she tried a different daydream. After all, this was her favourite time, when she could lie here in her own place with her own whisky and her own cat and dream of possibilities. She had to. She had to block the other thoughts out.

As the rhythm of those fading milk-pumps ran around her system and her left foot tapped it out, Lilia thought of someone else. She liked to think they would meet by chance – suddenly, joyfully – on a street: Paris, perhaps (because Lilia had loved to read old copies of *Paris Match* for her French exams). Yes, they'd meet on the Rue St Germain, or maybe a boulevard, any of those boulevards. At first they would be too startled to talk, the shock would freeze them, but soon it would be Juniper who would laugh and open her arms while Lilia rushed in and burrowed into that smell of tweed and dog. The street would be empty and they would walk, arms linked, to the Luxembourg Gardens. Here, Juniper would laugh again, and point out the wonderful line of fanned pear trees and how abundant they were. She'd pick one and hold it out and Lilia would bite into it. They'd find a pretty bar, Art Nouveau; yes, an Art Nouveau bar on the Left Bank. There they would drink Pernod and Lilia would giggle at the magic of it: how the wondrous little drink turned to opaque cloud once the water was added.

In her chair, Lilia licked her lips and the cat finally jumped into her lap.

Lilia had to settle herself again. She was truly fanciful tonight: she closed her eyes once more and rubbed the cat's ears.

It had been such a long time since he took a breath, the headiness of cat litter and coffee was a shock. A fat tortoiseshell growled from his mother's lap. Dieter shuddered. Death had given him a fear of cats.

He watched his mother, he often did.

She hasn't taken care of herself, he thought, not in the way I would — if that was my body. Dieter sighed; Ma had let herself go.

Gla-mour, he mouthed.

At least he hadn't aged. Not a wink, not a whisker: in appearance at least. Dieter was a boy, he wore shorts; his blond hair was cut to a short back and sides.

He sat on the floor by her chair, staring up.

Dieter tried to concentrate.

Today he was going to do it. He didn't know why he had chosen today to touch her. The passage of time in living terms; the hours, minutes, days, meant little to Dieter: it was simply a case of here he was and this is what he intended to do.

He grabbed her hand and she twisted on that armchair in her sleep.

Dieter smiled and sat up; he knelt in front of her like a little supplicant. He brought her hand to his lips. He pointed one of her swollen fingers out; he opened his mouth and then he bit. The cat hissed.

When Lilia woke to the cat scratching and biting her hand she pushed him off her lap.

'Bad, bad boy!' she said and she sucked the blood from the cut on her index finger. She was a little dazed and shocked: the cat was so fat and docile he had never done such a thing before. 'No supper for you!' she cried.

Later, as she brushed her teeth and picked out the pieces of meat, she watched the cat. He was back to his old self, preening his fur in the bidet, the shine of chicken skin glossy on his face because Lilia couldn't deny him. She looked at the plaster on her finger: it wasn't such a deep cut.

'I wash myself, you should wash yourself,' she told him, and she spat out her toothpaste.

She examined herself in the full-length bathroom mirror as she did every night. Her legs were wonderfully shapely; the stairs had seen to that. The rest, though, was bloated. The cream, the butter: the cheese; it had taken its toll.

It wasn't over yet: she was sure. 'Forty-one, I am only forty-one,' she said. Maybe she would change her hair: her white hair. In the next moment she was promising herself she'd write to Juniper, it was her turn after all. The last she heard, Juniper had begged a visit, 'because, really my dear, it is quite too long and life, as you know, is so very, very short.'

Lilia thought of her suitcase, waiting mouth open on the floor of her bedroom. She had brought it up from the basement yesterday evening: she was ready for something, though what she hardly knew. The lazy fat cat twirled in and out of her legs and purred.

'Yes, we are ready, it is time for bed, for sleep,' she said, and she switched off the bathroom light.

It was strange, for a moment – the moment between light and darkness – she thought she saw something in the bathroom mirror; it was behind her, a flicker, an outline.

It was a boy.

Lilia's heart swelled, she turned, because it could be true, because miracles do happen. The cat spat and hissed and she switched the light back on.

There was nothing there.

Lilia forced herself to swallow: she forced the familiar creep of sadness to her extremities, to her fingers, her toes, where it could always be within reach. She'd had too much whisky. She knelt down and picked up the big cat: he would sleep with her tonight.

'It is time,' she muttered, 'time for bed, time to sleep.'

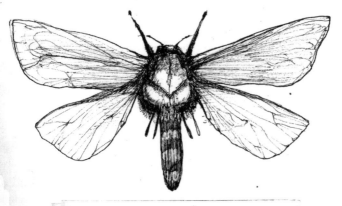

GHOST MOTH, male, hepialus humuli

Acknowledgements

Huge thanks to my editor Penny Thomas, and to my agent Veronique Baxter, and Laura West, at David Higham Associates. Also to Simon Hicks, Sarah Davies and Mick Felton at Seren. To the Hay Festival and Arts Council of Wales, I can't thank you enough for the International Fellowship year that gave me (among many other things) the chance to meet Eme De Mario in Xalapa, Mexico. Mario, thank you for these amazing illustrations, and bountiful thanks to Peter Florence, Lyndy Cooke, Becky Shaw, Cristina Fuentes La Roche, and María Sheila Cremaschi for the best festival support. I'm very grateful also to Nina Steingräber for the Yiddish and German translation, and to Silvia Gutiérrez for the English to Spanish translation. Thanks also to Claire Berliner, Andy Squiff at Squiff Creative Media and to Victoria Thorley for the wonderful moth on the cover.

Sugar Hall has been a long time in the making: Kamau Brathwaite, thank you for a fantastic education all those years ago in my beloved New York City. Junot Díaz, huge thanks for your brilliant stories in the same city.

Laurence and Joan – my tireless readers – you have great patience: also Joanie Philips and Eric Portman bless you for those early readings.

Many books have been helpful in researching *Sugar Hall*, in particular: Barbara Bush, *Slave Women in Caribbean Society, 1650-1832* (Indiana University Press), Kamau Brathwaite, *Motherpoem* (OUP), *Slavery and the British Country House* (eds Madge Dresser and Andrew Hann, English Heritage). I would also like to thank the British Empire and Commonwealth Museum in Bristol (now defunct), the International Slavery Museum in Liverpool, and London's Imperial War Museum (where I discovered Al Jennings singing on the BBC).

Stories of the Boy were told in my school playground when I was a knock-kneed girl. He haunted a local house – Littledean Hall – and he does to this day.

Extract from 'Limbo', by Kamau Brathwaite, from *The Arrivants: a New World Trilogy* with kind permission of the author.

Extract from *The Brief Wondrous Life of Oscar Wao* by Junot Díaz (Faber and Faber) with kind permission of the author.

Extract from *In Youth is Pleasure* (Enitharmon Press) with kind permission of the estate of Denton Welch.

Every effort has been made to identify copyright holders and seek permissions for all quoted material in this novel.

SEREN

Well chosen words

Seren is an independent publisher with a wide-ranging list which includes poetry, fiction, biography, art, translation, criticism and history. Many of our books and authors have been on longlists and shortlists for – or won – major literary prizes, among them the Costa Award, the Man Booker, the Desmond Elliott Prize, The Writers' Guild Award, Forward Prize, and TS Eliot Prize.

At the heart of our list is a good story told well or an idea or history presented interestingly or provocatively. We're international in authorship and readership though our roots are here in Wales (Seren means Star in Welsh), where we prove that writers from a small country with an intricate culture have a worldwide relevance.

Our aim is to publish work of the highest literary and artistic merit that also succeeds commercially in a competitive, fast changing environment. You can help us achieve this goal by reading more of our books – available from all good bookshops and increasingly as e-books. You can also buy them at 20% discount from our website, and get monthly updates about forthcoming titles, readings, launches and other news about Seren and the authors we publish.

www.serenbooks.com

1	2	3	4	5	6	7	8	9	10
11	12	13	14	15	16	17	18	19	20
21	22	23	24	25	26	27	28	29	30
31	32	33	34	35	36	37	38	39	40
41	42	43	44	45	46	47	48	49	50
51	52	53	54	55	56	57	58	59	60
61	62	63	64	65	66	67	68	69	70
71	72	73	74	75	76	77	78	79	80
81	82	83	84	85	86	87	88	89	90
91	92	93	94	95	96	97	98	99	100
101	102	103	104	105	106	107	108	109	110
111	112	113	114	115	116	117	118	119	120
121	122	123	124	125	126	127	128	129	130
131	132	133	134	135	136	137	138	139	140
141	142	143	144	145	146	147	148	149	150
151	152	153	154	155	156	157	158	159	160
161	162	163	164	165	166	167	168	169	170
171	172	173	174	175	176	177	178	179	180
181	182	183	184	185	186	187	188	189	190
191	192	193	194	195	196	197	198	199	200
201	202	203	204	205	206	207	208	209	210
211	212	213	214	215	216	217	218	219	220
221	222	223	224	225	226	227	228	229	230
231	232	233	234	235	236	237	238	239	240
241	242	243	244	245	246	247	248	249	250
251	252	253	254	255	256	257	258	259	260
261	262	263	264	265	266	267	268	269	270
271	272	273	274	275	276	277	278	279	280
281	282	283	284	285	286	287	288	289	290
291	292	293	294	295	296	297	298	299	300
301	302	303	304	305	306	307	308	309	310
311	312	313	314	315	316	317	318	319	320
321	322	323	324	325	326	327	328	329	330
331	332	333	334	335	336	337	338	339	340
341	342	343	344	345	346	347	348	349	350
351	352	353	354	355	356	357	358	359	360
361	362	363	364	365	366	367	368	369	370
371	372	373	374	375	376	377	378	379	380
381	382	383	384	385	386	387	388	389	390
391	392	393	394	395	396	397	398	399	400